Books by Brenda Hasse

Adult

On The Third Day

Young Adult

The Freelancer
Wilkinshire

Children

My Horsy And Me, What Can We Be?
A Unicorn For My Birthday
Yes, I Am Loved

A Lady's Destiny

~

Brenda Hasse

A Lady's Destiny

ISBN: 978-0-9906312-4-8 (pbk)
ISBN: 978-0-9906312-5-5 (ebk)

To Evan, Alexander, Adam, and Benjamin, with love

Chapter 1

THE GRAY WOLF'S breath appeared like wisps of fog in the frigid morning air as he trudged homeward to Tildenham. Rand's yellow eyes scanned the frosted trees and ghostlike bushes along the roadside as he preceded his master, who was accompanied by his father's knight, Sir Garrick. As Lord Edwin's ebony war horse punched his hoof through the ice of a shallow puddle, the wolf sidestepped and snapped his head to look over his shoulder toward the startling sound. Assured all was well, he returned his line of vision to the dirt road ahead and resumed his rhythmic gait.

A brisk breeze tainted with acrid smoke whistled through the branches rippling the wolf's fur. Rand raised his nose to inhale its scent. His paws stilled on the frozen ground. He lowered his head. The hair along his spine rose. Narrowing his eyes, he stared into the ashen distance, curled his lips to display his ivory teeth, and growled.

Lord Edwin reined Fulton as the pungent odor enveloped his nose.

"A campfire?" He looked down at his wolf, who continued to resonate his warning.

Sir Garrick brought his dapple gray horse alongside his young lord.

"Highwaymen?" The knight placed his forearm upon the pommel of his saddle. His chestnut eyes peered down the road as he strained to listen for any suspicious sound. A decade older than Lord Edwin, he looked to the wolf and wondered if his hearing was beginning to fail. He waited for his lord's assessment and would advise if necessary.

Lord Edwin scanned the roadside where robbers may have set up camp, but all was quiet and still.

"It's quite strong, too strong to merely be a dying campfire."

Rand sprang forward, darting down the road like a pig running from a butcher.

A quizzical glance was exchanged between the lord and his knight. They spurred their mounts into a gallop to follow. As they neared the edge of the woods, their eyes were drawn skyward to several charcoal plumes of smoke. Whatever was once afire continued to smolder.

The wolf outpaced the horses as the trio emerged from the woods and crested a hill to see Tildenham in the distance. Reining their destriers to a stop, the men stared at the charred remains of the once pristine village.

Lord Edwin's mouth fell agape as he scanned the destruction.

"My God, what happened?" He reined his horse as it pranced nervously, leaned forward, and patted Fulton's neck to calm him. His attention was drawn to swishing tails of several horses grazing in a nearby field. Small clusters of goats, cows, and geese dotted the field as well. Sitting upright in his saddle, he looked back to the village. Its skeletal foundations of blackened buildings appeared a total loss. Bodies littered the muddied ground like fallen leaves. "Why didn't Father defend them?"

His father, Lord Kester, upheld the reputation for being a kind provider for those who worked his land. Where other kingdoms housed their peasants in dwellings made of sticks and mud, Tildenham's peasants lived in well-constructed homes made of wood from its vast forest. Located outside the castle walls, the buildings had lined several dirt streets with a small village square for people to gather and socialize by a warm campfire.

Rand scampered from body to body in search of life while those who survived wandered the streets aimlessly looking for family and friends amongst the dead.

The young lord and knight proceeded through the village. Lord Edwin resisted the urge to cough as he passed through a plume of smoke reeking of ash and burnt flesh. He waved his hand back and forth in front of his face seeking fresh air.

Sir Garrick directed his horse around the contorted body of a man lying in the street. He looked to the cindered threshold where a home once stood and saw two young children clinging to each other for warmth. Their sooty faces, streaked by tears they had shed, stared at him.

Taking a quick headcount, Lord Edwin estimated a little over a score of the villagers survived. Several were injured. He watched two men load a woman's body into a horse-drawn cart while a young woman sifted through the rubble for anything salvageable.

Encouraging their horses toward the gatehouse, the drawbridge lay open and the portcullis hung at a crooked angle. As they crossed over the moat and entered the bailey, they discovered the destruction inside the castle equaled what they had encountered on the outside. Bodies littered the ground and nearly every crafter's building that lined the walls of the castle was destroyed. They reined their horses before the Keep. Its door hung ajar from its broken hinges. They unsheathed their swords as they dismounted.

"Lord Edwin!"

The lord and his knight turned toward the stable. One of its walls had been torn away causing its roof to sag in the center. Bryce, the stableboy, finished tying the lead of a horse to a post.

Lord Edwin lowered his sword and looked to the lad's sky-blue eyes.

"Bryce, what happened?"

The stableboy brushed his red hair away from his freckled face before gathering the reins of the horses.

"Barbarians, my lord. They dressed in leather and fur and spoke a language I couldn't understand. They arrived during the evening meal, went into the Great Hall, and began killing everyone." Bryce stroked the side of Fulton's face as the destrier became restless.

Sir Garrick's eyebrows rose, and his eyes widened.

"Everyone?" He looked toward the Keep.

Bryce peeked around Fulton's head to see the knight.

"All, but a few. I watched them enter the Keep. Then there was screaming. I freed the horses from the stable and hid to save myself. After the cries from the Keep grew silent, I heard screaming from the village before the barbarians rode away. There was nothing I could do, my lord. I would have lost my life as well." Bryce downcast his eyes to the ground and shook his head as if disappointed with himself.

Lord Edwin knew the lanky lad, only three years past a decade would have been struck down.

"You made the right choice." He patted the stableboy's shoulder hoping to ease the burden of guilt he carried.

"Thank you, my lord." Bryce watched the men turn toward the Keep. He knew what awaited his lord inside but thought it best to remain silent. As they disappeared through the doorway, he led the horses to the side of the stable to join the few he had managed to gather and tether. Securing their reins to a post, he paused to look at the devastation within the bailey.

Lord Edwin and Sir Garrick noted the wooden box filled with swords and daggers in the hallway before sheathing their swords and stepping over several bodies.

It had long been the Lord of Tildenham's decree of all who dined within the Great Hall to deposit their weapons in the box before feasting. Unfortunately, it left those within the room defenseless and vulnerable when the barbarians attacked.

Lord Edwin and his knight entered the large room, its grandness replaced by carnage. Charred scraps of tapestry dangled from the brass rods on the stone walls with shadowed scars of soot replacing the beauty once displayed. The portrait of the Lady of Tildenham hung askew over the carved stone fireplace. The dead lay atop tables and scattered upon the blood-soaked rushes on the floor like a tossed deck of playing cards.

The clicking of Rand's toenails on the stone floor announced his entry into the room. He sniffed several bodies before going to his master's side.

A servant girl appeared in the kitchen doorway. Recognizing the young lord, she wove her way around the bodies as she rushed toward him.

"Oh, my lord, I heard screaming, lots of screaming, and I could do nothing." Unable to keep her composure, she covered her mouth with her hand and began to cry.

Lord Edwin needed answers. He sighed, clasped the woman's wrist gently, and encouraged her to remove her hand from her face.

"What's your name?"

The woman slowed her breathing as tears continued to roll down her cheeks. She dried them with the edge of her soiled overskirt, calmed herself, and looked to her lord with bloodshot russet eyes.

"Isabel." She pulled a stray brunette curl away from her face, flipped the long strand over her shoulder, and brushed the wrinkles from her skirt in an attempt to make herself more presentable for her lord.

"Isabel." Lord Edwin hoped by repeating her name, he would cast it to memory. He stared at her face. *Maybe a score or more.*

"Did you hear any justification for the attack?"

"No, my lord. I was returning a crock to the larder when I heard screaming and shouting, so I hid behind a barrel of apples. When all was quiet, I crept out and had a look see here and upstairs." She scanned the room. "They ransacked the entire Keep as if they were looking for something."

Lord Edwin turned and looked up to the balcony toward the bedchambers. A body lay draped over the railing. *My God, Father, Mother.* He turned back to Isabel.

"Where are my parents?"

She pointed a shaking finger toward the High Table where two bodies lay covered by a tapestry remnant.

"They have been laid over there. I'm sorry, my lord."

Lord Edwin turned toward the place of honor where he usually joined his parents for the evening meal. He approached the High Table, stepped onto the dais, and pulled aside the scorched tapestry, letting it fall to the floor. His parents lay head to head with their eyes staring toward the ceiling. His father had suffered a stab wound to his chest and his mother's throat laid filleted open at its base. Lord Edwin raised his chin. He took a deep breath as the weighted responsibility of the kingdom settled upon his broad shoulders. Clenching his teeth while balling his fists until his knuckles turned white, he tried to calm his breathing. He wanted to pursue the murderers, hunt them down, and kill every one of them, but now was not the time. His garrison was dead and those who survived needed his guidance and protection.

He turned to face Sir Garrick and Isabel and forced himself to speak calmly.

"From this day forward, we shall no longer check our arms at the doorway for the evening meal. We shall be on guard to defend ourselves at all times."

Even though the young lord had yet to reach a score in age, Sir Garrick recognized the determination within his hazel eyes and hoped it was sustainable. If not, he would uphold his promise to his former lord and see that it was.

Chapter 2

WHITE FEATHERS FLOATED like snow falling from the sky as Lady Averly plucked a chicken for the evening meal. She was doing her best to put the soft down into a gunny sack for later use as bedding, but the feathers had a mind of their own.

Harry, her orange tabby, crouched on the stone floor. He sprang into the air, trapping a wayward feather within his paws.

"Thank you, Harry."

As a feather floated down toward her nose, she blew it back into the air while hastening her pace. Mentally reviewing the evening menu, she hoped it would please her father, Lord Burton. *Father seems distant as of late, often lost in thought as if something is weighing heavily on his mind. His hair near his temples has turned quite gray over the past few months too.* Lady Averly knew her stepmother, Lady Miriam, was to blame. *Her evil green eyes would curdle milk if she stared at it long enough.* She pulled another handful of feathers.

Lady Averly cared little for her stepmother, and even less so for her half-brother, Alger. At age eight, he would succeed her father as the Lord of Holbrook. Lady Miriam coddled, catered, and allowed him to do as he pleased. She often defended his inappropriate behavior. Everyone recognized his true nature as a spoiled brat.

The metallic bang of a copper pan crashing on the stone floor pulled Lady Averly from her thoughts. She held the naked bird up to the light to ensure it was clean of feathers.

"Mina, is the water boiling yet?" Lady Averly removed a pinfeather and checked the bird again.

The round freckled faced cook paused from chopping carrots. Her baby blue eyes enlarged as she looked toward her mistress.

"My lady, I forgot." Mina set her knife down and rushed to the large fireplace where an iron pot of water hung from a hook.

"Father seems a bit out of sorts lately. I thought some chicken soup would cheer him up. It's his favorite." Lady Averly set the bird on the table top, picked up the knife Mina had abandoned and sliced the chicken down the breastbone cutting it in half.

Harry rubbed his face against his mistress's leg, hoping to draw her attention, but Lady Averly was distracted by the cook's long strawberry blonde hair that fell toward the flames as she bent to see the level of the water in the pot.

"Mina, tie your hair."

Several years ago, a cook bent over a fire, setting her hair aflame. From that day forward, Lady Averly insisted all women tie their hair behind their head or stuff it under a cap.

Mina noted her lady's long golden locks tied neatly at the nape of her neck. Taking a leather strap from a hook on the wall, she bound her hair away from her face. Retrieving a towel from the mantel, she wrapped it around her hand before grasping the hot handle of the hook and rotating the pot over the fire to heat the water.

Lady Miriam entered the kitchen like a plague cast upon the land.

"Averly!"

Startled by the woman's high-pitched, raspy voice, Harry arched his back and hissed as he watched the wicked woman cross her arms over her chest and tap her foot impatiently on the floor.

"You seem behind. You know how your father wants his meal on time."

Glaring at her stepmother, Lady Averly set the knife on the table and picked up her cat to calm him.

Harry had grown from the malnourished orphan kitten she discovered several years ago while gathering chicken eggs. He became a permanent fixture in the kitchen, kept the mice population to a minimum in the Keep, and snuggled next to her for warmth at night while sleeping in her small chamber. Under her watchful eye, she ensured he was well cared for and often fed.

She nuzzled the top of his head and stroked his fur until he began to purr. Tearing a small bit of meat from a ham, she marched past her stepmother to place Harry on the floor outside the kitchen doorway before giving him the treat. She hoped the feline would make himself scarce while Lady Miriam continued with her tirade. Lady Averly placed her fisted hands upon her hips and sneered at the perfectly styled ebony hair on the back of her stepmother's head. Tempted to speak her mind, she refrained, having learned to do so years ago after being sent to the dungeon for punishment by Merle, the executioner who resembled a giant ogre. She returned to the table, picked up the knife, and chopped the chicken leg and thigh apart.

"The staff and I are working quickly and..."

Lady Miriam scowled.

"I don't want to hear your addle-pated excuse."

Lady Averly took a deep breath.

"Supper will be on time, as always." She secretly wished her father was absent from the meal, then she could intentionally delay it to spite the evil woman.

"Well, it looks to me as if you're running late, incompetent as always. Snap to it! And quit feeding that damn cat. He can go catch mice if he wants something to eat!" Lady Miriam's violet gown twisted and flailed behind her as she pivoted and left the room in haste.

The staff remained silent. They watched Lady Averly take deep breaths to compose herself, gather the chicken pieces, and toss them into a wooden bowl.

Mina went to her mistress's side.

"Don't worry, my lady, we'll have the meal ready on time."

Lady Averly looked at her friend's kind face before scanning the empathetic stares of her peasant friends. The women smiled reassuringly and nodded their heads in agreement. She forced a slight grin on her face as everyone returned to her assigned task. Taking a moment to admire the staff's efficiency, she sighed before dropping the chicken pieces into the pot of water that had yet to boil.

She selected some potatoes from a basket and returned to the table. As she diced them, she pondered a wishful thought. *I wonder how different my life would be if mother was still alive.*

Lady Averly was seven years old when she was called to her mother's bedside and watched as she expelled her last breath. The months that followed were sorrowful but pleasant. Her father tried to spend time with her daily. They would often ride their horses together. However, all happiness seemed to leave Holbrook on the day Lord Burton wed Lady Miriam and her stepmother took her rightful place as the Lady of Holbrook. She insisted her stepdaughter assume a more suitable role in servitude.

It's been a decade. Mother, I wish you were here.

Noticing her friend staring at nothing and lost in thought, Mina set a basket filled with loaves of bread upon the table next to the cut potatoes.

"My lady, what troubles you?"

Lady Averly glanced at her stout friend and grinned.

"Oh, life in general, I guess. I was thinking how everything has changed since Father married Lady Miriam. If Mother was alive, I would be living a life of royalty, dressing in pretty dresses, and receiving the respect of a true lady. Forgive me, my intention is not to demean anyone, but my stepmother treats me as if I'm the last on the list of priorities."

Mina's bulbous belly rose and fell as she chuckled.

"Well, at least you're on the list."

The cook's comment brought a smile to her lady's face as the two women continued with the preparation of the evening meal.

*   *   *

Lady Miriam entered the solar, a small room between her and her husband's bedchambers, and saw Lord Burton sitting in a chair with an open book in his hands. She stood before him, crossed her arms over her chest, and tapped her foot impatiently.

"I fear supper will be late again."

Lord Burton refused to look up from the book he was reading as his wife began pacing the room.

"My dear, Averly has always been prompt with the evening meal. You worry needlessly."

Stopping abruptly, Lady Miriam clenched her fist at her sides and stomped her foot.

"But you know how Alger gets cranky when he's hungry."

"In truth, he's become quite chubby lately. It may do him some good to miss the meal entirely." Lord Burton turned the page and tried to focus on his reading.

"Nonsense, you don't mean that! He's only eight. He will slim down once he grows into a man."

Then he will have to grow at least seven feet tall. Lord Burton closed his book with a snap. He knew he would have little peace until his wife's concern was addressed.

"I'll go and speak with her." He set the book upon a nearby table and stood.

"Good, she always listens to you." Lady Miriam watched her husband leave the room. Her mouth turned upward at one side, forming a sneer. "And tell her to quit feeding that cat of hers too!"

Chapter 3

SIR GARRICK LOWERED himself to one knee. Isabel curtsied. They bowed their heads to their new lord.

Even they understand the responsibility I've inherited. Lord Edwin exhaled.

"Rise."

They obeyed their lord's command.

He rotated to face his parents once again, placed the palm of his hand over his mother's unblinking eyes, and closed them before looking at his father's face. *Father, how am I to carry on without you when I have yet much to learn. I promise to uphold your honor and to do my best.* He placed the palm of his hand over his patriarch's blank orbs and pulled them closed. Removing the gold signet ring from his father's left pinky, he held it before his eyes and examined the engraved lion bookended by an inset ruby before slipping it onto his left pinky finger.

Lord Edwin placed his fisted hands upon his hips as he stared at his parents in their state of eternal rest. The ground frost made a proper burial impossible. The matter of the dead, all of the dead, needed to be addressed before any disease could set in and spread. He turned toward his knight.

"I need you to organize the survivors. Tell the women, children, and the injured to come to the Keep. Have a few of the men herd the animals toward the stable and the strongest, have them gather the dead and place them in a pile next to what remains of the village. They can begin by laying my parents in the graveyard and covering them with any dirt, straw, and stone they can find."

"Yes, my lord." Sir Garrick nodded and left the Great Hall.

Lord Edwin's eyes met the helpless stare of Isabel, who stood with her hands entwined nervously in her overskirt. Her eyes were bloodshot and puffy. Her hair was untamed and disheveled.

Over the years, Lord Edwin gave little thought to the staff's workload. He would go about his day eating delicious meals unaware of the cook's laborious preparations. The cleaning women prided themselves on the immaculate cleanliness of every room in the Keep. The peasants in the laundry ensured his soiled clothing magically appeared in his bedchamber shortly after they were gathered for cleaning.

Not quite certain what to tell Isabel, he looked down at Rand, who sat nearby. He patted the top of the wolf's head, gathering his thoughts before approaching the cook.

"Do you know if any other members of the staff survived?"

"If any did, then they managed to hide somewhere within the Keep or escape, my lord. Those who worked in the kitchen are dead."

Lord Edwin looked toward the kitchen portal. With commanding strides, he crossed the Great Hall and entered. His foot skidded on the slippery floor. Regaining his balance, he looked to his boots and saw a pool of blood beneath them. The stench of smoldering flesh forced him to cover his nose with his hand and glance in the direction of the fireplace where several bodies lay on its embers. His stomach soured and became queasy. He placed his other hand on his abdomen to calm it. Scanning the room, he saw overturned pots and wooden bowls with their contents strewn upon the floor amongst the dead.

Isabel stepped cautiously through the doorway and stood behind her lord. Rand entered the kitchen and sniffed a body.

Lord Edwin sensed someone behind him. He lowered his hands to his sides and turned to face the servant.

"Are you a cook or server?"

"I mostly serve the food, but also assist with its preparation when needed. The head cook lies there." She pointed at the floor to his right.

He looked at the woman's contorted body. Her soulless eyes stared back at him.

"Isabel." He turned away from the gruesome sight and looked at the servant who wiped a tear from her cheek. "Since you possess some kitchen experience, I need you to fill her position. The women who have survived will assist you in putting the kitchen into working order. I'll return shortly with Sir Garrick and we'll remove the dead. Meanwhile, please take inventory of our cooking supplies."

"Yes, my lord." Isabel curtsied as her lord left the room.

Lord Edwin crossed the Great Hall, ascended the staircase, and went to his parent's chambers. He pushed on his father's bedchamber door. It was bolted, but the solar door was ajar with its latch broken. His heartbeat quickened. *The treasury.* He stepped inside, noting the overturned furniture before turning to his right and passing through the arched opening in the wall to enter his father's bedchamber. Stepping over the crumpled rug, his eyes were drawn to the armoire with its doors ajar and its contents scattered about the floor. *Oh, God.* He hurried to the armoire and threw the remaining clothes upon the floor to reveal the back panel with its inlaid diamond pattern. Pushing the center-right diamond, the panel opened with a click. He pulled it wide to reveal a second wooden door. Lifting the latch, he entered the small chamber. A tiny window allowed natural light to illuminate the numerous chests lining the perimeter of the room. Lord Edwin sighed with relief, for they remained undisturbed.

He lifted the lid of the nearest chest, grasped a handful of coins, and let them cascade like a waterfall. *At least I have the funds to rebuild.* Closing the lid, he left the chamber.

After ensuring both doors were secure; he emerged from the armoire into the disheveled bedchamber that was now his. As if to escape the chaos, he went to the balcony entrance, opened the double glass doors, and admired the view overlooking the winding river and the forest in the distance while trying to avert his eyes from the devastation directly below. He wished his parents were alive and Tildenham was the majestic kingdom he remembered before leaving with Sir Garrick only a fortnight ago. Letting out a sigh, he returned to the bedchamber, shutting the balcony doors behind him.

The carved wooden bed with its four tall bedposts centered the wall opposite from the large fireplace. The impressive burgundy canopy with its curtains tied to each post offered warmth during cold evenings. Lord Edwin picked up the mattress from the floor and tossed it onto the bed. It would have to be made properly before nightfall. His foot brushed against something on the floor. It was one of his mother's gowns. He picked it up and inhaled its rose fragrance. Looking up to the ceiling, tears he was unable to hold back escaped the corners of his eyes and rolled down his face. He let the dress fall to the floor as he sat on the bed. *If only I'd been here...* The thought of saving his parents entered his mind, but then he reflected. *I'd be dead as well. Instead, I'm left here to carry on.* His heart ached, yet the hollowness within it was painless. He sat up straight and wiped away his tears. *Now is not the time to display weakness, for there are those who depend upon me.*

He stood and looked at the clothing strewn about the floor. It needed to be packed into trunks and moved to another chamber. *With so few women surviving, I may have to right the bedchamber myself.* A list of what needed to be addressed grew exponentially within his mind as he kicked the clothing into a pile. The rest of the room would have to wait until later, for the peasants were his priority. On his way through the solar, he picked up his father's overturned desk chair and set it upright.

Lord Edwin descended the staircase as the surviving peasants trickled into the Great Hall. They stepped over bodies and looked about, dumbfounded by the gruesome site.

Hearing footsteps behind him, Sir Garrick turned toward his lord.

"My lord, I have assigned men to collect the dead and herd the livestock inside the castle walls. Bryce and an elderly man are repairing the stable as best they can and trying to build a makeshift corral."

Lord Edwin slapped his knight on the shoulder and nodded approvingly.

"Good. How many men survived?"

"Only ten or so."

How do I run a kingdom with so few? Overwhelmed, Lord Edwin glanced toward the ceiling.

As if to read his lord's mind, Sir Garrick made a suggestion.

"Word can be sent to neighboring kingdoms offering an opportunity for freemen to come to Tildenham. Many hands will be needed for planting crops once the ground thaws and crafters to fill the shops once they are rebuilt." The knight paused to allow the contemplation of his suggestion before venturing on. "To rebuild our defense, a missive to the baron requesting men for the garrison should be considered as well."

"I agree." He looked to the askance eyes of the people within the room. They appeared tired. Their clothing scorched, hair singed and burns on their skin. He stepped upon the dais and waited for their murmurs to quiet before speaking.

"We have endured a great tragedy. I know you're tired, some of you are injured, but we must put this room in order before we rest tonight. Once done, we'll share a meal with whatever food Isabel and those who wish to help her can find. You'll sleep within this room until other accommodations can be made." He looked to his knight, who nodded his head approvingly and awaited further instruction.

Chapter 4

LADY AVERLY LADLED the chicken vegetable soup into a wooden bowl and centered it upon a tray. Hoping her father would be pleased, she hoisted the tray, resting the edge on the top of her right shoulder.

"Mina, could you dish up the remaining bowls for the High Table?"

"Yes, my lady." The chubby cook filled several wooden bowls with soup and placed them onto a large tray. An awaiting serving girl lifted the heavy tray to her shoulder and followed her mistress.

Pausing at the doorway, Lady Averly turned to ensure the trenchers were heaping with roasted vegetables and cuts of meat. Servants filled tin pitchers with ale and wine and hurried past her into the Great Hall to fill the empty mugs of thirsty attendants. The first batch of freshly baked sweet cakes was pulled from the stone oven and set on a table to cool.

She nodded her head with confidence and smirked, knowing everyone had helped to disprove her stepmother's accusation. Lady Averly left the kitchen with the serving girl following closely behind.

The Great Hall was filled to capacity as Lady Averly raised the tray above her head and squeezed her slim body between the backs of the men who were seated on benches at long tables. Glancing at the High Table, her father's face donned a proud smile. Unfortunately, her stepmother's face wore a sour scowl. Chubby Alger was sitting to the right of his mother, stuffing various flavored sweet cakes into his mouth. As always, Lady Miriam insisted the future heir of Holbrook receive dessert as his first course.

"Here you go, Father." Lady Averly set the warm soup before him, lowered her tray to the floor leaning against the table, and turned away.

Lady Miriam cocked her head to the side as she picked up her goblet of wine.

"Where's my soup?"

Lady Averly looked toward the wooden ceiling, widening her sapphire blue eyes and gritting her teeth before turning calmly toward her stepmother.

"As you can see, it's coming on the tray, on time." She emphasized by motioning with her hand in the direction of the serving girl struggling to weave her way between the seated men.

Lady Averly grabbed two bowls of soup from the tray as it was lowered by the servant. Secretly wishing she could throw the contents in her stepmother's face, she placed a bowl before Lady Miriam and the other before Alger but doubted the brat would eat it. However, if she omitted his serving, she was sure to be scolded. Taking another bowl from the tray, she set it before Sir Thomas, her stepmother's knight who sat to the left of her father.

"Thank you, my lady." Sir Thomas brushed his mousy brown hair away from his hazel eyes to admire every feature of her body boldly. He parted the whiskers of his long mustache, pulling it to each side of his mouth to reveal his full lips. He ran his tongue over them until they were wet with spittle.

Lady Averly recalled the aggressive encounter with the knight while alone in a hallway several months ago. Thankfully, Mina had entered, realized what was happening, and announced that she was needed in the kitchen.

To discourage his affection for her, she refrained from replying, nodded her head in acknowledgment, and turned toward her father.

"Is there anything else you need?"

"No, my dear." He ate a spoonful of soup. "Very delicious."

Lady Averly curtsied before picking up her tray, returning to the kitchen, and adding it to the stack upon the shelf. The sight of a beautiful place setting on the center table helped to calm her nerves. The pewter plate was filled with a sampling of the evening meal and a neatly folded linen napkin placed to the side with a fork atop. Even though her family treated her like a servant, the staff always respected her like royalty. As she sat upon the stool, she looked to the floor for Harry, but he was absent from the tidbit or two of meat she would usually share from her plate. *Perhaps he's hunting mice.*

The women in the kitchen busied themselves with refilling pitchers of ale and wine and pulling more sweet cakes from the oven.

"Thank you, everyone. I appreciate your thoughtfulness, truly." She picked up her goblet and sipped the warm, red wine spiced with cinnamon and clove.

"Averly!"

Nearly choking on her wine, she returned her goblet to the table. Narrowing her eyes at the kitchen doorway, she dreaded answering the screeching summons. Begrudgingly, she rose from the stool and went to the Great Hall.

Guests had lowered their conversations to whispers as Lady Averly entered and wove between the backsides of men, making her way to the High Table once again.

Lady Miriam pushed her soup bowl forward.

"This is cold, and so is Alger's soup. Bring us another bowl and make certain it's hot this time."

Lady Averly peeked at her half-brother's bowl. He had yet to sample the soup. Glancing at the brat, he smiled and pushed mushy sweet cake through his teeth. She looked to her father for support, but he kept his eyes downcast at the food upon his plate. Pressing her lips together, she refrained from speaking as she glared at her stepmother and half-brother, picked up their bowls, and returned to the kitchen.

Throwing the contents of the bowls into the slop bucket, she ladled the last of the soup from the pot into the bowls, returned to the Great Hall, and dropped them upon the High Table causing some of the steaming soup to spill onto the tablecloth.

Lady Miriam's green eyes flared, and her mouth fell agape in response to her stepdaughter's impertinence.

"I can assure you, it's hot." She turned to her half-brother. "Alger, if you bother to eat the soup at all, do take care not to burn your tongue." Lady Averly pivoted swiftly and returned to her meal.

She plopped onto the stool and ate a bit of meat only to discover it was cold. Assuming her entire meal was likewise, she pushed her plate away and picked up her goblet.

Mina glanced at her lady as she transferred sweet cakes onto a trencher.

"My lady, you must eat."

Lady Averly swallowed a mouthful of wine hoping to numb her frustration.

"If it wasn't for Father, Harry, and you, I think I would run away."

"Run away? To where?"

"I don't know where. Anywhere but here. For as long as that hag is in charge, my prospect for happiness seems quite miserable and hopeless."

"Oh, my lady, you're only ten and seven. Things shall turn around. You'll see."

Chapter 5

A BRISK WIND whipped Lord Edwin's black wool cloak away from his body. He pulled it around himself and looked skyward at the threatening gray clouds as he walked to the gatehouse. *A storm is brewing.*

With daylight fading into darkness, it was imperative to close the entrance of the castle for the protection of those residing within.

Accompanied by his knight and his wolf, Lord Edwin entered the gatehouse.

The peasant men, who were eager to assist their lord, stepped aside to allow him to inspect the pulley systems of the portcullis and drawbridge.

A man stepped forward to report his assessment.

"It won't budge, my lord. The mechanisms are wedged in place and the chains are broken. More than likely it was the intention of the attackers to ensure the portcullis would remain open for their escape. If we were

32

to lower the portcullis, it will be difficult with so few men to lift it again. The chain must be repaired. With the blacksmith dead and his building in shambles, a quick repair is unlikely."

Rand stood in the doorway as if frozen. His ears perked toward a noise in the distance.

Lord Edwin knew little of the workings of the gatehouse, so he trusted the man's evaluation.

"We have no choice. The entry will have to remain open."

Sir Garrick stepped forward and scrutinized the sabotaged devices.

"We cannot close either of them?" The knight's concern was apparent.

Lord Edwin looked down at the stone floor in contemplation. He came to a simple solution and looked toward the men.

"A blockade in front of the opening would at least be a deterrent."

The men nodded their heads in agreement as one stepped forward.

"We'll gather what we can find and do our best, my lord."

"Very well." Lord Edwin exited the gatehouse. Sir Garrick and Rand followed.

Two men entered the bailey, leading an empty horse-drawn cart toward the stable. They had taken the bodies from the Keep and added them onto the growing pile of dead outside of the castle wall.

One of the men stopped and bowed respectfully.

"We buried your parents as best we could, my lord."

"Thank you." Lord Edwin planned to visit the graves and pay his respects later.

The trio followed behind the cart as they walked toward the Keep. Lord Edwin tried to recall each building as he passed its rubble. It was easy to distinguish where the blacksmith was located with its anvil protruding from the ash like a soldier refusing to yield.

"So much is ruined." Lord Edwin sighed.

His knight glanced at the young lord but remained silent. He had seen worse in his lifetime and knew all was not lost unless they were attacked while being defenseless.

The peasant men brought the cart to a stop next to the stable. Bryce came forward, unhitched the horse, and lead it inside for the night.

Noticing the stable roof dipped slightly at its center, Lord Edwin followed the stableboy for a closer inspection. He spotted a cracked beam and could see gray clouds through the holes where the roof was missing. Bryce and the men had managed to reconstruct the wall with whatever boards they could find suitable. *It'll have to do for now.*

The stableboy went to the well carrying an empty bucket as his lord exited.

"Bryce, we need a beam to support the center of the roof." Lord Edwin looked to the sky as the lad paused and looked toward his lord. "I think it may be best to put as many animals as you can into the stable. Overcrowd them if necessary. The little shelter it can give them will be better than none." He began walking toward the Keep.

"Yes, my lord." Bryce filled the bucket from the well. The peasant men, overhearing their lord's request, searched in the rubble for a suitable beam.

Noting the Keep's large doors hung askew, Lord Edwin and Sir Garrick examined the hinges. The thick iron was sheared in several places causing the doors to hang loosely from the stone wall.

Sir Garrick tapped on the wooden doors with the pommel of his sword to ensure they were solid before offering his assessment.

"It's beyond repair for tonight. The hinges will either need to be remade entirely or once we obtain a skilled blacksmith, he may be able to repair them. Until then, the best we can do is to close the doors as tightly as possible." He knew his solution gave those inside the Keep little protection should another attack occur. "Perhaps we should take turns at guard."

"I agree."

Rand preceded his master as the trio entered the Keep.

As the Lord of Tildenham and his knight stepped into the Great Hall, he saw a ladder leaning against the wall with a woman atop tearing down the charred remains of a tapestry.

Isabel looked up from the tabletop she was washing. She tossed the rag into the bucket of dirty water and went to her lord's side.

"My lord, I've taken inventory. They pillaged what they could, but in their haste, they failed to find the other storage room. With so few of us left, I believe we can get by on dry goods, cheese, and wine. Oh, there's also fruit in the barrels. They took all of the meat." Isabel waited for his reply.

"Thank you. I'll go hunting tomorrow to replenish what was taken. For tonight, just a simple meal will have to do."

"Yes, my lord." Isabel curtsied. She turned to a peasant woman, asked her to finish wiping down the tables, and went to the kitchen to ensure the village women were baking bread and reorganizing the storage room. She would instruct them to begin preparing the evening meal.

A clatter to his left drew Lord Edwin's attention. He watched as two women struggled to place his mother's carved wooden chair at the High Table. He went to the women's aid.

"Only one chair will be necessary." He placed his father's chair at the High Table, removed his mother's chair, and set it on the floor against the wall behind the dais.

The women bowed their heads as their faces blushed. One stepped forward.

"Our mistake, my lord."

"No apology necessary. Your effort is appreciated. Thank you."

The women curtsied and busied themselves elsewhere.

The blood-soaked rushes from the stone floor were stacked outside the Keep's doorway and would be taken to the pile of the dead in the morning. Once the floor was mopped, new rushes were spread to absorb any remaining dampness. A large fire was built in the fireplace to remove the chill from the room. The remaining tables and benches were turned upright and washed for the evening meal. With the day ending, ladders were set aside for the night with the intention of scrubbing the blackened walls in the new day's light. Women replaced the broken tallow candles in the candelabras while a young lad waited patiently, holding a stick with its tip afire. He handed it to a woman, who lit each taper, illuminating the room with a golden glow.

Once everyone in the bailey had entered the Keep for the evening, Lord Edwin and Sir Garrick closed and barred the Keep's broken doors.

The Lord of Tildenham paused inside the Great Hall and scanned the survivors, noting the few who lay on pallets recovering from their injuries. Sir Garrick stepped next to his lord and stood with his arms crossed over his chest and his legs shoulder length apart. He nodded his head in approval as he looked about the Great Hall.

"Much better, my lord. Quite cozy and clean."

"Yes, it will have to do for now." He looked at his mother's portrait over the fireplace. It had been straightened and hung properly.

Isabel emerged from the kitchen carrying a tray of wooden plates and goblets in one hand and a large wooden bowl of freshly baked bread in the other. Women, who had helped prepare the meal, followed with trays of cheese, cut apples, and pitchers of wine.

"I'm sorry, my lord. This is the best we could do for tonight." Isabel set the tray and bowl upon the end of a long wooden table.

Lord Edwin scanned the table.

"It looks wonderful and greatly appreciated. Thank you."

Everyone gathered around the table and waited for Lord Edwin to seat himself first.

Isabel filled two plates with food and went to place them upon the High Table.

"Isabel." Lord Edwin called, halting her progress, for he understood her intention.

She stopped and looked toward him.

"My lord?"

"Sir Garrick and I will be joining everyone at this table." He motioned toward the long table. "Including you, and those who helped prepare the meal." He knew the staff took their meals in the kitchen, but not tonight. It was necessary for everyone to feel safe and be together after such a tragic event. He lowered himself to a bench and Sir Garrick sat across from him. A woman came forward with two goblets, filled them with wine, and set them before the men.

The men, women, and children looked to one another before sitting hesitantly as instructed.

Isabel set the plates before her lord and knight. All remained uncomfortably silent as she handed a plate and goblet to each person before seating herself.

The pitchers of wine and trays were passed, tankards and plates filled, and whispers were shared between those who sat next to one another.

Sir Garrick leaned forward and spoke quietly.

"Perhaps you should give a word of encouragement to get us through this trying time, my lord."

The Lord of Tildenham considered his knight's suggestion, but no words came to mind.

"What should I say?"

"Something positive, uplifting."

Lord Edwin lifted his full tankard from the table and stood. Muttered conversations stopped, and all looked toward their lord as he began to speak.

"Many of us have lost loved ones. For reasons we do not understand, we've survived. Perhaps we've been left behind to rebuild, to make Tildenham great once again. I'm thankful and proud to join you at this very table, to share a meal as we reflect and celebrate the lives of those we've lost. Let's be encouraged by what we've accomplished today and will continue to do in the future. Godspeed to our loved ones who are no longer with us and may they watch over us from above as we continue our journey through life." He lifted his tankard in a toast, as did everyone at the table. Many nodded their head, and a few wiped a tear away from the corner of their eyes before Lord Edwin resumed his seat.

If anyone was uncomfortable sharing a table with royalty or felt confined by the Keep's walls, he had set them at ease. Conversations began to fill the room as they ate their meager meal.

Sir Garrick broke off a bit of bread.

"Well done, my lord." He tossed the crust into his mouth.

"Thank you."

"The bread is excellent. My compliments to the cooks." Sir Garrick raised his tankard in a toast and winked at the women.

Several of the women nodded, blushed, and smiled at the knight's kind words. They tilted their heads toward each other as they whispered and glanced in his direction.

For a man of his age, many would describe Sir Garrick as quite handsome with his charcoal hair and chestnut eyes. His devilish smile displayed pearly white teeth and caused dimples to form in his cheeks. He was tall with broad shoulders and muscular from years of wielding a heavy sword. It was a burning question among many of the women as to the reason such a fine man who had reached the age of a score and ten remained unmarried.

Lord Edwin glanced at the people sitting at the table as he reached for his goblet. *They seem content.* After taking a sip of wine, he paused with his mug in midair and looked toward the intimidating lord's chair at the High Table. However unprepared he may be, he had become the Lord of Tildenham with the survivors depending on his guidance and leadership. Setting his drink upon the table, his attention was drawn to the sound of someone clearing their throat.

The room grew quiet. A peasant man spoke the words many were thinking.

"My lord, with so few of us to work the fields, how will we plant enough crops to see us through next winter?"

Lord Edwin took the time to swallow the food in his mouth.

"I understand your concern. With the planting season only a month's time away, I will appeal to freeman from other kingdoms. Until they arrive, we'll focus on rebuilding the village for you and those who come to work the soil and help make Tildenham sustainable once again."

Many nodded in agreement with their lord before continuing with their meal.

"Again, well done." Sir Garrick picked up his mug and took a swig.

Encouraged by the compliment, Lord Edwin ventured to lay out his agenda.

"We must visit the mill tomorrow to ensure we have the lumber to rebuild. Before any disease can spread, the rushes must be added to the pile of dead and set afire. With so few of us, we can't afford to lose one person from any disease that may spread."

"I agree, my lord. We may need to send someone for seed for the fields. I assume what was saved for planting has been lost."

"I fear so as well." Lord Edwin was thankful he had enough coin to purchase what may be needed. He only hoped other kingdoms had ample seed to spare at market and freemen to work the fields.

Chapter 6

WITH THE EVENING meal ending, the servants of Holbrook removed the empty trenchers from the tables, took them to the kitchen, and tossed them into a bucket for the pigs' breakfast.

Lady Averly dipped the used mugs into a basin of steaming water and set them on a shelf upside down to dry.

A servant entered the kitchen carrying a tray of collected mugs. She set down on a nearby table.

"My lady, Lady Miriam has requested your presence."

Lady Averly sighed.

"Thank you." She wiped her wet hands on her overskirt and made her way through the crowded Great Hall. The devilish smirk on her stepmother's face made her leery as she approached the High Table.

Lady Miriam looked toward her husband before she spoke.

"Well, shall you tell her, or shall I?"

Those within the Great Hall paused in their conversations and servants stood still. Lady Averly looked from her stepmother to her father.

"Tell me what?"

Lord Burton glanced hesitantly at his wife and then to his daughter with an expression of sympathy masking his face.

Alger began to laugh and point his finger at his half-sister as he bit into another sweet cake.

Lord Burton opened his mouth to speak but paused in search of the proper words to sugarcoat his daughter's predicament. In his attempt to stall for time, he was interrupted by his impatient wife.

"We have accepted a rather generous offer for your betrothal, a very large sum indeed." Lady Miriam giggled and brought her hands together with a clap.

Lady Averly's mouth dropped open as she stared at her stepmother. Alger laughed louder.

"I knew she would be surprised, Mother."

Lady Averly found it difficult to breathe. *Are my ears deceiving me? Please, Father, it can't be true.* She stared at her father with her mouth still agape.

Unable to withstand his daughter's inquisition, he cast his line of vision downward to his tankard before taking a drink.

"Father? When and to whom?" Lady Averly recalled the countless conversations she had with him expressing her desire to know her husband's character and nature before committing to a marriage.

Lady Miriam answered for her husband.

"Oh, it doesn't matter. His family has accepted you as their son's bride while giving us a very large dowry."

"Father?" Lady Averly hoped he would confess the story to be false. His kind eyes reluctantly stared into hers.

"I'm sorry, my dearest, but the contract has been signed. I've been informed and reassured that you will find great pleasure in your new kingdom. Averly, I wish you every happiness with your husband." He sighed as if defeated. "More so than if you were to remain here." He glared at his wife, insinuating his reasoning.

Lady Averly looked back to her stepmother, who seemed quite pleased with herself as she smiled and chuckled. Lady Miriam lifted her tankard from the table and paused before taking a celebratory drink.

"Oh, and your wretched cat scratched Alger today. I had him killed so he can no longer hurt anyone." Lady Miriam kissed the chubby cheek of her son.

Glaring at her half-brother, Lady Averly noticed a tiny scratch on his right cheek. Knowing the child's mean disposition, she was certain Harry had lashed out in defense. Unable to keep her emotions in check any longer, angry tears welled in her eyes. Refusing to give her stepmother the pleasure of witnessing her crumbling composure, she turned abruptly and retreated to the kitchen. Safely inside the portal, she leaned against the stone wall, crossed her arms over her chest, and allowed her tears to silently cascade down her cheeks.

The women's conversations quieted as empathy filled their hearts for their mistress. Noticing the silence within the room, Lady Averly wiped the tears with her overskirt, grabbed several mugs from a tray, and resumed washing. There was little doubt in her mind that those within the room had overheard her announced misfortune.

Mina took dirty mugs from the tray, dunked them in the tub, and went to Lady Averly's side.

"My lady, don't give up hope. Perhaps your father is right." She tried to console as she placed the mugs upon the shelf to dry.

"She killed Harry." Tears spilled onto Lady Averly's cheeks. She grabbed more mugs, rinsed them, went to the shelf, and slammed them into place. Clenching her teeth, she turned to her friend. "My stepmother sold me to the highest bidder, but I'll show her."

The servants paused in their duties and glanced in the direction of their lady.

Mina scanned the room as she lowered her voice.

"What do you plan to do?"

Lady Averly waited until those within the kitchen returned to their duties before she whispered.

"To leave, tonight, and ensure she never receives a single coin."

"Oh, my lady, do not dare."

"Give me a good reason why."

"It's too dark to travel during the night, especially for a lone woman. Your horse could stumble, or you may fall victim to highwaymen. No telling what they'd do to you. Oh, and you haven't set foot outside the castle walls for over a decade."

"That's more than one reason." Lady Averly scowled. "I can keep to the woods, remain out of sight."

"But, where will you go? You've no destination or arrangements."

"At this point, I don't care where I go or the lack of arrangements. All I know is that I must leave. I've had enough of my stepmother, my bratty half-brother, and their vindictive, demeaning treatment. I'm a lady, not a servant. No offense."

"None taken, but you shouldn't go alone. It's unsafe."

"I don't want anyone to suffer the wrath of my stepmother if, heaven forbid, I'm caught and returned. I must do this alone. Perhaps I can pass as a freeman, a servant, and find employment. With any luck, I'll find a place to hide away and never return." She wiped the tears away from her cheeks.

Mina displayed a hesitant smile. Anyone involved in her mistress's escape would be severely punished, if not drawn and quartered. The cook stared into Lady Averly's determined bloodshot eyes.

"I can see your mind is set and you'll not be persuaded otherwise. I can hardly blame you. Let me gather some supplies for your journey. I'll have Emmet ready your horse."

"Thank you, Mina." Lady Averly grasped her friend's forearm conveying her appreciation.

Chapter 7

A GUST OF wind sputtered snow through the casing of the window within Lady Averly's tiny chamber. The last of winter refused to relinquish its grip on the land and allow spring to decorate the earth with a carpet of green.

She pulled her mother's portrait from beneath the bed. Her stepmother threatened to destroy it if it was displayed upon the wall. Lady Averly untied the twine, removed the oilcloth, and angled the painting toward the single flickering candle on the rustic table. It was true. She resembled her mother, even down to her golden locks of hair. She traced the outline of her mother's chin before returning the portrait under the bed and dressing in several layers of her warmest peasant attire. She lifted her skirts and strapped a dirk to her calf before folding her cloak over her arm and picked up her gloves. Lady Averly looked to the crude wooden bed with its lumpy mattress and recalled the countless times she had changed its straw, the small table below the window with its lonely chair, and the iron pot she filled with embers to heat it during the winter months. She blew out the taper before lifting the bolt on the door and easing it open. Pausing in the shadowed hallway, she listened for footsteps to ensure she was alone before closing the door hesitantly with the hope the latch would make only the slightest of clicks as it was pulled shut.

Candles atop tall candelabras flickered as she passed through the hallway. Her soft-soled boots made it easy to move silently past the solar and through the corridors as she walked toward the sally port.

As she drew near the door, she saw Mina's distraught face illuminated by the single lit taper she was holding.

"My lady, the weather has taken a turn for the worse. I wish you'd reconsider."

Afraid her friend's voice may have been heard by someone, Lady Averly glanced over her shoulder. The hallway remained empty. Guilt seeped into her mind as she thought of her father. *Will he miss me?* Leaving him in the care of her stepmother was unavoidable. *It was his decision to marry her.* Lady Averly took a deep breath, let it out slowly easing her conscious, and turned back to Mina.

"No, I must go now. They'll not expect me to leave during such a storm. It may help to delay their search and give me more time to distance myself from Holbrook."

Mina exhaled, knowing she had done her best to dissuade her lady and friend.

"Very well, I've packed some food and wine. Emmet has strapped it to your saddle." Mina watched as her mistress put on her cloak and gloves before embracing her friend farewell. "Oh, do take care."

"I will, I promise. Tell Emmet to report my horse missing from the stable. I don't want him implicated in any way." Lady Averly flipped the fur-lined hood atop her head as Mina pulled open the sally port. They shielded their faces against the stinging sleet whirling through the door.

Emmet looked upward to the open portal. The lad's teeth chattered as he gripped the bridle tightly to steady the chestnut mare. He had thoughtfully positioned the horse beneath the sally port and waited as his lady settled upon the saddle.

"Thank you, Emmet." Lady Averly wrapped her cloak around her, clasped the reins, and encouraged Nelly forward into the blustery winter night.

"You're welcome, my lady." The stableboy boosted himself up through the doorway and into the welcoming warmth of the Keep. Mina watched her mistress disappear into the blinding snow before closing the door and barring it shut.

Lady Averly peeked beneath the edge of her hood in search of the road lined with evergreens, but all she saw was whirling snow. A shiver ran up her spine as the wind whipped her cloak away from her lap. Retrieving its edge, she pulled it across her body and tucked it under her thigh. Lowering her hood over her face, she trusted her horse to find her way.

As if Nelly shared the same desire as her rider, she lowered her head and punched her hooves through the crusted snow, trudging her way across the open field toward the road where the trees offered shelter.

Neither traveler knew where they were going but pushed forward through the moonless night, distancing themselves from Holbrook as the snow continued to fall, covering them with a blanket of white.

Chapter 8

TILDENHAM'S PEASANTS ROTATED the duty of adding logs to the enormous Great Hall fireplace to keep the room cozy and warm throughout the night. Many found it difficult to sleep with the wind whistling through the cracks of the Keep's doors and hallways like moaning spirits.

The clicking of Rand's toenails on the hallway stone floor forewarned his master. Lord Edwin opened his eyes and sighed as he lay in bed. He looked to the bedchamber window. The snow continued to fall from the gray morning sky. As the rhythmic clicking stopped, he looked to the doorway where the wolf was crouched with his tail wagging.

Lord Edwin sat up in bed.

"Don't you dare."

Ignoring his master's playful warning, Rand dashed across the room and leaped onto the bed to greet his master with several sloppy licks to his face.

"Oh, you win." Lord Edwin rose and dressed for the day.

Sleepy-eyed survivors watched the Lord of Tildenham and his wolf descend the staircase. A morning meal was brought forth from the kitchen. Everyone sat together and ate. Lord Edwin leaned across the table toward Sir Garrick.

"The stable's roof was weakened during the attack and the weight of the snow could cause it to give way."

Bryce joined the conversation.

"My lord, I'll check the roof and see to the animals."

Lord Edwin looked toward the eager lad who sat a few seats down from Sir Garrick.

"I appreciate your offer, Bryce, and the earnestness in which you perform your duty, but I fear the depth of the snow may be difficult for even me to reach the stable."

Rand nudged his master's elbow, hoping to receive a portion from his meal. Lord Edwin gave him a piece of cheese, which he gobbled up quickly.

"Yes, my lord." Bryce accepted the compliment graciously. He and the men had propped the roof as best they could. However, he agreed with his lord's concern for the animals.

It was close to midday when those within the Great Hall watched their lord, knight, and a few men exit the room and remove the bar of the Keep's door. Sir Garrick placed the palms of his hands on one edge of the door while a man held the opposite edge in place by gripping the bracket for the bar. Sir Garrick pushed, but the portal remained closed. Men stepped forward and placed their shoulders on the door.

"Together now." Lord Edwin took his place alongside the men. "Push!" The relentless storm opposed their intrusion.

"Again!"

A flurry of snow swirled through the crack as it creaked open. Sir Garrick peeked outside.

"My lord, the snow is nearly halfway up the door."

The men continued to push until it widened enough to allow someone to pass.

Bryce stood at the end of the hallway watching helplessly.

"My lord, I should go. I can fit easily through the doorway opening."

Lord Edwin grabbed a cloak from a nearby hook on the wall, donned it, and signaled the lad to come forward. He grasped the stableboy by the shoulder.

"Put some wood on the fire while I'm gone. I'm certain I'll need a good warming upon my return." He gave Bryce's shoulder a grateful squeeze. "Men, close the door behind me." He ordered as he stepped into the snowy blizzard.

Raising his hands to shield his face from the stinging snow, he lumbered through the knee-high accumulation toward the stable. Lord Edwin kicked aside a drift that blocked the door of the stable, unbolted it, and pulled it open. He backed into the stable and closed the door. He turned and nearly bumped into the rump of a horse. The shelter was crowded with cows, sheep, pigs, and horses. The ducks and geese were nestled in the straw in one corner. A dusting of snow covered the backs of the animals as the wind pushed it through the gaps between the boarded walls and roof.

Shielding his eyes from the sprinkling snow, Lord Edwin scanned the repairs to the roof. The chickens in the rafters clucked nervously as they peered down at him. He tested the added support beam. It remained solid under the additional weight of the snow. Most of the animals seemed comfortable, and perhaps thankful, to be within the confinement of the small, protective space. *At least they're out of the storm.*

Lord Edwin broke the layers of ice in the buckets to ensure they had water to drink. He opened a burlap sack of grain and dumped small piles of it onto the stable floor. The supply of hay for the horses, goats, and cows seemed adequate.

He patted Fulton's rump before returning to the door and pushing it open with his shoulder. The wind slammed it shut behind him. He replaced the bar to ensure it remained closed. With the wind at his back, he was forced to quicken his steps toward the Keep. Lord Edwin pounded on the door with his fist and squeezed through the portal as it opened. He shook the snow from his cloak and looked to Bryce, who was staring at him with askance eyes for his report.

"The repairs to the stable are holding. The animals are safe and still have food and water. Well done."

The stableboy breathed a sigh of relief and smiled with pride. Some of the men tousled his hair and patted him on the back.

Lord Edwin hung the cloak on the peg before turning to his knight.

"The snow is knee high and the drifts are much higher. The wind has yet to calm. No sense going out to hunt. The deer will be bedded down. It's best if we can get by with whatever food is in storage."

"I agree, my lord."

The Lord of Tildenham and his knight joined the others in the Great Hall. Bryce added another log to the fire and looked toward his lord, who nodded in appreciation. Happy and content, many within the room busied themselves with cleaning, sewing, and entertaining the children.

*   *   *

The resonant chattering of her teeth forced Lady Averly to open her sapphire eyes, widening them to bring the unfamiliar roadside into focus. The gray sky above indicated it was daylight, but which day? Her nonstop escape from Holbrook had been a day, or maybe two or three. She positioned herself on the saddle to relieve her aching bottom.

The wind continued to swirl around them as they followed the road, but it no longer possessed the stinging bite as before. *Did I doze off? God, please let me be a long distance from Holbrook.*

Unable to feel her extremities, she glanced at her hand to see if it was still holding the reins and her feet to verify they were in the stirrups. She noticed the snow had blown away from the dirt road exposing a rough coating of ice.

A gust of wind whipped her hood off her head. She reached to replace it as Nelly lost her footing and fell to the ground.

Taking a moment to realize what had happened, Lady Averly lay on the road staring at the grayish sky. Breathing deeply, she tried to force air back into her aching lungs.

Nelly pulled on the reins in her mistress's hand as she struggled to regain her footing. Fearing her horse would kick or step on her while attempting to stand, Lady Averly released the reins, rolled away from her horse, and managed to find her footing within the snow on the side of the road.

"Whoa." She patted Nelly's neck until her horse stopped struggling and lay upon the ground with her legs folded beneath her. Lady Averly held onto the mare's mane as she stepped cautiously toward the horse's head.

"You're tired." Lady Averly stroked Nelly's face. "So am I." Glancing up and down the road, she saw it was empty of travelers. "I wonder where we are. Wherever it is, we better keep moving."

Once she was certain she had her footing, Lady Averly pulled on the reins, encouraging her horse to stand. Nelly whinnied as she rose to her feet and limped as she stepped forward.

"Oh, no. Don't be injured." Lady Averly led her mare to the side of the road. She ran her hand down each leg before lifting it to search for a stone in Nelly's hooves. Unable to discover the source of Nelly's lameness, she examined each hind quarter and discovered blood dripping from a cut on the left side. Lady Averly searched the area where they had fallen and spotted a sharp shard of ice with its edge tipped with blood.

I need to find a safe place for us to rest. She peered down the road from which she came. Thankfully, it was void of travelers.

Assuming her horse should no longer bear a rider, she led Nelly along the side of the road where they were assured to keep their footing in the snow.

They had walked for several hours when Lady Averly thought she heard distant hoofbeats. She halted her horse abruptly, listened, but discovered only silence. In her tired state, she wondered if the sound she heard was Nelly's echoing gait. Her attention was drawn to her mare's ears as they flipped backward and forward like a loose shutter. *An approaching rider.* Her heartbeat quickened. *We need to get off the road.* She yanked on the reins, hurried her step, and searched the roadside until she spied a narrow pathway veering into the woods. Wading through the knee-deep snow, she pulled Nelly to her side, turned, and kicked the snow to cover their trail. She paused to listen. The sound of hoofbeats confirmed an approaching rider.

She scanned the snow-dusted winter foliage for a place to hide and spied a group of evergreens a good distance down the pathway. Tugging the reins to encourage Nelly forward, she trudged toward the greenery, hoping it would provide the necessary cover for them, that is if she could reach it in time. With her horse in tow, they wove between leafless bushes and trees as the sound of hoofbeats grew louder. Lady Averly looked over her shoulder as she pulled on the reins, tripped, and braced herself with her hands as she fell forward. Rising, she ignored the snow that clung to her body and forced her legs forward. Her breathing labored as panic became the adrenaline she needed for the remaining distance. Shielding her face from the evergreen branches, she pushed through the boughs and entered a clearing within the circle of pines. As her horse joined her, the branches closed behind Nelly's rump, concealing them safely inside.

Lady Averly listened as she stroked her horse's velvet nose to keep Nelly quiet. The hoofbeats of the rider's horse were close. She prayed to remain undiscovered as her mare's ears rotated toward the rhythmic sound. Lady Averly drew her dagger from its sheath and readied for an attack. *I'm not going back to Holbrook.* She held her breath and listened. Nelly pulled away from her mistress and began to eat the needles of the evergreen. With her horse showing little concern for the hoofbeats as they faded, she assumed they had remained undetected.

Returning her weapon, she looked to the tops of the trees swaying in the wind as she brushed the snow from her cloak. Placing her hand on her grumbling stomach, Lady Averly untied the leather pouch Mina had packed with food, parted the branches of a pine tree, and entered the sheltered darkness to its trunk. She looped the reins on her wrist while Nelly pawed the ground and nibbled on the sprouting spring grass.

The brown needles beneath the umbrella of branches were absent of snow and provided a soft cushion for Lady Averly to sit upon. She leaned against the trunk, opened the pouch, and peeked inside to find a flask of wine, a loaf of bread, cheese, dried meat, and a few sweet cakes. *Oh, Mina, you are such a dear.* She found an apple at the bottom and tossed it to her horse. Nelly bit into it with a resounding crunch.

Lady Averly wrapped her cloak around her tightly and buried her feet in the bed of dry needles for warmth. In comparison to the noisy chatter echoing from the Great Hall of Holbrook, she welcomed the sounds of nature as she dined. *I hope the worst of the storm has passed. Heaven knows if I'm able to survive much more of its wickedness.*

She returned the uneaten food to the pouch and laced it shut. The red wine soothed her concerns as she leaned her head back against the trunk of the tree and closed her eyes.

Chapter 9

LADY MIRIAM LOOKED up from her embroidering to see a servant girl enter through the open solar door carrying their midday meal on a tray. It dawned on her that her stepdaughter, who normally brought their meal, had failed to visit them for the past several days and was absent from the evening meals too.

"Where's Averly?"

Lord Burton looked up from his account book at the servant. He tried to recall the last time he saw her too.

"Is she ill?"

"I don't know, my lord and lady. I'm just doing as I'm told." The servant set the tray of food and two tankards of spiced wine on the small table next to the Lady of Holbrook, who pulled her needle through the cloth.

Lady Miriam selected a scone and nibbled on its corner.

"Tell her to come here at once."

"Yes, my lady." The servant curtsied before leaving the room, closed the door behind her, and quickened her pace to the kitchen. She rushed toward Mina while wringing her hands in her overskirt.

"Lady Miriam is asking for Lady Averly. What shall we do?"

Mina had informed the kitchen staff of their mistress's decision and swore them to secrecy. Everyone had covered for her for as long as possible. They hoped to allow her time to distance herself from Holbrook, but it looked as if time had run out.

"I'll go and tell them." Mina washed her hands and tidied her hair. The women in the kitchen watched with concern as the head cook left to break the news to the Lord and Lady of Holbrook.

Mina tried to rehearse what she would say to them as she ascended the staircase and walked hesitantly toward the solar. She stopped before the closed door, took a deep breath, and exhaled before knocking.

"Enter."

The command was muffled. Mina opened the door and stepped into the room.

Crumbs fell out of Lady Miriam's mouth as she spoke.

"Who are you?"

"My lady, my name is Mina. I'm the head cook."

Lord Burton closed the account book before inspecting the tray of food as if uninterested in the cook's reply.

"Where's my daughter?"

"My lord, she's not here."

Lady Miriam picked up a tankard to wash down the food in her mouth.

"Well, that's obvious. Where is she?"

Mina hesitated in her reply. *The direct approach would be best.*

"She's gone."

Lady Miriam choked on her wine. She coughed and gasped for air as she returned her drink to the table. Her eyes began to tear. Her face reddened.

"Gone?" She cleared her throat to remedy the hoarseness in her voice. "Gone where?"

"I don't know, my lady."

Lord Burton looked toward the cook.

"Has she gone on an errand?" He selected a cut of meat from the tray, placed it into his mouth, and looked toward the cook for her reply as he chewed.

Mina sighed.

"No, my lord, she's left Holbrook. It's my understanding that her plans are to never return."

"But she must return!" Lady Miriam sprang from the chair and turned to her husband. "The dowry for the betrothal will be lost!"

Lord Burton held up the palm of his hand to his wife in a request for silence and addressed the cook.

"Mina, when did she leave?"

"The other night, during the storm, my lord."

Lord Burton's eyebrows drew together.

"Do you know why she left?"

"There were many reasons, my lord." Mina glanced toward Lady Miriam before continuing. "But I believe the betrothal may have pushed her to the point of making the drastic and desperate decision to leave Holbrook."

"Well, she has no say in the matter. That's for us to decide." Lady Miriam began pacing the room.

Lord Burton rose from his chair and looked out the frosted solar window. The storm had calmed. *Could Averly have survived? Could she have found shelter?* He looked to his wife.

"Calm yourself, my dear. I'll send a search party to retrieve her." He directed his attention to the cook. "Thank you, Mina. That will be all."

Lady Miriam glared at the cook.

"What do you mean 'that will be all'? It's obvious she aided Averly. She should be punished!"

Lord Burton ignored his wife.

"That will be all, Mina."

"Yes, my lord." The head cook curtsied before turning to leave the room. Mina exhaled as she stepped into the hallway and closed the door. *That went well. Oh,*

I wish Averly could have seen her stepmother's face. She chuckled as she made her way to the kitchen.

Mina's entrance was met by inquisitive stares. Their questions would have to wait. She redirected the staff before returning to the goose she was plucking. With the meal preparations running smoothly, her thoughts drifted to her friend. *I pray she's in good company and will remain undiscovered.*

A shiver went down her spine, for the thought of Lady Miriam's vengeance upon her friend's return would be severe. *Lady Averly's future would be bleak indeed. She may be better off dead.* The cook made the sign of the cross on her body before continuing to pull feathers. She would instruct the staff to eavesdrop on conversations to obtain information about Lady Averly's fate.

Chapter 10

LADY AVERLY'S EYES snapped open as her body rocked back and forth. Momentarily disoriented, she soon realized Nelly was tugging on the reins in search of food.

"How much time have I wasted?" She grabbed the pouch of leftover food, crawled out from beneath the branches, and looked skyward. It was still daylight. The snow had stopped, and the wind seemed to be subsiding. *We need to find shelter.*

She checked Nelly's wound. It was crusted with blood. Lady Averly tied the pouch to her saddle before pulling the reins and leading her horse out of the evergreens. She climbed atop, decided to avoid the icy road, and follow the trail to wherever it would lead them.

*   *   *

With their quivers filled with arrows and strapped to their backs, Lord Edwin and Sir Garrick carried their longbows and waded through the snow toward the stable. Rand followed in their footsteps.

Bryce stood in the doorway with their readied war horses.

"At least the deer will be easy to track." Sir Garrick strapped his longbow to his saddle. "That is, as long as the weather holds." He looked to the threatening sky.

"The snow is quite deep. Let's hope they're able to move." Lord Edwin finished attaching his longbow to his saddle and climbed atop Fulton.

Hoping for fresh venison, Bryce chimed in, "If they're hungry, they may be forced to do so, my lord." He released his hold on the bridles as Sir Garrick climbed atop his horse.

Lord Edwin nodded to the stableboy as he reined his horse.

"Let's hope they're hungry then." He headed toward the gatehouse with Rand leading the way. Men were able to clear an opening in the blockade for them to pass.

The stableboy watched the small hunting party of three depart.

"Good luck my lord, Sir Garrick!"

Both men raised their hand as a silent acknowledgment to the stableboy's farewell.

Bryce grabbed the edge of the stable door, closed it tightly, and returned to his duties.

*   *   *

Lady Averly continued to scan the thick trees, underbrush, and evergreens for a hunter's shack as she directed her horse to follow the path that seemed endless. She looked to the sky fearing darkness would soon fall, forcing them to spend another night in the cold.

As her mare crested a small hill, a gray wolf stepped from the woods onto the path, locked his yellow eyes upon them, and growled.

Nelly tossed her head upward, rearing in fright. Unable to stay in the saddle, Lady Averly tumbled to the ground and landed face down in the snow. She lifted her head, brushed the snow away from her eyes, and watched her horse disappear into the woods. The wolf curled its lips, displaying sharp white teeth, and lowered his head as it took a step toward her. Lady Averly's heartbeat quickened as the canine inched closer. She rose to her hands and knees before standing cautiously. She scanned the snow along the edge of the path, searching for Nelly's hoofprints and found them a step or two forward to her left. When the wolf paused momentarily, she darted into the woods.

71

Following Nelly's tracks, she ignored the leafless branches scratching her face as she pushed her legs through the snow. Lady Averly looked over her shoulder hoping to distance herself from the wolf but discovered she was alone. She turned and walked backward, slowing her pace while searching the woods for the beast. Her feet were knocked out from beneath her as she fell over a snow-covered log and landed on her back. Her head hit something with a resounding thud. Darkness seeped into her line of vision. She lay motionless in the clearing while attempting to focus on the cloudy sky and catch her breath.

Lady Averly turned her head to the side, reached beneath her hood, and touched the rising lump. *Oh, am I bleeding?* She put her hand before her face. It was absent of blood.

Her peripheral vision caught a shadowed movement. Afraid the wolf may have found her, she rotated her head hesitantly toward it. Her vision blurred momentarily before refocusing on a woman in a dark blue gown sitting upon a limestone bench. The woman's violet-blue eyes stared at her and a smile appeared on her kind face.

"*All is as it should be.*"

Lady Averly heard every word the woman said even though her lips remained still. Trying to clear the fuzziness from her mind, she squeezed her eyes shut and opened them wide before staring at the woman who looked at something above Lady Averly's head.

Tilting her head backward to follow the woman's line of sight, Lady Averly ignored the sharp pain as the lump on her head pressed against the rectangle stone base. Upon it stood a towering angel with its wings partially unfolded, arms outstretched, and gentle face staring down at her. Her body tensed momentarily before she realized it was a statue.

A resinous growl to her right announced the arrival of the wolf. Lady Averly looked to the woman for help, but the bench was empty. As the wolf stepped toward her, she stood uneasily, backed away from the advancing beast, and into the statue's protective arms.

"Rand! Enough!"

The wolf froze in place. His growling ceased, but he continued to stare at her.

Lady Averly glanced in the direction of the tall man who stood on the edge of the woods. He held Nelly's reins. As he pushed his way through the saplings, a branch caught the edge of his black cloak revealing his forest green tunic. He kicked aside a drift of snow with his knee-high black boots and walked into the center of the clearing. His curly brunette hair tousled in the breeze and his hazel eyes seemed to question her reason for being in such a place. She noted the longbow strapped over his shoulder. *A hunter.*

"Come."

Lady Averly wondered if the man was addressing her before watching the wolf join his master on the opposite side of the clearing.

"He means no harm." Lord Edwin patted Rand's shoulder and looked about. "I forgot about this place. Mother often came here. It was her sanctuary away from the chaos of the Keep."

Ah, royalty. Lady Averly turned away from the statue and took a step backward. She stared at the angel's face. Its expression seemed solemn and forlorn.

"I can see why. It's lovely." She touched the throbbing bump on her head.

He noted her peasant clothing and assumed she was one of the villagers who had survived the attack. However, the expensive cloak she was wearing was of a quality owned by royalty.

"You have a lovely cloak."

Lady Averly looked to her garment and groaned inwardly at her mistake in wearing it. She failed to realize it would raise suspicion.

"I didn't steal it if that's what you're implying. It was a gift." She told the truth, for her father had given it to her.

He knew the cloak had never belonged to his mother and accepted her explanation with a nod of his head. *A gift from whom.*

"It matters not." Noting her bluish lips and flushed cheeks, he assumed she had hidden somewhere since the attack. "I'm pleased you're alive."

Lady Averly was unsure of what to say in reply. She nodded her head and remained silent.

"Well, we need to return to the Keep where you can warm yourself and have something to eat." He steadied her horse and cupped his hands to boost her into the saddle.

As she drew closer, she noted his clothing trimmed with gold thread. *Royalty.* His face was sincere. She placed her foot into his hands and soon found herself atop Nelly.

Lord Edwin led her horse through the woods with the wolf loyally walking by his side. They came to a pathway where an ebony stallion was tied to a tree. He handed the reins to her, untied Fulton, and climbed atop. Lord Edwin searched the woods.

"I was with Sir Garrick. We separated to hunt. Perhaps he has returned ahead of us." He reined his horse and led the way down the trail.

Emerging from the fringe of the woods, they crossed an open field and approached the charred remains of the village. Lady Averly reined Nelly to a stop. Her mouth fell agape.

"What happened?" She saw where buildings once stood, but now it was nothing more than ash and rubble amongst the snow. The castle's walls were scarred with black soot. *Where has he taken me? What kingdom is this?*

Lord Edwin turned in his saddle to see the reason the woman had reined her horse. Her face was masked with disbelief. He directed Fulton in a full circle to stand parallel to her horse and sighed.

"I was away at the time and was told barbarians were responsible for the attack." He encouraged Fulton forward.

Lady Averly touched her heels to Nelly's underbelly to follow.

Lord Edwin glanced at her profile as her horse came alongside Fulton.

"There are only a few dozen or so men, women, and children who survived. Until the village can be cleared and rebuilt, you will join the others and reside in the Keep."

They directed their horses through the village at a slow pace. Lady Averly tried to identify where structures once stood and averted her eyes from the snow-covered pile of dead in the distance.

"My father used to say, 'Even during this difficult time, we must remain optimistic and believe our kingdom shall prosper once again.'" Lord Edwin looked toward her and shrugged his shoulder. "In truth, we have no other choice."

They exited the village, crossed the drawbridge, and entered the bailey.

Lady Averly tried to imagine the kingdom's magnificence prior to the attack as she observed what was left of the shops within the castle walls.

Bryce came forward from the stable as the pair reined their horses. He grasped Nelly's bridle and patted her nose.

"My lord, this isn't one of our horses." His blue eyes scanned the full length of the mare. "My, she's a beauty though."

The Lord of Tildenham dismounted and gave Fulton a pat on the rump before stepping toward Lady Averly's horse. Unassisted, his destrier entered the stable, eager for his bucket of oats.

Lord Edwin noticed the dried blood on the hind quarter of the mare. He paused to touch the wounded area before looking to Lady Averly for an explanation.

"She fell onto a chunk of ice."

Bryce looked to where his lord stood.

"I'll see to it, my lord."

"Thank you, Bryce." Lord Edwin helped Lady Averly from her horse. "You failed to introduce yourself. Your name please."

She took a step backward to look up to his hazel eyes that waited for her reply. *What hurt will it do to tell him my name?* She decided her title would remain a secret.

"Averly."

"Well, Averly, go into the Keep and warm yourself by the fire."

She curtsied and turned toward the large door of what she assumed was the Keep.

Lord Edwin admired the elegance and grace in her stride as she walked away. He returned his attention to the stableboy, who had taken Nelly's reins where they rested upon the saddle, pulled them over the horse's head, and walked to the rear of the mare to examine the wound.

"Bryce, has Sir Garrick returned?"

The freckle-faced stableboy pulled his red hair aside to examine Nelly's wound before untying the satchel from the saddle and handing it to Lord Edwin.

"Yes, my lord, and he brought back a large buck."

"Good, very good. He had better luck than I at providing meat for our meal tonight." He patted the mare on the rump as he passed behind Nelly. *However, I believe I've outdone him by returning with a wayward citizen of Tildenham, and one who is quite beautiful as well.*

Rand was in a playful mood and pranced in front of his master as if trying to block his way.

Lord Edwin crouched, spread his palms wide, and bounced from side to side. The wolf growled playfully and turned his head toward each hand, anticipating which palm would touch his head first.

Lady Averly stood before the threshold of the Keep. The door was closed. She turned to see what was upsetting the wolf and grinned at its playful antics with his master.

Lord Edwin touched the side of Rand's head before looking into the woman's sapphire blue eyes and smiling.

Lady Averly's grin faded as she became self-conscious of his hazel eyes staring into hers. She turned away and knocked on the door. A peasant man opened the portal and stepped aside, allowing her to enter. She smiled in appreciation and walked into the hallway. The peasant raised his hand toward her in a silent offer to take her cloak. She pulled it closer to her body.

"No thank you. I'd rather wear it until I'm warmed."

Conversations echoed from the end of the hallway. She hoped a warm fire awaited her in what she assumed was the Great Hall.

Lord Edwin tapped Rand's head with his right and then his left avoiding the snap of his jowls. Grabbing Rand's head with both hands, he messed his hair, released, and clapped his hands together.

"Let's go." Lord Edwin ran into the Keep. Rand scampered after his master.

Chapter 11

LADY AVERLY STEPPED from the hallway into the warmth of the Great Hall. She lowered her hood revealing her golden blonde hair, glanced around the large room, and inhaled its fresh clean scent. Her attention was drawn to ladders against the stone walls. The women atop were scrubbing the blackened scars of where she assumed a tapestry was formerly displayed. She was pleased to see men holding the base of each ladder to ensure the safety of those at the top. A staircase to the left led to the second floor with a balcony overlooking the room. An old woman, the storyteller, sat in a corner with children sitting on the floor around her. She noticed the High Table on the raised dais with its lonely wooden chair. *Strange, only one.* Centered on the opposite wall was a grand fireplace. Its intricately carved stone mantel and warm crackling fire beckoned her forward.

Lord Edwin stepped beside her.

"There's an empty bench by the fire." He nodded his head toward the vacant seat.

She looked up into his face as Rand brushed against her cloak on his way to the kitchen with the hope of receiving a bit of meat. A woman stepped forward and accepted the satchel from Lord Edwin before entering the kitchen.

"Thank you." Lady Averly removed her gloves, approached the empty bench, and exhaled as she sat. She held her stiff, frigid hands toward the warmth of the flickering flames. The oil portrait hanging over the mantel seemed to stare back at her. The woman was dressed in a lovely deep blue gown decorated with an intricate design of black beading. Her eyes were a violet-blue and her hair the color of charcoal. *She seems familiar. A guest at Holbrook perhaps?*

Lady Averly closed her eyes as the warmth of the fire seeped into her bones and her weary body relaxed. A tap upon her shoulder forced her to lift her head upward and look at the kind, wrinkled face of a peasant woman, who was holding a tankard of hot spiced red wine before her.

"Thank you." She cupped the warm mug between her hands, brought it to her lips, and sipped the brew as the woman nodded her head and left.

A little girl approached Lady Averly and sat next to her on the bench.

"What's your name?" The child tilted her head to one side as she watched the mug tilt upward.

Lowering the mug to her lap, Lady Averly looked into the big brown eyes of the little girl who was the picture of innocence with her tousled blonde hair and worn clothing.

"My name is Averly. What's your name?"

"Glenna."

"How old are you, Glenna?"

"Four. My Mommy and Daddy are in heaven."

"I'm certain they're at peace. A wise woman once told me, our loved ones are always watching over us even though we can't see them." Lady Averly thought it was best to change the morbid subject. "How do you like staying in this big room?"

"I like my house better. The bad men burned it."

"Why?"

The little girl shrugged her shoulders.

"Don't know." Glenna brushed the fur on Lady Averly's hood. "It's soft."

Lady Averly took another sip of the wine. Her shoulders ached. In fact, her whole body ached. She looked to the hunter, who chatted with another man, possibly a knight.

"Who are those men?"

Glenna looked in the implied direction.

"Oh, that's our new lord, Lord Edwin. The bad men killed his parents too. The other man is Sir Garrick."

Uncertain of which kingdom she had trespassed, she pressed further for information.

"I'm sorry. My head is a bit fuzzy." Lady Averly tried to make light of her lack of knowledge. "What is the name of this kingdom?"

Glenna assumed Lady Averly may have lived in the opposite end of the village where she seldom played.

"Fuzzy, that's funny. It's Tildenham, remember?"

"Yes, now I remember. Thank you, Glenna." Lady Averly watched the lord and his knight converse. They appeared to be close friends.

The little girl displayed a kind smile before getting off the bench.

"You're welcome." She joined the children on the floor and listened to the storyteller.

A chill sent a shiver through Lady Averly's body. She tried to steady the quivering mug as she brought it to her lips. Goose pimples puckered her skin, yet she felt warm, very warm and the lids of her eyes became heavy.

"Dear, are you well?"

Lady Averly blinked lethargically and looked up into an aged, round face framed by gray wispy hair. It was the storyteller.

"I'm not sure."

The elderly woman placed her arthritic hand beneath Lady Averly's chin, the other on her forehead, and tilted her face upward to examine her eyes.

"Oh, my dear, your eyes are glassy. I believe you have a fever. Perhaps you've caught a chill." The old woman lowered her hands, looked to her lord, and walked away.

Lady Averly watched as the storyteller approached Lord Edwin and waited patiently for a break in the men's conversation before speaking. She returned her gaze to the flickering flames and took another sip of wine. With little food in her stomach, the drink made her head feel light and detached. She wanted to close her eyes and sleep.

As the men's conversation ended, the Lord of Tildenham and his knight looked toward the storyteller.

"Yes, Patrice." Lord Edwin gave the woman his undivided attention.

"My lord, the young woman by the fireplace is ill. She has a fever."

Lord Edwin stared at Lady Averly as he tilted his head toward the storyteller.

"Do you know her?"

"She's a stranger to me, my lord, most likely not from our village." Patrice glanced toward Lady Averly.

Lord Edwin recalled the way she carried herself, the fine cloak, and the unknown horse. He suspected she may have a connection to royalty, but from where, and why was she dressed in peasant attire? Perhaps she was a prisoner left behind after the attack.

"Please ask Isabel to ready a chamber, one with a fireplace in order to keep the room warm."

"Yes, my lord." Patrice curtsied slightly before heading to the kitchen.

Sir Garrick crossed his arms over his chest as he stared at Lady Averly's back.

"I hope she isn't contagious."

Lord Edwin glanced at his knight before drawing a conclusion.

"Perhaps she hid in the woods during the attack and, God willing, endured the wickedest of weather. More than likely she's just caught a chill."

A pair of women crossed the Great Hall and ascended the staircase to the bedchambers above. Lord Edwin assumed the cast iron pot carried by one of the women contained hot coals to start a fire within the bedchamber's fireplace. He approached Lady Averly, stood before her with his feet shoulder width apart, and crossed his arms over his chest. He looked down at the top of her head.

"I've been informed that you're unwell."

Lady Averly tilted her face upward to the masculine voice.

"This wine is very good." She peeked through her heavy eyelids with a slight grin on her face.

He placed his fingers under her chin to steady her head and scrutinized her features. She seemed a little flushed, her eyes were half open as if in pain, and she was warm to the touch.

"I'm having a bedchamber readied for you. You'll rest there until you're well."

"Are you always so bossy?" Her inquiry was slurred as she pulled her face away from his hand.

"When one is intoxicated, such as yourself, then I'm in a better position to decide what is best. Now, up with you, let's get you to bed." Lord Edwin took a step backward to allow her room to rise.

Lady Averly tried to stand while keeping both of her hands on the tankard. Unfortunately, her legs refused to comply. She plopped back down upon the bench and giggled.

"I can't stand up."

Lord Edwin glanced at his knight, who motioned for him to offer his assistance.

"If I may be so bold, Averly."

He placed his arm under her knees, the other behind her back, and scooped her into his arms. Her petite and delicate body rested against his broad chest.

"You didn't spill my wine. Well done, my lord." She took another swig and leaned her head against his shoulder.

Lord Edwin glanced at his knight, who was smiling. Sir Garrick raised his eyebrows several times teasingly.

The Lord of Tildenham scowled as he passed his knight on the way to the staircase.

Sir Garrick smirked.

"She's a keeper, I think."

Lady Averly whispered in agreement.

"Yes, I am."

Overhearing her response, Lord Edwin smirked as he ascended the staircase in search of the prepared room.

One of the peasant women stepped into the hallway from the bedchamber. She set the iron pot upon the floor outside of the door before seeing the pair coming toward her.

"In here, my lord." She stepped aside and motioned toward the open bedchamber door. The room was on the opposite side and several doors down the hallway from Lord Edwin's bedchamber.

"Thank you." He passed by the woman, entered the room, and set Lady Averly upon the edge of the freshly made bed. He took the tankard from her hands and set it on the nightstand. Looking at the fireplace, he saw flames wrapping around the logs. A small armoire was against the wall adjacent to the door. He realized the women returned to their duties leaving him alone with Lady Averly.

"It's small, but it'll do." He placed his fisted hands on his waist as he watched her look about the room.

Lady Averly's mouth dropped open.

"Small? Sir, you jest. This room is huge."

Lord Edwin knew the room paled in comparison to his bedchamber, but in her current condition, he refrained from the pointless argument.

Lady Averly tried to remove her boot. It slipped off much quicker than she anticipated. She fell back upon the bed and smacked her head upon the stone wall.

"Ouch! Not again." Cupping her hand over the aggravated spot, she felt another lump rising. She tossed her boot across the room and giggled.

"Let me see what you've done." Lord Edwin helped her sit up and examined her head. "You have a lump. The skin isn't broken."

"That's the wrong one. I hit my head on the statue earlier." She placed her hand upon his and moved it to her newest injury. "There."

He searched for the second lump amongst the silky stands of golden hair and found a smaller one.

"I think I better remove your other boot for you." He knelt upon one knee, clasped her calf, and felt a dirk beneath her skirt.

She lifted her leg off the floor and extended it, nearly kicking him in the face. He removed her boot, tossed it next to the other, and removed the dirk before easing her foot to the floor. He set the dirk on the nightstand.

Lady Averly tried to unclasp her cloak. In her intoxicated state, the difficulty of the task was beyond her capability.

"I can't get this off." She blew a strand of hair away from her face and looked to Lord Edwin for assistance.

He unclasped the silver fastening. Helping her to stand, he removed the garment from the bed and tossed it onto the chair next to the fireplace. Reaching with his free hand, he pulled back the covers of the bed.

"In you go." He waited patiently as she lowered herself to the bed and lay on her side. He pulled the blanket over her shoulder. Spying the second blanket at the foot of the bed, he unfolded it and spread it over her as well.

"Thank you, my lord. You're too kind." Unable to fight the calming effects of the wine any longer, she closed her heavy eyelids.

"You're welcome. I'll send Isabel to watch over you." As he left the bedchamber, he reached for the door to close it behind him and paused to admire her beauty. She looked like a delicate porcelain doll, so fragile and easily broken. *How she survived alone in the woods during such a storm is a credit to her character.* He pulled the door until he heard it shut with a click.

Chapter 12

AN INCESSANT RATTLING within the bedchamber pulled Lady Averly from her sleep. She opened her eyes a mere crack and saw the backside of a woman shadowed in the amber glow of the fireplace and watched her skirt sway back and forth like a pendulum as she stoked the fire in the darkness. She closed her eyes, shivered, and expelled fervid air through her nostrils.

Candlelight permeated her eyelids as she heard the woman set something upon the nightstand. As a hand pressed upon her forehead, Lady Averly opened her eyes to see the illuminated concern upon the young woman's kind face.

"Hello, Averly. My name is Isabel." She moved her hand to Lady Averly's cheek. "You poor thing, you're burning up. I'll see if I can make you some peppermint tea." Isabel removed the top blanket from the feverish woman.

Lady Averly's throat was sore. When she spoke, her voice sounded like the croak of a frog.

"Mm...yes, peppermint, thank you, Isabel." She let her eyelids fall shut.

Before leaving the bedchamber, Isabel hung the dirk in the armoire in fear Averly, in her delirious state, may harm herself. She scurried through the hallway, paused at the balcony to overlook the evening meal in progress in the Great Hall, and looked to the table below in search for her lord. She descended the staircase and stood patiently waiting for his conversation with Sir Garrick to end.

Lord Edwin looked toward the cook.

"Yes, Isabel."

"My lord, I'm very concerned, very concerned indeed. Averly is quite warm. I know of nothing else to do except steep some peppermint tea and bathe her with cool water."

"Please do your best and keep me informed of any change in her condition." He glanced to the balcony.

"Yes, my lord." Isabel hurried toward the kitchen.

*   *   *

Trenchers heaping with meats and vegetables were placed on tables as the evening meal in the Great Hall of Holbrook began. A candelabra's flames danced as Sir

Thomas passed it swiftly and seated himself on a bench at the High Table. He leaned toward Lord Burton.

"My lord, we've searched. Lady Averly is nowhere to be found."

Lord Burton paused with his tankard halfway to his mouth.

"Have you searched everywhere, including the fields and woods?"

"Yes. Even though the conditions were quite challenging, the garrison combed the kingdom thoroughly. I'm sorry, my lord, but there was no sign of her."

Lady Miriam slammed her fist upon the table.

"No sign of her!"

Conversations quieted as many looked toward the High Table. Realizing she had made a spectacle of herself, Lady Miriam looked to those within the room, smiled sheepishly, and picked up her tankard of wine. She turned to her husband after taking a sip and insisted through clenched teeth, "Burton, they must search again."

"My dear, it's impossible to have the men search in the dark of night without risking their lives. At this point, we can only pray she found shelter and is safe." Lord Burton dismissed his wife by turning toward Sir Thomas. "Thank the men for their effort." He reached for his tankard.

"Yes, my lord." Sir Thomas selected a large portion of meat from a tray. He leaned toward Lord Burton and lowered the volume of his voice. "The stableboy said her horse is missing from the stable. I fear she may have traveled further than we assumed."

Lord Burton took a lengthy sip of wine before speaking.

"We'll widen the search in the morning."

Lady Miriam slammed her tankard upon the table.

"Morning? She may not be alive in the morning."

Lord Burton set his tankard upon the table. The crow's feet at the corner of his hazel eyes deepened as he glared at his wife.

"We've no guarantee she survived the storm. If you hadn't insisted we sell her off to the highest bidder, perhaps she wouldn't have run away."

Lady Miriam lowered her voice to a whisper.

"But the dowry is huge. We would live comfortably for the rest of our lives."

"Mommy, I want another sweet cake." Alger shoved the last bite of his fourth dessert into his mouth.

"Yes, dear, we'll get you more." She raised her hand signaling a servant before turning back to her husband for his reply.

Sensing a loss of hope, Lord Burton drained his tankard and held it toward a nearby serving wench, which she promptly refilled.

"We may be forced to accept the worst, my dear."

Chapter 13

LORD EDWIN TAPPED his knuckle on the bedchamber door, took a step backward, and waited with fisted hands on his waist. Rand pranced up the staircase and joined his master.

Isabel removed the damp cloth from Lady Averly's forehead and dropped it into the bowl of water on the nightstand before rising from the chair, opening the door, and curtsying.

"My lord." She stood aside.

Stepping into the bedchamber, his eyes were drawn to the patient lying in the bed. Rand lay down before the fireplace.

"How's Averly?"

"Not very well, my lord. Her fever has yet to break. I tried to get her to drink some tea, but she would take no more than a sip." Isabel returned to the chair next to the bed, retrieved and wrung out the cloth, and dabbed it on Lady Averly's face.

Lord Edwin joined the servant. He glanced at the full mug of tea on the nightstand.

Isabel folded the cloth into a rectangle, placed it on Lady Averly's forehead, and neatened the blanket.

"I've stripped her down to her chemise and covered her with the thinnest blanket to help cool her body. She continues to shiver as her fever rises. If it goes much higher, I fear she may expire." Isabel sighed. "She must have gotten chilled to the bone to have contracted such a wicked illness."

He knew the cook had missed the evening meal to tend to Averly.

"Go and eat. I'll sit with her for a while."

"Thank you, my lord." Isabel returned the cloth to the basin, picked up the mug of cold tea, and left the bedchamber, closing the door behind her.

Lord Edwin sat in the vacated chair and scanned Lady Averly's pale complexion. He touched the back of his hand to her face. She was hot, very hot. Unsure of what he should do, he imitated what Isabel had done. He rinsed the cloth, squeezed out the excess water, and washed Lady Averly's face.

There was a knock at the door.

"Enter."

Sir Garrick stepped into the room.

"How is she?"

"Her fever has yet to break. She's very warm." He folded the cloth and placed it on Lady Averly's forehead. "I know little of healing, but Isabel believes she may expire if her fever continues to climb."

"Let's hope it doesn't come to that." Sir Garrick scrutinized the woman's face. "Strange, I don't recall her as a resident of the kingdom and neither do the peasants. I mean to say, it would be difficult to forget a woman who possesses such beauty."

"I don't recall her either."

"But when you think about it, when do we have time to pay much attention to those in the village?"

"True, but she would be difficult to overlook." Lord Edwin turned the folded cloth over on her forehead. "Averly."

Sir Garrick read his lord's mind.

"A pretty name for a pretty woman."

Moments stretched by as they stared at her angelic face. The uncomfortable silence in the room brought the Lord of Tildenham back to the matter at hand. He looked to his knight.

"Did you need something?"

"If you intend to sit with her for a while, I'll take your shift to guard."

"Thank you."

Sir Garrick grasped his lord's shoulder.

"I hope she improves soon."

"As do I." He looked to his knight, who nodded his head before leaving the bedchamber and closing the door.

With so few surviving the barbarian's attack, Lord Edwin needed everyone's able hands to help rebuild Tildenham, including hers.

The dying embers crackled and popped drawing Lord Edwin's attention toward the fireplace. He rose from his chair, selected a log from the stack on the floor, and placed it atop the ashen embers. A moan murmured from behind him. He turned to see Lady Averly wince as if in pain. Returning to the chair, he rinsed the cloth and replaced it on her forehead. She opened her eyes and looked toward him.

He placed the back of his hand against her cheek. "How are you feeling?"

"I ache." Her voice was raspy and dry.

Isabel knocked on the door before opening it a crack and peeking into the room.

"Shall I sit with her again, my lord?"

"Isabel, could you first prepare another mug of your peppermint tea with honey, please. Her throat sounds raw. Perhaps add something to ease her aches as well."

Lady Averly looked toward Isabel. Her voice a raspy whisper.

"White willow."

Lord Edwin and Isabel looked toward her, both surprised by the request. The cook wondered if the woman was a healer.

"My lord, I've more tea steeping in the kitchen. If we have white willow, I'll add some to the tea."

Lord Edwin nodded.

"Thank you."

Isabel left the bedchamber door open as she went to the kitchen.

Lord Edwin flipped the cloth over and placed it upon Lady Averly's forehead again. She closed her eyes.

"Will this ache ever end?" She arched her back and turned her head toward him as if pleading for help.

Lord Edwin knew little about healing. He hoped the white willow would bring her comfort. He thought of only one pointless suggestion until Isabel returned.

"Try to focus on something else."

She opened her eyes and looked into his golden-flecked orbs trying to determine if he was sincere.

"Such as what?"

He pulled her left arm from beneath the thin blanket and laid it upon the bed.

"Focus on my touch." He placed his index finger upon her forearm and traced its length.

She watched his hand move back and forth between her elbow and wrist. She fought the urge to pull away from his forwardness, all the while knowing she had little strength to do so. The sensation was unnerving, tickled somewhat, but was pleasant and oddly calming. She allowed her eyes to close.

Lord Edwin remained silent as he continued to trace his finger along her arm. She did not seem repulsed by his touch. He turned the cloth over and replaced it upon her head.

"Here's the tea." Isabel entered the room unannounced. "We had some white willow too. Let's hope it eases her pain."

Lord Edwin pulled his finger away from Lady Averly's arm as if being caught doing something inappropriate.

"Good, very good." He took the cloth from her forehead and put it in the basin. "Averly, let's get you sitting upright. You need to drink some of this tea." He reached under her shoulders, lifted her to a sitting position, and sat on the bed behind her for support.

The thin blanket fell away from her chest. Too weak to care, she hoped her modesty was preserved by the dim light within the bedchamber.

Isabel brought the mug to her lips and tipped it at an angle ever so slowly.

Lady Averly lifted her right hand to steady the tankard and sipped the tea. It soothed her throat. When she had enough, she turned her head away and lowered her hand.

Lord Edwin stood and lowered Lady Averly's head to the pillow.

Isabel placed the tankard on the nightstand before pulling the blanket over Lady Averly's chest.

"Maybe you'll be able to drink some later, but for now you should rest." Isabel waited for her lord's instructions.

Lord Edwin smiled. Their eyes locked upon one another.

"I'll leave you in Isabel's care."

"Thank you." Lady Averly blinked her eyes lethargically.

"Rand." The wolf joined his master as they departed the bedchamber, shutting the door behind them.

Isabel sat in the chair and rung out the cloth of excess water.

Lady Averly sighed and drifted off to sleep.

Chapter 14

LADY AVERLY OPENED her eyes. The only light in the room was the amber glow of the dying embers in the fireplace. She glanced toward the shadowed figure sleeping in the chair next to the bed. It was Isabel.

Lifting her hand to her face, Lady Averly brushed away the damp strand of hair clinging to her cheek. She ran her tongue over her dry, cracked lips and looked to the nightstand, hoping to find something to quench her thirst. She assumed the tankard next to a basin contained the tea she drank earlier.

Rolling onto her side, she extended her hand and touched the handle with her fingertips. She could not grasp it. Her head seemed to float momentarily, and her vision blurred as she eased herself upright against the headboard. The blanket fell away from her chest exposing her damp muslin chemise to the coolness of the room.

Lady Averly picked up the tankard from the nightstand, reached her finger inside, and discovered it to be half full. Bringing it to her nose, she smelled peppermint before taking a sip. The tea was cold, but it didn't matter. She gulped down the mug's contents. After returning it to the nightstand, she reached for the blankets folded at her feet, covered herself, and snuggled within the warmth of the bed. Her body continued to ache. *I hope the worst has passed.* She stared at the glowing embers. Her thoughts turned to Holbrook.

Surely Father realizes I've left by now. Poor Mina, Lady Miriam probably riddled her with questions.

Isabel straightened in her chair and leaned forward.

"You're awake?"

Lady Averly turned her head toward the cook.

"Yes."

The cook placed the back of her fingers to Lady Averly's cheek.

"You're still warm, but much cooler. And damp. Good, your fever has broken." She noticed Lady Averly's dry and cracked lips. "Would you like more tea?" She reached for the empty tankard and looked inside.

"I drank it while you were sleeping."

"Then I'll go fetch more. I imagine you're hungry too." She rose from the chair. "I won't be long." Isabel left the door ajar as she exited the bedchamber.

Alone in the room with the crackling embers as her only company, Lady Averly closed her eyes, but the silence was soon interrupted by a rhythmic tapping on the stone floor echoing from the hallway.

A pungent, warm breath on her face caused her to open her eyes. Rand's nose was nearly touching her nose.

"Hello, Rand. What are you doing awake at this time of night?"

Lord Edwin entered the bedchamber.

"He's helping me. I was on my way to relieve Sir Garrick of guard duty when I saw your bedchamber door open. Isabel said your fever broke. That's good news." He sat in the vacated chair. Rand turned toward his master. Unsure of what to say, Lord Edwin patted the wolf's shoulder.

Lady Averly shivered.

Lord Edwin looked toward the fireplace and rose.

Rand watched as his master took the poker and rustled the coals before placing two logs upon them.

"Thank you, my lord." Lady Averly watched as he returned the poker and resumed his seat.

"You're welcome."

"I understand your parents were killed during the attack. I'm sorry for your loss."

"Thank you." He stood as Isabel entered the bedchamber carrying a small wooden tray.

"I don't know what you fancy, Averly, so I brought a variety of food for you to choose from. Not only did I bring tea, but I thought a cool drink of watered ale would be to your liking too." Isabel crossed the room and stood beside her lord.

Lady Averly pulled herself upright, leaned against the headboard, and for modesty sake, ensured the blanket remained over her chest by tucking it tightly under each arm.

"Thank you, Isabel."

The cook stepped in front of Lord Edwin

"Excuse me, my lord." She set the tray upon the chair before taking the basin of water from the nightstand and exiting the room. Rand sat, hoping to share a tidbit or two of venison he detected on the tray.

Lord Edwin lifted the tray from the chair and displayed it before her.

"Care for something to eat?"

"No thank you, but I would welcome something to drink."

He set the tray on the nightstand, picked up the tankard of ale, and presented the handle toward her as he sat. *Sir Garrick will have to wait a few more minutes to be relieved of duty. I'm certain he will understand the justification for my delay.*

"Thank you." The cool watered ale refreshed her dehydrated body, but after several gulps, the tankard was lowered away from her mouth.

Lord Edwin took the mug as she released it and set it upon the nightstand.

"I think you should pace yourself. It's been a while since your stomach has had anything in it."

Lady Averly sighed as she licked her lips to moisten them.

He placed the tray of food on her lap.

"You should try to eat something to regain your strength. I, on the other hand, need to get to my post. Sir Garrick will be eager to get some sleep." He stood. Rand looked to Lady Averly's lap.

She perused the tray of food before looking to Lord Edwin.

"My lord, thank you again. I truly appreciate all you've done for me."

Lord Edwin nodded his head in acknowledgment before leaving the bedchamber. His faithful wolf remained fixated on the plate of food.

"Rand!" The call echoed from the hallway. The wolf seemed to sigh before leaving the bedchamber.

Lady Averly selected a wedge of bread, dabbed it in the small dish of butter, and took a bite. The bread tasted like unsalted porridge. *I'm certain my illness has affected my tongue's ability to taste.* She washed it down with a sip of tea before returning it to the tray. As she set the food on the nightstand, goosebumps puckered on her arms. She snuggled beneath the covers and watched the flickering flames of the fire until she fell asleep.

Chapter 15

BEAMS OF SUNLIGHT radiating through the window forced Lady Averly to shield her eyes as she awoke. Finding herself alone in the bedchamber, she rolled onto her side and pulled the blankets over her shoulder, enclosing herself in the warmth. *Ah, I can't recall the last time I slept past the break of dawn.* She sighed. Her body was less achy, and her fever had subsided.

Cherishing the solitude of her luxurious room, she listened to the echoing conversations from the Great Hall. The merriment reminded her of Holbrook's chattering kitchen staff. *I miss them, especially Mina. But I can't go back. I must either move on to another kingdom or remain within Tildenham. Until I decide what to do, I can work in the kitchen to earn my keep.* She glanced at the nightstand. The plate of food was still there. *Perhaps I should try to eat something.* She sat up, reached for the tray, and set it in her lap. The bread made a hollow sound when she tapped it.

"A little stale."

The wedge of cheese was crusted around the edge. Breaking off a piece and popping it into her mouth, she admired the fine details of the bedchamber while she ate. The woodwork was exquisite. The bed was large enough for two, carved with the finest craftsmanship and fitted with soft linen sheets and wool blankets. She imagined the number of dresses the armoire could hold. The room was a far cry from the tiny, bare chamber she was accustomed to at home. *I could get used to this.*

She knew the reason for her isolation. Residing within the room's luxury could not continue once she was well. Others may become resentful of any preferential treatment displayed by their lord. Like everyone else, she would sleep on a pallet in the Great Hall.

Lady Averly drank the contents of both tankards but soon regretted doing so as her need to use the garderobe became apparent. She returned the plate to the nightstand and leaned over the edge of the bed in search of a chamber pot. She did not see one in the shadowed darkness. Hearing approaching footsteps, she sat upright quickly and, for modesty sake, ensured the blanket covered her thin chemise.

The door opened silently. Lord Edwin peeked into the bedchamber to find her awake.

"How are you feeling?" He stepped into the room.

"I believe my fever has gone."

He walked to the head of the bed and held the back of his hand toward her cheek.

"If I may?"

She agreed with a slight nod of her head before he touched her cheek.

"Yes, you're much cooler." He moved the palm of his hand to her forehead. It was cool to his touch. "Good." He noted her damp hair.

Self-conscious of her current hygienic condition, she tucked her untidy hair behind her ears to make it more presentable. Her bladder reminded her of its urgency.

"Where's Isabel?"

"She's busy in the kitchen." He went to the fireplace, stirred the embers, and added a log before turning toward her with the poker still in his hand. "Since she's the only kitchen staff member who survived the attack, she's taken over the responsibility of supervising our meals."

"Oh, then I've kept her from her duties." A pang of guilt wretched her heart as she glanced toward the open portal before looking back to Lord Edwin. "I'm sorry."

"There's no need to apologize. You were ill and needed someone to watch over you." He replaced the poker on the hook and approached the bed.

Lady Averly bit her bottom lip before looking at the open door.

Noting her uneasy behavior, Lord Edwin was curious.

"Is there something you needed?"

"Well, yes." She cringed inwardly as she looked to the tall lord towering over her. "I need to use the garderobe." Her face blushed.

"It's at the end of the hallway." He made light of the personal request.

Lady Averly wished Isabel could assist her, but her need outweighed her modesty. She pulled back the covers to swing her feet to the floor, unaware her chemise rose to mid-thigh.

Catching a glimpse of her naked legs, Lord Edwin looked toward the window, allowing her time to straighten her garment. He kindly changed the subject.

"Looks like a nice day today."

Lady Averly pulled her chemise over her legs as she looked around the bedchamber.

"I believe so." She crossed her arms over her chest hoping to retain some form of modesty.

"Where is my cloak?"

Lord Edwin looked around the room.

"Perhaps it's in there." He opened the armoire door. It was empty. "Maybe Isabel had it washed." He closed the door, pausing a moment with his index finger vertically upon his lips and then pulled it away before he spoke. "However, I've something you may borrow until we find it." He left the room and returned moments later carrying a lovely burgundy brocade robe folded over his arm.

"Here, try this on." He held the robe open before her.

She eased herself to the edge of the bed and stood abruptly. A black fog seeped into her line of vision. After blinking several times and taking a deep breath, she turned her back toward him and inserted her arms into the robe. The sleeves hung past her hands much like her father's robe did when she was a little girl. She pushed them up over her wrists before folding the sides of the robe over her body, tying the belt with a cross and tuck, and inhaling a sandalwood scent that seemed to wrap around her neck. Several inches of the robe's hem lay upon the rug.

Lord Edwin took a step backward, noted the droopy shoulders and sleeves. He admired her small waist and the curvature of her hips.

"Perfect." He refrained from smiling.

Lady Averly held her arms out to her sides and examined the fit of the gown. She chuckled to herself, knowing she must look silly. Turning toward him, she caught a glimpse of the sarcastic smirk mocking her humorous appearance and tried not to laugh.

"It's a beautiful robe. Thank you for lending it to me."

"My pleasure." He motioned his hand toward the open door. "I'll point you in the direction of the garderobe."

He exited the room. Lady Averly lifted the front of the robe from the floor and followed. She stepped from the rug to the cold stone floor.

"Oh my."

Lord Edwin paused in mid-step and turned around.

"What's wrong?"

"All is well. I was only startled. The floor is quite cold."

He looked down at her dainty, bare feet.

"As you can see..." He pointed to the other end of the hallway.

She leaned out the doorway and peered in the direction he indicated. It was farther than she anticipated.

"If you'll allow me to be so bold, I'll carry you." He didn't wait for her reply before scooping her into his arms and cradling her close to his chest.

"Oh! But..."

Her body became rigid. She kept her hands in her lap and tried to avoid looking up to his face.

Sensing her uneasiness, he decided to make light of the situation.

"There, problem solved." He walked the distance, set her down before the chamber, and opened the door. A single candle burned within the tiny room to light her way.

"Thank you." She tiptoed inside and shut the door.

Once she emerged, he scooped her into his arms again. As he carried her back to the bedchamber, he broke the silence between them.

"Over the next few days, I'd like you to rest in your bedchamber. You need time to recover from your illness."

Lady Averly looked into his hazel eyes.

"But, my lord, shouldn't I be helping in the kitchen?"

"Not until you regain your strength. Isabel can find some needlework to occupy your time or would you prefer to read a book?" *Can she read? Most peasants can't.*

She had to agree with his reasoning. A few days to regain her strength would be wise.

"I've never had much time for needlework and fear my stitching would fall far short of the talented women within the Keep. I would prefer to read."

Lord Edwin entered her bedchamber and lowered her gently to the rug. Ensuring she was steady on her feet, he moved the chair next to the window where she could utilize the natural sunlight for reading.

"This should do well." He looked to the window to ensure the chair was in the optimal location. He motioned for her to sit.

Dragging the robe behind her like the train on a wedding dress, she went to the chair, sat as instructed, and wrapped the garment around her legs to keep them warm.

Lord Edwin took a blanket from the bed and handed it to her.

"I'll return shortly."

Lady Averly spread the blanket upon her lap and brushed away the wrinkles. Unsure where the library was located within the Keep, she strained to listen for Lord Edwin's returning footsteps. The only sound she heard was the crackling logs in the fireplace. She looked to the window, admiring its natural light. *An excellent place to read a book.*

Moments later, Lord Edwin returned with two books.

"Not knowing what you prefer to read, I chose two of my personal favorites." He handed her the leather-bound books.

"Thank you." She glanced at the titles before setting them on her lap. "I apologize for keeping you from your duties."

"No apology necessary." Wanting to remain in her company, he searched for a topic of conversation, but his mind was blank. "Well, I'll leave you to enjoy your books. Good day."

"Good day, my lord."

Lord Edwin left the bedchamber in search of Isabel.

Rand met his master at the bottom of the Great Hall staircase and followed him to the kitchen. Pausing in the doorway, Lord Edwin scanned the room for Isabel.

Women pulled loaves of bread from the oven while others went about various tasks. Rand raised his nose and sniffed the tantalizing aroma.

It took Lord Edwin a few moments to locate the head cook and go to her side.

"Isabel, when you have a moment, could you please have someone prepare a bath for Averly."

She looked up from the bread she was forming into a loaf.

"Yes, my lord."

"Thank you." He slapped his thigh twice as he left the kitchen. Rand followed obediently.

Exiting the Keep, Lord Edwin shielded his eyes from the bright spring sun reflecting off of the melting snow. He sloshed through muddy puddles as he walked by the charred remains of crafter's shops and ducked under the droplets raining down from the rooftop of the stable.

Sir Garrick and the peasant men awaited their lord's arrival at the woodshop, or what was left of it. They were eager to begin reconstruction.

Sir Garrick nodded his head toward an elder peasant, who displayed an unscathed board.

"My lord, we're in luck." The man smiled, knowing his news would please his lord. "We discovered a stack of lumber behind the remnants of the woodshop. Somehow it was spared from the fire."

Lord Edwin brushed his palm over the surface of the board. He looked to the stack of unscathed lumber.

"Good. It's a start." He turned to see Bryce holding the bridle of a horse hitched to a wagon. "We'll begin by repairing the stable and constructing a smaller building for the chickens, ducks, and geese. Let's get it loaded." Lord Edwin grabbed the edge of the board and helped the man place it into the back of the wagon. While some of the men loaded the lumber, others gathered what tools they could find in the rubble.

Lord Edwin looked to the gatehouse. It offered little protection. The repairs would have to wait until he found a blacksmith and reconstructed the shop. He had little knowledge of the craftsman's trade and the requirements for the building. He watched as the last board was loaded.

Bryce directed the horse and wagon toward the stable. The men began clearing the debris for the new building and stacked the rubble to one side. A wooden bucket of nails was retrieved from a peg in the stable. It was a small start toward reconstruction, but it was a start nevertheless.

*   *   *

"We need to search again." Lady Miriam paced the solar.

"I've sent another search party along the roads and to nearby villages. She couldn't have traveled far during the storm." Lord Burton turned a page in his account book.

Lady Miriam stopped suddenly and glared at him.

"What will we do if she isn't found?"

"I'm not thinking that far ahead. Not yet anyway." He refused to be distracted from his analysis of their financial predicament.

"You may want to do so. Our coffers have become very low as of late." Lady Miriam resumed pacing.

"I'm quite aware of the fact."

"I hate to miss out on such a large dowry." She turned toward him with her fisted hands upon her hips.

Lord Burton looked up from the account book and glared at his wife.

She widened her eyes and smiled like a cat that just swallowed a canary.

"What if we find an imposter to replace her? Her betrothed will never know the difference."

Lord Burton sighed. *She's taking this matter a bit too far.* He was growing weary of her incessant prattling.

Lady Miriam began to pace while she thought out loud.

"Perhaps I should begin interviewing women. There's so much to do. She must possess an educated way of talking, walking, and knowledge of all subjects."

Lord Burton closed the account book.

"You'll do no such thing. My dear, calm yourself. We'll find her."

Lady Miriam glared at her husband, for she truly had her doubts.

*   *   *

A peasant woman emptied a bucket of warm water into the bathtub.

"Thank you." Lady Averly was all too familiar with the laborious task of boiling water, filling buckets, and lugging them up several flights of stairs. She recalled the countless baths she had drawn for her father, stepmother, and bratty half-brother, and wondered if they ever appreciated the back-breaking effort on her part.

The last bucket of warm water was dumped into the tub. The woman nodded with a smile before leaving the bedchamber, closing the door behind her.

A twinge of guilt resonated within her conscious as she stared at the inviting tub. *How very strange to have someone draw a bath for me.* She picked up the basket of fragrant soaps, comb, and stack of linen from the bed and set them on the seat of the chair before pushing it next to the tub.

Lady Averly took off the robe and hung it in the armoire. She slipped her chemise over each shoulder and let it fall to the floor. Stepping out of the garment, she tested the water with her hand. *Ah, perfect.* Submerging herself, she leaned her head on the back of the tub, exhaled, and allowed her body to relax. A bath was one of the few pleasures she was able to enjoy at Holbrook, even though she had to draw it herself.

A knock on the door caused her body to tense. She raised her head from the edge of the tub and crossed her arms over her chest.

"It's me."

Lady Averly relaxed, recognizing the voice of the cook.

"Come in, Isabel."

The door creaked open and the cook entered.

"Your clothes are in the laundry, your boots have been brushed clean, and I brought clothes and a clean

121

chemise for you to borrow for now." Isabel set the clean clothes on the bed and the boots on the floor. She stoked the fire and picked up the soiled chemise from the floor.

Lady Averly returned her head to the rim of the tub.

"Thank you. I hope drawing my bath wasn't too much trouble for the kitchen staff."

"There is always a pot of hot water over the fire. We both know that filling the tub always takes some effort, but well worth the work." Isabel admired the long, blonde locks hanging like a silky golden waterfall over the edge of the tub.

"Let me wash your hair before I go. Sit up." Isabel set the laundry on the bed and picked up the empty mug from the nightstand.

Lady Averly sat up and exhaled as Isabel poured warm water over her head. She tilted it backward as scented soap was lathered and then rinsed from her hair.

"Lean back and I'll comb out the tangles." Setting the tankard on the chair, Isabel picked up the comb from the basket.

Lady Averly looked over her shoulder.

"I don't want to keep you..."

"Oh, it will only take a moment. Lean back." It was a simple kindness offered by the cook.

Lady Averly complied, closed her eyes, and thought of the many times Mina had combed out her hair.

She hoped her friend's assistance in her escape would remain a secret and free from punishment.

"Finished." Isabel selected a linen and wrapped the wet hair in a towel before lathering a cloth with the same soap. "Lean forward and I'll scrub your back."

"Thank you." Lady Averly opened her eyes and did as requested. She imagined the sweat and grime washed away with each pass of the soapy linen.

"Will you need help getting dressed?" The cook dipped the mug in the water and rinsed away the scented suds.

"I believe I can manage. Thank you."

Isabel picked up the laundry from the bed and the tray of stale food from the nightstand.

"Then I'll return to the kitchen. A midday meal must be prepared and taken to the men. I'll send someone up later to remove the tub."

"Thank you, Isabel." Lady Averly finished the remainder of her bath unaccompanied.

Chapter 16

LADY AVERLY PULLED the leather lacing of her forest green bodice tightly and knotted it securely. She straightened a muslin overskirt over her brown wool skirt and stepped to the window. Glancing up at the sun, she marked it at near midday.

Green patches in the distant fields peeked through the melting snow. The charred remains of buildings punctured the carpet of white like fingers reaching toward the sky.

She peered down into the bailey. Men were busy constructing a small building and repairing the stable. A man carrying a board lost his footing and fell to one knee. Lord Edwin came forward and helped the peasant rise from the ground.

As if he could sense her staring at him, Lord Edwin turned and looked toward her bedchamber window. He smiled and nodded his head in acknowledgment.

She smiled politely. Guilt gnawed within her as he turned away and resumed his work.

I should be doing something to earn my keep.

A knock sounded upon her bedchamber door.

As she turned away from the window, her hand bumped the top book stacked upon the nightstand. It fell to the floor. She bent to retrieve it. When she stood too quickly, a wave of dizziness overtook her. She clutched the edge of the nightstand to steady herself as she blinked and widened her eyes to clear her blurry vision. The knock sounded again.

"Enter." She bid as she returned the book to its proper place.

Two boys, about a dozen years of age each, nodded their heads respectfully as they entered the bedchamber carrying wooden buckets. They remained silent as they dipped each bucket into the cooled bath water and carried them out of the room.

Lady Averly picked up the mug and the basket of soaps from the chair and exited her bedchamber. She saw the boys walking toward the garderobe. *Good. The shoot probably needs a thorough rinsing.* She turned toward the Great Hall and peered over the balcony. The room was vacant. Descending the staircase, she heard the merry chattering echoing from the kitchen. Standing in the doorway, she observed the women working collectively.

Isabel stood next to the fireplace stirring a large pot. She looked to the doorway.

"Averly, what are you doing up and around?"

"I thought I may be able to help with the food preparations." She entered and set the mug near a washtub. "In truth, I'm not used to being idle and have grown quite bored."

Isabel was aware of Lord Edwin's desire for the woman to remain in her bedchamber over the next few days. The paleness of her face justified his reasoning. However, she also understood Lady Averly's point of view.

"I could use some help stirring this pot." Isabel retrieved a stool and set it next to the fireplace. Patting the seat to encourage Lady Avery to sit, she handed her the wooden spoon as she accepted the basket of soaps and placed it upon a shelf before moving to a table to cut the venison into cubes.

Lady Avery peeked into the large iron kettle. The soup was boiling. The warmth of the fire brought to light her proximity to the flames. She pulled her hair and skirt as far away from the fire as possible. Looking at each woman in the room, their hair was worn loosely. The unnerving memory of the woman set aflame gave her the courage to speak her mind.

"May I make a small request?"

Isabel scooped the venison pieces into a bowl and dumped them into the soup.

"Yes."

"I once worked in a kitchen where I saw a woman's hair catch fire. We made a habit of tying our hair to avoid such an accident reoccurring."

Isabel scanned the women in the room. Some had stopped working and began pulling their hair away from their face. She wiped her hands on her overskirt.

"Let me see what I can find to tie our hair." Isabel took a linen from a nearby shelf and tore it into long strips. She handed a tie to each woman, who secured her hair.

Lady Averly accepted the ragged-edged strip of fabric.

"Thank you." She balanced the wooden spoon on the edge of the pot and tied back her hair before returning the spoon to the bubbling broth.

Women brought bowls of chopped vegetables to the pot and added them while Lady Averly continued to stir.

*   *   *

Conversations resonated throughout the Great Hall of Holbrook. Lady Miriam tapped her index finger on the High Table as she stewed over the loss of the dowry. She leaned toward her husband.

"With Averly still missing, what do we do now? You won't let me find a replacement. How long do we have before we must return the signed contract?"

"We have time, my dear. Calm yourself. We will find her." Lord Burton looked toward the approaching servants, who carried trays of food and filled tankards with ale or wine.

A stranger dressed entirely in black entered the room. He approached the High Table, bowed.

Lady Miriam glanced at her son's plate. Only one sweet cake remained. She selected a variety of food from a tray and added it to his plate.

Lord Burton's attention was drawn to the man who stood before him. He was tall, muscular, and broad-shouldered. His piercing sepia brown eyes stared at him, unblinking.

"Who are you?" Over the years he had become leery of lone travelers. Many of them were freelancers hired for a substantial fee to kill a kingdom's lord.

"My name is Doran."

"And what do you want, Doran?" He sat back in his chair, placed his elbow upon its arm, and leaned against his fisted hand.

"May I request a night's stay? I'll leave tomorrow for my next destination."

Lord Burton visually scanned Doran from the ebony hair on the top of his head to his black boots. He noted his leather breastplate, the lethal sword at his side, and several dirks on a belt extending from his right shoulder to left hip.

"What service do you provide? Your occupation?" Lord Burton doubted the stranger would tell the truth, but it was worth posing the question.

Doran understood the Lord of Holbrook's assumption. He had been mistaken for a freelancer many times before.

"Several kingdoms have been attacked over the past few months. I've been ordered by Baron Vinson to follow their trail of destruction, find their location, and report back to him. He intends to stop the barbarians by whatever means possible."

Lady Miriam turned her attention away from her son and looked at the visitor in earnest. *I can't believe our good fortune.* She leaned toward her husband and whispered.

"Could he search for Averly for us?"

Her husband nodded his head in affirmation.

Lady Miriam clenched her teeth.

"Then we must employ him. Now." She scrutinized the stranger from head to toe.

Convinced the man was telling the truth, Lord Burton lifted his tankard from the table.

"I'll grant you one night's stay. However, I wish to speak with you after you've satisfied your appetite and quenched your thirst." Lord Burton motioned toward the tables of the Great Hall.

"Thank you, my lord. I look forward to our conversation." Doran found an empty seat on a bench and selected a chunk of meat from a trencher as he waited for the empty tankard before him to be filled.

Chapter 17

THE MEN OF Tildenham knocked their muddy boots against the wall of the Keep removing the excess dirt before entering. After all, it was their lord's residence and they were temporary guests. They slapped each other's shoulders in recognition for a job well done. The shed for the smaller animals was finished. Fresh straw from an unscathed mound in the field was spread inside, and the animals resided comfortably in their new shelter.

The candelabras illuminated the Great Hall with golden light. Several mouthwatering trays of food and pitchers of ale and wine were brought forth from the kitchen as Lord Edwin sat at the table.

Lady Averly carried baskets of fresh bread and placed one upon the table before Lord Edwin.

"Up and around, I see." He watched as she placed a second basket on the center of the table. Her face lacked color. A peasant woman handed him a mug of warm wine. He accepted it with a nod of his head.

Lady Averly smiled shyly as she walked to the other end of the table and set the last basket of bread upon it.

"Please sit." He gestured with his hand to the seat across from him before taking a sip of his drink.

Lady Averly tilted her head to the side in acknowledgment and did as the Lord of Tildenham requested. A platter of meat and vegetables was placed between them as Sir Garrick sat next to his lord.

Unaccustomed to eating in the company of others, Lady Averly kept her eyes downcast at the tabletop. Her attention was drawn to the tankard before her as it was filled with wine.

"Did you like the books?"

Conversations at the table quieted. Lady Averly blushed before looking into the askance eyes of Lord Edwin.

"Yes, but I've read both of them before." Her honest answer slipped between her lips without realizing her admission. Many at the table turned their head toward her, for it was uncommon for a peasant to possess the ability to read.

Lord Edwin stared at her.

"Both?"

Well, I guess I've said too much. Since I'm in this deep, I might as well be honest.

"Yes." She picked up her tankard, trying to make light of her admission.

"Who taught you to read?" Lord Edwin dug further for the truth.

Isabel offered a response, even though it was an assumption.

"A priest."

Surprised by the cook's response, Lady Avery glanced to where she was seated several seats down from Lord Edwin.

"A priest?" He pried for confirmation of the suggestion.

Lady Averly redirected her attention to the Lord of Tildenham.

"Isabel is correct. It was a priest." Lady Averly took a sip of wine.

"And where did you get the books? Not exactly a topic a priest would have an interest in reading."

"From him, but in all likelihood, he borrowed them from someone or perhaps they were a gift he received." She hoped her answer satisfied his curiosity as she tore a portion from a loaf of bread and set it on her plate. Lifting her chin, she stared at his inquisitive face defiantly.

Fully aware of Lady Averly's silent challenge, Isabel leaned forward and glanced at her lord's face, which conveyed interest and intrigue. The cook looked down at her plate to conceal an all-knowing grin on her face.

*　　　　*　　　　*

"You want me to find your daughter?" Doran needed clarification.

Lord Burton sighed.

"Yes, she is ten and seven, long golden blonde hair, dark blue eyes, and quite stunning actually. She resembled her mother, God rest her soul."

Lady Miriam scowled at her husband before turning toward Doran.

"She ran away the night of the recent snow storm. We believe she was on horseback since her mare is missing."

"Is there any indication she's still alive?" Doran recalled being held up in a pub during the wicked spring storm. He found it difficult to believe a seventeen-year-old woman could have survived.

"Yes, she must be somewhere." Lady Miriam paced the solar.

Lord Burton scowled at his wife's overzealous insistence.

"Since neither she nor her horse has been found, we assume she's alive. Perhaps she found shelter, or someone took her in." Lord Burton offered the information and the positive assumption. Biting one of his fingernails indicated otherwise.

"There must be a lot at risk, for this is an unusual request and your desperation for her return is obvious." Doran looked from Lord Burton to Lady Miriam.

Lady Miriam stopped pacing and turned toward the guest.

"Why would you think such a thing?" She giggled as she crossed her arms over her chest. He had come too close to the truth. She waved her hand flippantly to excuse her nervousness and resumed her pacing.

"Forgive me, my lady. I didn't mean to pry." Doran observed Lord Burton bite another fingernail as his wife paced the floor and fidgeted with her hair.

Lady Miriam turned her back to Doran, opened a book lying on a table, and closed it again.

"Well, getting back to the matter at hand." She looked over her shoulder. "Will you accept the assignment?"

"Yes, though finding her is highly unlikely. With freemen moving from kingdom to kingdom, people have been known to conceal their identity, some indefinitely."

Lady Miriam turned to face Doran.

"What's your fee?" She hoped it would be a small sum. After all, her stepdaughter was nothing more than a profitable inconvenience.

"My priority is to carry out my orders. If I happen to discover your daughter along the way, I may have to travel a great distance to return her to Holbrook." Doran hoped to fetch a large bounty for the unwelcomed detour.

"I see." Lady Miriam turned to her husband. "What do you think, my dear?"

Lord Burton took matters in hand. Grabbing paper, quill, and ink from his desk drawer, he scribed the description of his daughter and the betrothal justification for her return. Tearing off the bottom quarter of the paper, he scribbled the amount he would pay for her return.

"I believe you will find this reward adequate." He handed the missive to Doran, who looked at the amount and refrained from smiling.

Chapter 18

WITH EACH MOUTHFUL of food, Lady Averly's strength increased. *A bit more rest and a few more meals and I'll be back to my old self again.* She kept her eyes downcast, hoping to avoid the inquisitive lord sitting across from her. After taking a sip of spiced wine, she averted her eyes to the other end of the table, politely ignoring the conversation between Lord Edwin and Sir Garrick.

A few of the women rose and began collecting dirty dishes. Under the watchful eye of Lord Edwin, Lady Averly stood, gathered the dishes nearest to her, and entered the kitchen in search of a slop bucket. She stepped aside as a peasant woman wrapped each hand with a linen towel, went to the fireplace, and lifted the iron kettle filled with boiling water from a hook over the fire. The woman poured the hot contents into an oval, wooden tub before returning the kettle to the hook. A repetitive scratching sound caused Lady Averly to turn and watch a woman scraping the remnants from a plate into a large bucket. *Ah, there it is.* Lady Averly dumped the scraps from the dishes and tipped the mugs upside down over the container before submerging them into the hot water of the tub.

Isabel entered the kitchen carrying platters of leftovers from the meal.

"Averly, you shouldn't concern yourself with the dishes. We can get it." The cook's kind face was masked with concern.

Lady Averly hated to admit, but the small effort she had made seemed to drain her energy quickly.

"I feel I should earn my keep, just like everyone else." She washed a plate, inspected it for cleanliness, and leaned it against the others on a shelf to dry.

"Very well, but don't overdo it." Isabel wrapped the leftover bread in linen before placing it upon a shelf in the storage room.

The sound of music drifted into the kitchen from the Great Hall. Lady Avelry rinsed the last tankard, set it with the other dishes, and stood in the doorway wiping her wet hands on her overskirt. She leaned her shoulder against the wall as she watched the residents of Tildenham.

The elderly women sat close to the fireplace. Their needles bobbed up and down as they pulled their thread through the embroidery cloth while tapping their feet to the music. Men's laughter erupted at a nearby table. Lady Averly watched as a man stood and pantomimed his dramatic story. At its conclusion, the men erupted with laughter. She imagined the tale was crude in nature and assumed an overindulgence of ale or wine contributed to their loud merriment. Across from them, a man sat on a bench and played a horn pipe while another beat rhythmically on a drum. The center of the Great Hall had been cleared of furniture. She smiled as she watched several people dance a merry jig. Those who were seated upon the benches stomped their feet and clapped their hands in time with the music.

She grinned as Rand sat on the floor next to his lord. His eyes narrowed with each rhythmic pat of his master's hand upon his head. Sir Garrick had taken her vacated seat.

Upon finishing his conversation with his knight, Lord Edwin's attention was drawn to the beautiful woman standing in the kitchen doorway. Displaying pearl white teeth, she smiled as she watched the peasants dance. *She's amused.* It pleased him to see her happy. He scanned the Great Hall. *Everyone is happy.* He looked back to Lady Averly. *I believe there is more to you than you have led us to believe. You seem well educated, but to have read both books?* He had his doubts. *You dress like a peasant. It's apparent you're comfortable working in the kitchen, not a trait of royalty.*

The dancers clapped their hands as the tune ended. The musicians nodded in appreciation before beginning the next song at a slower tempo. Many of the men chose a partner for the dance.

Sir Garrick followed Lord Edwin's line of vision, grinned, and leaned across the table toward him.

"Go ahead."

Lord Edwin redirected his attention to his knight.

Sir Garrick raised his eyebrows teasingly and smiled.

"Ask her to dance."

"With her recent illness, I fear she may not be up to it."

"It's a slow tune. She shouldn't get too tired from a spin or two around the room." Sir Garrick lifted his tankard to his lips and drank.

Lord Edwin looked back to Lady Averly, who appeared intrigued by the dancing couples.

A woman laughed as her partner whirled her about the floor. Lady Averly grinned as she watched them pass by. She caught sight of Lord Edwin. Their eyes locked. Her smile faded as she grew uncomfortable under his stare. Luckily, another dancing couple passed by, allowing her to look away and break the trance between them.

Perhaps a turn around the room would be to her liking, Lord Edwin convinced himself before rising.

Rand stood and wagged his tail.

"Come here, boy." Sir Garrick slapped the palm of his hand on his thigh as he watched Lord Edwin approach the lovely lady. Rand obeyed the knight's request, went to his side, and sat.

Out of the corner of her eye, Lady Averly saw the Lord of Tildenham walking toward her. She brushed away imaginary wrinkles from her overskirt and fidgeted with its edge between her fingers. Pulling her shoulder away from the wall, she stood upon both feet as he stopped before her.

"Is all well with you?"

She forced her down cast her eyes to meet his.

"Yes."

"Then would you care to dance?" He pivoted his body and motioned with his left hand toward the dance floor.

Lady Averly stared at his right elbow he offered as an escort. The idea was enticing. She hesitated.

Lady Miriam made a point of keeping her preoccupied with duties in the kitchen instead of allowing her to enjoy the entertainment and partake in the dancing. She recalled peeking at the twirling couples from the kitchen doorway hoping to someday be one of them.

"I don't know how."

He lowered his elbow, finding it difficult to believe her admission.

"Truly?"

"Truly. I was never given the opportunity."

"Then let this be your opportunity, with me." He held out his hand and waited.

She looked at his palm, then his sincere face, and placed her hand within his.

The dancing couples parted to make room for their lord and his partner.

Afraid he was missing out on the excitement, Rand pranced toward his master as if he expected to join in the dance as well. Isabel, who sat on a nearby bench, was able to coax the wolf to her side, patted his head, and gave him the attention he sought.

Lord Edwin placed his left palm upon Lady Averly's waist. He felt her body jump as if his touch had scalded her. He held her right hand in his and lifted it to shoulder level.

Lady Averly looked to the other the couples. The women had their left hands placed upon their partner's shoulders. She did the same but was unsure as to what she should do next.

"Look at me and follow my lead." Lord Edwin waited for her eyes to meet his.

She took a deep breath, tilted her face upward, and looked into his hazel eyes. *Heaven help me.*

Lord Edwin stepped to the right and guided her in the direction of his movement.

Lady Averly followed his lead but entwined her foot between his and tripped. She removed her hand from his shoulder to brace herself for the fall.

Lord Edwin held her securely, steadying her within his arms. He stood still while she regained her footing.

"Sorry." Her cheeks reddened before daring to look into his eyes. She returned her hand to his shoulder.

"No apology needed." Lord Edwin smiled kindly. He looked toward the musicians. "May we slow the tempo a bit, gentlemen?"

"Yes, my lord." The drummer's rhythm slowed.

Lord Edwin took a step. She followed his lead.

"Very good." He glided her about the room without a misstep.

As her confidence grew, her body relaxed, and she smiled.

Lord Edwin returned her smile knowing she felt at ease.

Others in the Great Hall watched the young couple whirl around the room.

As the music ended, Lord Edwin released her hand and removed his from her waist. He bowed respectfully. Lady Averly curtseyed.

Rand's ears perked. He went toward his master.

"Thank you for the dance." Her gratitude was sincere. "It was as enjoyable as I imagined."

He placed his hand on the small of her back and guided her toward a bench.

"You're most welcome." Lord Edwin felt Rand brush against his leg. He reached down and patted the wolf's head.

Lady Averly scanned the room. The children were lying on pallets covered with blankets. They would soon close their eyes and fall asleep. With her health improved, she thought her isolation should come to an end.

"My lord, I'm feeling better now. Perhaps I should sleep in the Great Hall tonight."

"You're still recovering. It would be best for you to remain in the bedchamber for the time being."

"But, my lord, I'm unaccustomed to such fine quarters."

"Nevertheless, you've been ill and need a quiet place to rest."

The musicians began an upbeat tune.

"Thank you." She glanced to the balcony with the intention of retiring.

Lord Edwin motioned toward an empty bench facing the dance floor. He waited for her to sit before joining her.

"You're welcome."

She sat on the nearest bench and focused on the footwork of the dancers who stepped lively to the music. She doubted her ability to learn such a quick step. As the hour grew late, she put her hand over her mouth to hide a contorted yawn.

The attempt failed, for her movement drew Lord Edwin's attention. After suffering from such an illness, he imagined her need for rest. She had surprised many by rousing so soon, let alone working in the kitchen. He admired the determination in her character.

She placed her hands on her lap. Her eyelids grew heavy. Even though she may have embarrassed herself with the stumble, she was proud of her accomplishment for the evening. As the tune ended, she looked toward Lord Edwin.

"I believe I shall retire. Thank you again for the dance. Goodnight." She rose from the bench.

Lord Edwin stood.

"Good night. Sleep well."

She nodded her head in affirmation and ascended the staircase. Her feet ached, and her legs labored to climb each step. As she turned in the direction of her bedchamber, she looked over the balcony. Lord Edwin was staring at her. She displayed a slight smile, turned into the hallway, and went to her room.

Chapter 19

AS DAYLIGHT PEEKED over the horizon, Doran rose and dressed quickly while lost in thought. *The sooner I can find the barbarians, the less death, and destruction they can cause.* His plan was simple. He would follow their trail of devastation until he came upon them, predict which kingdom they would strike next, and inform the baron.

He strapped on his sword, giving little thought to the Lord and Lady of Holbrook's request. The chance of finding the young lady was slim. However, if he discovered her, the bounty would enrich his coffers nicely.

Averly. More than likely she has assumed another name to retain her anonymity. He helped himself to a selection of meats, cheeses, and bread from a tray on a table in the Great Hall and went to the stable.

Emmet paused with his pitchfork of hay in midair as he watched Holbrook's visitor enter the stable. The stableboy pushed his blonde hair away from his blue eyes.

"Good morning, sir. Shall I ready your horse?"

Doran recognized the stableboy, a lad maybe ten and four.

"Yes."

Emmet tossed the hay into a stall, propped the pitchfork against a wall, and retrieved the saddle and bridle. He disappeared into a stall and within moments reappeared leading the horse by its reins.

"He's been fed and watered."

"Thank you." Doran took the reins from the lad and climbed atop his horse. He encouraged it forward with a touch of his heal to its belly, establishing a slow gait toward the gatehouse. He reined his horse occasionally and questioned those within the kingdom for any rumors they may have heard from traveling merchants. The blacksmith informed him of an attack on Heywood but was uncertain when it occurred. He thanked the blacksmith for the information, trotted his horse over the drawbridge, and followed the road through the village, heading southward toward Heywood.

*   *   *

Lady Averly slept longer than she had intended. She rolled onto her side and saw a folded stack of her clothes upon the seat of the chair. She assumed Isabel had stepped silently into her bedchamber and placed them there without waking her. She got out of bed, went to the chair, and held each item before her, examining its condition.

"It looks as if they made the trip unscathed." Refolding them, she opened the armoire and discovered her cloak hanging upon a peg. *My cloak.* Next to it hung her dirk. *I thought I had lost this.* She touched the weapon. *Apparently not.*

Touching the fur on the edge of the hood, thoughts of her adventure away from Holbrook came to the forefront of her mind. *I wonder if I've traveled far enough away from home. I don't even know where I am. If I left Tildenham, I may end up traveling in a circle and find myself back at Holbrook or cross paths with the barbarians.* She sighed. *I wonder if Nelly has healed from her injury.*

Lady Averly set the clean clothes inside the armoire before dressing in the clothes she had worn the previous day and pulling on her boots. Looking out the window at the overcast sky, she folded her cloak over her arm as she left the bedchamber.

The Great Hall was empty as she passed through it. Stepping into the doorway of the kitchen, she nearly bumped into a woman carrying a bucket of water.

The woman curtsied.

"I'm sorry. Just on my way to do some cleaning."

Lady Averly turned to watch the woman walk away while backing into the kitchen.

Isabel kneaded the bread dough on the floured tabletop, looked to the cloak over her arm, and wondered if the woman was leaving Tildenham.

"Good morning, Averly. I saved you some breakfast." The cook nodded her head toward the table.

Lady Averly saw a tray of buttered porridge with cream, toasted bread, and hard-boiled eggs. Her stomach grumbled.

"Thank you." She pulled a stool out from beneath the table, placed her folded cloak on the seat before sitting, and began to eat. *This feels somewhat familiar, kind of like home.* She watched the women go about their duties while she ate. After biting into the toasted bread, she retrieved a mug from a shelf and filled it with ale from a nearby pitcher.

"Isabel, is there anything, in particular, I can help prepare today?" She returned to her seat and sipped the ale.

"Nothing now, but this afternoon will be quite busy. Your help would be greatly appreciated, that is if you'll return by then." She added more flour to the table top and rolled over the dough before looking to Lady Averly for an answer.

"I'd like to visit my horse to see if her injury is healing properly. As it's been several days since I've seen her, she may think I've abandoned her. I promise to return soon to help with preparations." She ate a spoonful of porridge as she watched Isabel form the dough into a loaf.

The cook glanced at Lady Averly. *So, she has a horse. Not many peasants own a horse, especially a woman.* Isabel reached into a bowl and selected a slightly wrinkled apple.

"Perhaps this will mend any hurt feelings she may have." Isabel set the apple on the table before Lady Averly and smiled.

"Thank you. I'm sure Nelly will appreciate the treat."

After finishing her breakfast Lady Averly cleared her dirty dishes, grabbed her cloak and the apple, and headed for the stable. She stepped outside into the chilly day and pulled her cloak around her.

Bryce heard the creak of the stable door. He looked toward the brightness that filled the front of the stall as he placed some hay in the wall rack for a destrier. He poked his head around the back end of the warhorse and looked toward the doorway as it closed.

"Is there something you needed?"

Oh, a familiar face. Lady Averly remembered the lad from her arrival at Tildenham.

"Hello. I came to check on my horse." She looked from horse rump to horse rump as she passed each stall until she found her chestnut mare.

"She's been fed and watered. I've given special attention to her cut and used a salve on it." Bryce pointed to the wound covered with a sticky goo. "It's healing nicely." He stood outside the stall and watched as Lady Averly entered and examined the wound.

She touched close to the injury. *No swelling or puss. Cool to the touch. Good.* She smoothed the hair on Nelly's thigh before turning to the stableboy.

"I can see she's in good hands."

Nelly pulled her nose out of a bucket of oats as she continued to chew and looked toward her mistress. Lady Averly squeezed between her horse and the wall of the stall. She stiffened her fingers, placed the apple in the palm of her hand, and presented the treat.

Nelly's lips curled around the apple. She bit into it with a resounding crunch. Her head bobbed up and down approvingly, keeping time as she chewed.

Lady Averly stroked her horse's neck as the mare turned toward her bucket and resumed eating oats.

Bryce moved aside to allow Lady Averly to step out of the stall.

"She's a fine mare, a good-natured one at that too."

"Yes, she's a lifesaver." *More than you know.*

The stable door opened, and Rand trotted in.

"Good morning, my lord. We're just discussing the care I've given Nelly." The stableboy motioned toward the chestnut mare.

Lord Edwin paused in mid-step as his eyes met the defiant sapphire orbs of Lady Averly.

"Well, good morning to you both."

Lady Averly patted Nelly's rump as she stood before the Lord of Tildenham.

"Yes, my lord, he's done a fine job."

Lord Edwin nodded to the stableboy.

"As always."

Bryce anticipated his lord's request.

"Shall I ready Fulton for you, my lord?"

"Please." Lord Edwin looked toward Lady Averly. "Would you like to join me?"

Bryce took Fulton's bridle from a peg on the wall and went to the warhorse's stall.

"That depends on where you're going." She entertained the idea of a gentle morning ride but worried it may keep her away from her promised duties in the kitchen.

"I'll be inspecting Tildenham for repairs and ride to the mill in the woods. We'll return before midday."

She sighed. *The fresh air may do me some good.*

"Is Sir Garrick accompanying you?"

"No, he's seeing to another matter."

"Then yes, I believe I'd like to join you."

"Bryce...." Lord Edwin began.

The stableboy called from the stall as he fastened a buckle on Fulton's bridle.

"I'll ready her horse as well, my lord."

Lady Averly turned toward the warhorse's stall as the stableboy emerged. He pulled the blanket and saddle from the top of the stall wall, saddled the horse quickly, and backed Fulton into the aisle. Lady Averly watched in awe as the large ebony warhorse walked by her.

"I failed to realize the enormous size of your horse. Nelly pales in comparison." She watched Bryce tie the destrier to a post outside of the stable. Rand went to the destrier's side and sat.

Lord Edwin looked to his horse.

"He's just over seventeen hands high. It gives me a defensive advantage. More leverage and a better angle when necessary."

"I dare say I'd have difficulty climbing atop of him." She thought out loud.

Lord Edwin looked down at the petite woman standing beside him.

"I could give you a hand up if you wish to try him on for size." He chuckled.

She analyzed the distance from the top of the warhorse's back to the ground.

"I'll decline your offer. If I ever fell from his back, I'd surely suffer an injury."

Bryce led Nelly out of the stall.

"I believe her injury isn't severe, so she should be fine for a gentle ride. It may even do her some good."

The clouds parted as Lord Edwin and Lady Averly followed the stableboy out of the building and into the bright morning sunshine.

A patch of green foliage at the base of a charred fencepost drew Lady Averly's attention. Curious, she brushed away the surrounding debris to reveal a spring flower pushing up through the soil. *Strange.* She stood and looked at the area to the right of the stable.

Lord Edwin clasped his hands together to assist her onto her saddle, but when he anticipated her acceptance, Lady Averly had walked away. *What can she be doing?* He stepped to her side and looked over her shoulder.

"If I recall correctly, they're red tulips. They were her favorite."

Amongst the clutter of charred wood and ash was a walkway leading to a stone bench at the rear of the garden. Once protected by a fence, the plants were now singed and trampled.

She turned toward Lord Edwin.

"This was your mother's garden?"

"Yes, she grew a variety of flowers and put them in vases in nearly every room of the Keep. It was a welcomed change of color and fragrance after a long, dank winter."

Fulton stomped his foot impatiently. Lord Edwin glanced at his horse before suggesting.

"Perhaps we should be on our way."

Chapter 20

MUDDY WATER SPLASHED from beneath the horses' hooves as the warmth of the morning sun melted the remaining snow.

The gray wolf kept pace ahead of his master, who slowed his horse to equal Nelly's gait. Lord Edwin reined Fulton before the anvil surrounded by rubble.

"If I knew the requirements for the blacksmith, I'd restore this building next."

Lady Averly examined the rubble of the dwelling. She saw rings from barrels, an abandoned anvil, and the head of the hammer where the blacksmith had left it at the end of his workday. Its handle, once made of wood, had turned to ash and disappeared amongst the rubble.

"It's eerie, like a moment frozen in time." She sighed. "I believe, my lord, every blacksmith has their own tools. Much of what remains is from the former blacksmith. All he would need is a forge and bellows."

Lord Edwin rested his forearm upon the pommel of his saddle and looked toward her.

"You have knowledge of what must be restored?"

Lady Averly chuckled.

"Yes, when I was younger I would visit the blacksmith often to escape the responsibility of my duties." *And my stepmother's wrath.*

"Good. Then perhaps you should supervise its reconstruction." Lord Edwin had grown weary of the destruction. He longed to see Tildenham restored to its former beauty as soon as possible. Reining Fulton, he directed him toward the gatehouse.

Taken back by his statement, she hesitated before reining her horse to follow.

"Me?"

He glanced over his shoulder with a devilish grin upon his face.

They crossed the drawbridge entering the village at a leisurely pace. Rand darted about, sniffing each charred object. Most of the residences were a total loss even though an occasional fireplace stood intact.

Lady Averly reined her horse. She stared at a mangled and tattered handmade doll lying on the ground. Fighting back the tears, she imagined the joy it had brought to the little girl, looked at the nearby rubble, and wondered if the child had survived.

Lord Edwin peered into the distance. The large mound of victims from the attack had been reduced to ash. It had slipped his mind. He was thankful someone had taken the initiative to incinerate them before any disease could spread. He heard Lady Averly talking to herself, reined his horse in a circle, and brought Fulton aside her mare.

Overcome by grief, she dismounted, picked up the toy, and brushed it off. *Looks to be salvageable.* She strapped it to her saddle before resuming her place upon her horse.

"How could they do this?"

Lord Edwin spoke his mind.

"It's a nonsensical reality. Be that as it may, we must stay positive; focus on the future, and the endeavors it may bring. As history proves, we'll get past this hurtful time within Tildenham and move forward with each board we nail and each stone we mortar in place."

His words conveyed determination. His stare was intense. Lady Averly nodded her head in agreement. She wondered how he would accomplish such a daunting task.

"It seems as if everything has been destroyed."

"Except our will to move forward, our honor, and pride."

"Of course, but where will you get the supplies to rebuild?"

"I pray the pillagers have left our mill unscathed. Are you feeling well enough to ride the distance to the woods?" Lord Edwin pointed in the general direction.

She saw the tinting of green and yellow buds on the naked forest branches. *Looks inviting.*

"Yes, but I need to return in time to help prepare the evening meal."

He smiled.

"I'll have you back in time."

They rode out of the village, across an unplowed field, and followed the grass-covered road into the woods. Leaving the destruction behind them, their ride was calming and peaceful, except for the scurrying of a rabbit or squirrel crossing their pathway with Rand chasing closely behind.

At the end of the road was a small stone building nestled by a stream. Its gentle current rotated the waterwheel. Neatly cut and stacked lumber was next to the building.

Lord Edwin exhaled with relief as he reined Fulton to a stop.

"Just as I hoped, supplies to rebuild."

Lady Averly reined her horse. She looked to the stack of lumber, back to the destroyed village, and considered the momentous task. The gatehouse drawbridge and portcullis were still inoperable. She turned toward Lord Edwin.

"But what if the attackers return? How will you defend what you rebuild?"

Lord Edwin understood her concern. It was a topic he had discussed with his knight as well.

"Sir Garrick and I believe the barbarians have pillaged Tildenham thoroughly. They will continue their destructive journey until they have ravaged nearly every kingdom they encounter before returning to their own land. At present, the gatehouse offers little protection. Until the repairs are made to the mechanisms of the drawbridge and portcullis, we are vulnerable. Beginning construction within the castle walls gives our efforts some protection." He sighed. "With all of the destruction surrounding us, we need to begin rebuilding, to do something to remove the blackness spread throughout Tildenham."

Lady Averly nodded in agreement.

Lord Edwin continued, entrusting her with his plan.

"Once the gatehouse has been repaired, I can send word to the baron and request men-at-arms to replace those we have lost. I'll also offer work to freemen."

"But, my lord, if other kingdoms have also been attacked, there may be a high demand for their skills. You may receive little response to your request."

"True, but eventually they'll migrate once they've completed their work at other kingdoms. We can begin building the dwellings for the crafters and use them as temporary housing until they arrive."

Rand barked, drawing their attention.

Lord Edwin looked in the direction of his pet.

"More than likely he's cornered a rabbit." He reined his horse toward the woods with Lady Averly following.

They wove between trees and dodged budding low branches until they emerged into a shadowed clearing to see Rand sitting before a bench.

Lady Mary lowered her outstretched hand from the wolf and looked toward her son. She smiled. *All is as it should be.* Rand lifted his paw toward the apparition as if to shake hands.

Lady Averly scanned the area.

"This is where you found me." She whispered as she recognized the clearing.

Lord Edwin recalled the day vividly. He had been hunting when he encountered Nelly. He backtracked her hoofprints to the clearing and discovered Lady Averly lying on the ground in a disheveled state.

"Yes."

As if heaven itself was shining down upon the angel, a sunbeam broke through a cloud, enlightening its face.

The vague memory of an angel statue appeared in Lady Averly's mind. Her father had commissioned the angelic guardian to overlook her mother's grave. Lady Miriam forbade her to visit it. She often looked out of the Keep's window to view it on a distant hill. She looked to Lord Edwin.

"Is this a gravesite?"

"No. To my knowledge, those who have passed are buried in our cemetery located north of the castle, except for those who died during the last attack."

Lady Averly understood the need for the cremation. She looked toward Rand. He stared directly at a spot above the bench, closed his eyes, and raised his nose as if someone was patting him on his head. She had a faint memory of a woman sitting on the very same bench, or was it just a dream? *As cold as I was, she may have been a figment of my imagination. But the woman in the painting. I wonder.* Curious, she posed the question.

"Who's the woman in the painting above the fireplace in the Great Hall?"

"My mother, Lady Mary. My father's portrait is above the fireplace in my bedchamber. Why do you ask?"

Dare I tell him that I saw her sitting on the bench? Lady Averly decided to keep the matter to herself.

"Just curious. She's quite beautiful."

Lord Edwin whistled. Rand looked toward his master.

"Come." He turned his horse around, as did Lady Averly, who glanced behind her at the bench to ensure it remained empty.

Rand took one last look toward the bench before scampering away.

On the trail once again, Lord Edwin looked across the field at the distant cemetery. With putting Tildenham in order and addressing his lordly duties, he had neglected to visit his parents' graves. Or had he avoided it? He reined his horse to a stop.

Lady Averly brought Nelly alongside the ebony warhorse.

"If you don't mind, I'd like to stop and pay my respect to my parents." He nodded in the distance at the two mounds of stone on a small hill.

She assumed he may want to be alone while he paid his respects.

"Shall I return to the Keep? Isabel is sure to need my help soon." She looked to him for his reply.

Lord Edwin stared at the graveyard with its grass-covered mounds and mournful trees sheltering the souls of those who rested peacefully.

"It's a depressing site. Even though I believe their souls reside in Heaven, it's difficult not to focus on the loss buried within the ground." He looked toward her. "I'd appreciate your company."

"Very well." She hesitated before adding, "My lord."

Lord Edwin touched his heel to his warhorse's belly. Fulton trotted forward. Lady Averly's mare followed without any encouragement.

After crossing the field, they reined their horses at the graveyard entrance and dismounted.

"It's so peaceful." Lady Averly patted Nelly's neck.

"More like eerily quiet." Lord Edwin glanced up at the few trees within the cemetery in search of birds, but there were none. He stepped inside the stone walls, glanced at the graves as he passed by, and stopped in front of the side by side graves covered with stone.

Lady Averly passed a grave that was short in length. She assumed a child lay beneath the mound.

"I believe this is them." Lord Edwin knelt upon one knee and bowed his head.

Lady Averly stood quietly behind him. *It would be nice to place flowers upon their graves. Unfortunately, they have yet to bloom.* She bowed her head as she made the sign of the cross. Overcome by the loss of life surrounding her, tears welled in her eyes as she thought of her mother. She wiped them away from the corner of her eyes as she turned to leave. She glanced over her shoulder and paused as she heard Lord Edwin speak.

"I'm sorry I wasn't here to help defend Tildenham. I promise I will fulfill the role as its lord to the best of my ability. Please watch over me from above and guide me in each challenge I face. I'll always try to do what is right for the kingdom and its people. May you rest in peace." Lord Edwin rose and followed Lady Averly out of the cemetery. They climbed atop their horses and returned to the castle.

Rand stood on the drawbridge waiting for his master. As he spied the couple riding toward him, he turned and entered the bailey.

As the wolf passed by the doorway of the gatehouse, Sir Garrick stepped outside and waited for Lord Edwin to cross the drawbridge. He soon came into view.

"My lord, a moment of your time."

Lord Edwin reined Fulton, dismounted, and slapped his warhorse on the rear. Fulton trotted toward the stable. He looked to Lady Avelry.

"I'm needed here. I'll see you at the evening meal."

Lady Averly nodded as he turned and entered the gatehouse. She encouraged her horse toward the stable.

Bryce took Nelly's reins as she dismounted.

"With Fulton returning to his bucket of oats, I figured you would be close behind."

"You assumed correctly. Thank you, Bryce." She unstrapped the doll from the saddle and headed toward the kitchen. She held the doll before her. *Perhaps I can soak you in a tub of soapy water and mend what is damaged.* She brushed back the wayward strips of rags that made up the doll's hair before hanging her cloak on a peg in the Keep's hallway. *I know a little girl who will enjoy playing with you.* She headed toward the kitchen.

Chapter 21

LORD EDWIN JOINED the men in the gatehouse.

"My lord." Sir Garrick presented a splintered board. "We discovered the pulleys of the portcullis were merely jammed with pieces of broken boards. It took some doing. We removed the fragments, and all is in working order once again." He tossed the board aside. "However, it doesn't offer much security. It can be easily raised by several strong bodied men using poleaxes beneath the lowest crossbar and a log or such for leverage. The chains on the drawbridge have several broken links. Until we can repair them, the drawbridge will remain open."

A young man stepped forward. He brushed back his shaggy, thin brown hair and stood tall.

"My lord, I began my apprenticeship with the blacksmith a few months ago. I watched him closely as he created chain links. I'm a quick study and believe I can make the repairs if we can find the iron amongst the rubble of the blacksmith shop."

Lord Edwin stared into the eager blue eyes of the apprentice.

"Your name?"

"Coleman, my lord."

"Your age?"

"Ten and six."

"Well Coleman, let's go see what we can find." Lord Edwin led the group of men to where the blacksmith shop once stood. "Keep a sharp eye for anything that may be of use."

A heavy hammerhead was found near the anvil and needed a new handle. Several tongs, pieces of iron, and chisels were discovered beneath the ashes too. The forge appeared operable even though its chimney had collapsed.

Lord Edwin stood before the collected goods lying upon the ground. He looked to the apprentice.

"Do you have what you need to make the repairs?"

Coleman walked around the gathered items, picked up a chisel, and examined the iron made by the former blacksmith. He looked to his lord.

"I believe I can manage, my lord."

"Good." He turned to his knight. "I need you to assist Coleman. It may take the strength of both of you to bend the iron."

"Yes, my lord." Sir Garrick nodded to the apprentice indicating they would get the job done.

Lord Edwin looked to the men who awaited his orders. Across the bailey were several destroyed crafter's shops.

"I'll have Bryce hitch a horse to a wagon, two if there is a second one available. You and you," pointing to two of the men, "come with me. The rest of you, begin clearing the rubble of the blacksmith shop and the buildings across the way. With any luck, we will have new buildings started and an operable drawbridge by the end of the day."

He hoped Bryce could find two wagons, one for clearing the rubble and another to go to the mill and retrieve the lumber to rebuild.

*   *   *

Lady Averly stood at the center table of the kitchen kneading bread. She had made several loaves earlier that had risen and were baking in the oven.

She admired the kitchen, for it was unlike the dark one at Holbrook. A large southern window filled the room with natural light. Potted herbs and an aloe plant flourished on its windowsill. Her hands stilled as the memory of her mother came to mind.

Her mother was ill. She asked for her father's permission to visit the apothecary in the woods for a remedy to make her mother well. He granted her request on one condition, his knight must accompany her. The apothecary, an old woman, probably knew there was little hope for her mother, but offered several remedies. Even after her mother's passing, Lady Averly continued to visit the apothecary and learn her ways.

Isabel chopped potatoes at another table. She glanced at Lady Averly from the corner of her eye.

"You're not from around here, are you?"

Pulled from her thoughts, Lady Averly looked in the cook's direction.

"What makes you think that?" She added flour to the tabletop and continued to knead.

"I don't remember you from the village, but then again, most of my days are spent here, in the kitchen." Isabel selected another potato from a wooden basket.

Lady Averly shrugged her shoulders.

Isabel pressed, hoping for an answer.

"Were you captured by the barbarians and escaped?"

"No." She almost chuckled at the idea. "In all honesty, I believe they prefer to execute their prisoners."

"Then you must be running from something or someone."

Lady Averly shaped the dough into a loaf, deciding it was best to remain silent.

Still not satisfied, Isabel cut into the potato and continued her assumptions.

"Ah, indeed, you're a lady, but I have yet to figure out how you acquired your cooking skills. Most ladies of rank never set foot in a kitchen unless it's to give orders."

"Let's just say I was forced to do so." Lady Averly thought the smidgeon of truth would satisfy the cook's curiosity.

"Well, you've learned quite well. I've never seen such fine loaves of bread."

"Thank you." Lady Averly set the loaf aside to rise. She took the wooden paddle from the hook on the wall and removed the freshly baked loaves from the oven.

The cook tossed the potato pieces into a bowl, selected another from the basket, and paused to look at Lady Averly.

"What's your favorite dish to make?" Isabel ran the knife through the spud.

"Pastries. They seem to complete a meal."

Isabel thought for a moment.

"I like to make egg noodles. My grandmother and I would make them together." Isabel grinned at the pleasant memory.

Lady Averly looked toward the cook and grinned.

"Shall we make some and add them to tonight's soup?"

Isabel looked inside a nearby basket.

"We need eggs. Maybe the hens are sitting on some. Even duck or goose eggs will do."

Knowing she must wait for the unbaked loaves of bread to rise, Lady Averly took the doll from the bucket of water, wrung out the excess, and placed it on a stool near the fire. She wiped her hands on her overskirt.

"I'll go see if there are any."

Isabel pointed with the tip of her knife to a basket hanging from a peg on the wall.

"Take the basket hanging over there."

With the basket in hand, Lady Averly exited the Keep. She inhaled the fresh air, tilted her face skyward, and welcomed the warmth of the sunshine. Men were clearing the remains of a building as she passed by them on her way to the new coop.

Chickens scratched and pecked the ground as she walked between them. Ducks and geese were leery of her proximity as they conjugated outside of their new home. The coop was solidly constructed with a small opening on one side for the animals to come and go as they pleased. A wayward goat looked toward her as it chewed whatever it had found to eat.

Opening the door, she backed into the coop, closing the door behind her, turned, and bumped into the steadfast chest of Lord Edwin, who grasped her small waist to help stead her from the impact.

Lady Averly took a moment to realize what had happened. She looked up into the hazel orbs staring down at her.

"Oh, my lord, I didn't see you there. I'm sorry."

He grinned.

"No harm was done." He held her for a moment longer than necessary before letting his hands drop to his sides. "I was checking to see how the fowl liked their accommodations." He turned and looked about the coop.

Inhaling the smell of new lumber, she put the basket on the crook of her arm. The men had built stacked nesting boxes for the fowl to lay their eggs. The ducks and geese preferred to nest at the ground level, while the chickens used the upper boxes.

"It's very nice." She went to the nearest nesting box. "I came to see if there are any eggs."

"Good luck in your search. I must return to the men." He nodded and left.

After searching the empty nests, her basket contained only two chicken eggs and one duck egg. Several of the laying geese hissed their objection to her intrusion. She had experienced wicked pinches from geese many times before and did her best to avoid their long reaching beaks.

The pinging from a hammer resounded within the bailey as she exited and looked toward the noise to see Sir Garrick gripping a pair of tongs while a young man struck a piece of iron that glowed vibrant orange. She closed the door to the coop and returned to the kitchen.

After dropping the last of the chopped potatoes into a bowl, Isabel looked to the doorway to see Lady Averly enter.

"Find any?"

"A few." She tilted the basket for the cook to peek inside.

"They'll do." Isabel retrieved the container of flour, salt, and a large wooden bowl. She put the dry ingredients in the bowl before adding the eggs and stirring. The cook searched the room but failed to find what she needed.

"Averly, could you go to the larder and get the goat's milk?"

Lady Averly entered the storage room. Mice scampered out of sight. She retrieved the vessel and gave it to the cook, who poured in the correct amount into the bowl. When the dough was soft, not sticky, she sprinkled flour onto the table surface and dumped the noodle dough in the center. Adding more flour to the top, she rolled it with a rolling pin until the dough was a thin rectangle. Sprinkling flour upon it once again, she rolled the opposite long sides inward. Isabel selected a sharp knife.

"Now, we slice it." She cut the rolled dough into slices. When she was finished, she lifted the dough spirals upward until they uncurled.

"The noodles need to dry before going into the soup." She straightened and laid the noodles in rows upon the table. "Well, the preparations are done for now." Isabel looked about the room, confident everything was in order for the evening meal.

Lady Averly picked up the doll from the stool. It was slightly damp.

"Then I'll return later and help serve." She left the kitchen in search of the basket of sewing supplies in the Great Hall. She sat on the bench next to it. After selecting a needle, thread, and a pair of scissors, she began to sew and listened to Glenna sing to herself while she played with the rushes upon the floor. The song was a lullaby. She pictured the child's mother singing it to Glenna as she went to sleep at night.

After finishing the repairs, Lady Averly straightened the doll's dress and overskirt.

"Glenna."

The little girl stopped singing and went to Lady Averly's side. Her eyes widened as she looked at the doll held before her.

"I found this in the village. I cleaned her as best I could. Would you like it?"

Glenna nodded her head as her tiny hands reached for the doll and cradled it within her arms.

"Thank you, my lady."

"You're welcome." Lady Averly smiled as Glenna returned to her spot on the floor and began to sing the lullaby to the doll.

*　　　*　　　*

The sun had dipped below the horizon as Doran arrived at the kingdom of Heywood. The castle appeared to be intact. The village was destroyed. He passed peasants, who stared at him with weary eyes while they cooked their meals over open fires and children huddled together for warmth.

Doran stopped at the gatehouse. He was questioned before given permission to enter the castle. He reined his horse at the stable and entered the Keep. The Lord of Heywood indicated the attack occurred more than a fortnight ago. He was offered a tasty meal and given a room for the night.

Chapter 22

WITH EVERYONE'S APPETITE satisfied, the men visited while they sipped on their tankards, the women sewed by the fire, and the children played in the Great Hall of Tildenham. With the successful repair of the portcullis and drawbridge, a sense of security eased Lord Edwin's mind.

Lady Averly moved her queen into striking position.

"Checkmate."

Lord Edwin examined the playing board. His King was trapped.

"Well done." He smirked at the sheepish grin upon her face.

"Thank you. It has been a while since I've played."

"You seem to recall the game quite well." He looked toward Glenna as she approached them.

"Lady Averly, my dolly has a hole in her dress." Glenna stuck her finger through the tear as she stood before them.

A noble title? Lord Edwin assumed the child misspoke.

"I missed one? Let me see."

Glenna pulled her finger from the hole and handed it to Lady Averly.

Lord Edwin leaned over the table.

"Isn't that the doll you found in the village?"

Lady Averly glanced in his direction.

"Yes, it cleaned up quite well and only needed a few repairs." She turned her attention to Glenna. "We should find a scrap of fabric and make her another dress."

"Oh, that would be lovely." The little girl's brown eyes sparkled.

Lord Edwin grinned at the child's excitement.

"I believe Mother has plenty of fabric to choose from in her sewing chamber. Perhaps a suitable scrap can be found."

Glenna gasped as she looked to her lord. Lady Averly was impressed by his kind offer.

"That's very generous of you, Lord Edwin. What do you say, Glenna?"

"Thank you, my lord."

Lady Averly touched the top of the child's head and stroked her long sun-bleached blonde hair.

"Well done. We must always remember to be polite. I'll repair your doll once you retrieve a needle and thread from one of the women who are sewing by the fireplace."

Glenna skipped away.

Lady Averly watched the child approach the women before turning back to Lord Edwin. He was staring at her.

"I suppose you think it silly to rescue such a toy, but as you can see, it means a lot to her." She straightened the doll's rag hair.

"I don't think it's silly." He continued to stare, conveying his sincerity.

She looked into his hazel eyes.

"I feel it's important to restore normalcy as much as possible." She tilted her head to one side and looked to the doll as if embarrassed to have shared her opinion.

He smiled.

"I agree."

Glenna returned with the needle, thread, and a beautiful pair of embroidery scissors that once belonged to Lady Mary. She sat on the bench next to lady Averly and watched as she threaded the needle.

In very little time, the repair was done. Lady Averly snipped the thread and handed the doll to Glenna.

"Thank you, Lady Averly." The child stretched her arms wide and wrapped her arms around Lady Averly, who embraced the little girl in earnest.

"You're welcome. Please return these." She gave Glenna the sewing items. "And thank them." She smiled as she watched the little girl do as she was told.

Lord Edwin leaned over the table toward her.

"Lady Averly?" He emphasized "lady" in a whisper intended for her ears only.

Her smile faded. She knew he was expecting an honest answer. Even Isabel suspected her true title.

"It seems Glenna has bestowed the title upon me." She made light of the subject as she forced a grin upon her face.

He was intrigued. *It would be convenient if she has the blood of royalty running through her veins. She's quite beautiful and her disposition is an amiable quality as well.*

"Then I shall do the same." He grinned in return.

She thought it best to change the subject.

"If the weather is nice tomorrow, would you be offended if I try to put your mother's garden in order?"

"Offended? I'd be honored." He tried to camouflage a yawn with his hand. His attempt failed as she watched him lower his hand to the tabletop.

"It's been a long day. You and the men have accomplished a lot."

"It's nice to see the progress, even if it is in small strides. With the drawbridge temporarily repaired, men are rotating watch in the gatehouse and allowing Sir Garrick and I to get some much-needed rest."

"As they should." She looked to the knight, who sat at another table with some peasant men.

Lord Edwin picked up his rook and rotated it between his index finger and thumb.

"I must confess, even when I lay my head to sleep, my mind refuses to do so. I think of the buildings that must be reconstructed within the bailey and the skilled workers needed to make candles, ale, and others as well. The village must have several of the dwellings constructed before I can send word for needed freemen." He paused in thought as he looked at the peasants in the room. "It's a bit overwhelming."

Lady Averly admired his handsome profile. *It's a daunting task, but not impossible.* She smiled.

"I think you have a good plan. Under your guidance, my lord, Tildenham shall flourish once again." She returned her chess pieces to their starting position.

Lord Edwin rested his left elbow on the table and placed his chin within his fisted palm as he returned his chess pieces as well.

Lady Averly noticed the gold ring on his pinky finger.

"You have a lovely signet ring. Your father's, I assume."

Lord Edwin removed his fist from beneath his chin and extended his fingers.

"Yes."

She extended her hand, palm facing upward toward him.

"May I examine it more closely?"

He placed his fingertips within her dainty hand.

Lady Averly clasped his fingertips and lowered her face toward the ring.

He studied the features of her delicate face while she tilted his hand toward the flickering light of the candelabra and inspected the quality of the etched lion and rubies.

"It's lovely." She released his hand.

"Thank you." Lord Edwin laid his hand upon the table and nodded his head toward the chess board. "Care for a rematch?"

Lady Averly reached for a pawn and made the first move. She hoped she was able to stay awake long enough to see the game through to its completion and wondered if he would be able to do the same.

Across the room, Sir Garrick kept a watchful eye. Isabel approached him, carrying a pitcher of ale.

"Sir Garrick, would you care for a refill?"

The knight held up his empty mug to the cook.

The cook filled the tankard, set the pitcher upon the table, and looked toward Lady Averly.

"She's pretty isn't she?"

"Very. It's a pity she isn't royalty, for I believe his lordship has taken quite a fancy to her." He sipped his ale.

"My guess, she's royalty all right, wherever she came from." Isabel collected several dirty tankards from the table before returning to the kitchen.

Sir Garrick glanced at the pitcher of ale the cook had left for him to empty. He took another swig from his tankard as he watched the couple closely.

"Royalty?"

Chapter 23

AFTER A GOOD night's rest, Doran sat at a table in the Great Hall of Heywood. He spooned porridge into his mouth while eavesdropping on the conversations. Reaching across the table, he lifted a wedge of cold meat pie from a platter and kept his eyes downcast while he took a hefty bite. A man to his left shared an exaggerated tale about the voluptuous and attractive red-headed woman who had warmed his bed during the night. Across the table, another discussed hand to hand combat.

A man to his right spoke of a barbaric attack on Heywood. Doran paused with his meat pie midway to his mouth and turned to the bearded man.

"Do you know how long ago and in which direction they traveled after the attack?"

"A few weeks back. Rumor has it they went toward Lowell. It's to the west, about a three days ride."

Doran knew his inquiry was a long shot, but it was worth posing the question.

"I've been asked to search for a fair lady with golden hair that goes by the name of Averly. Do you know if she is in Heywood?"

The men glanced at each other before looking toward him. They shook their heads, confirming his suspicion.

*　　　　*　　　　*

Lady Averly had slept in again. *Perhaps I should ask Isabel to wake me each morning.* She dressed quickly, hoping to have risen early enough to help with breakfast. She peeked over the balcony to see women collecting dirty dishes from the tables. Many had eaten and begun their day. She entered the kitchen to see her breakfast upon a table.

"I apologize, Isabel. I thought I had risen early enough to help with the morning meal."

"No need to apologize. Just sit yourself down and eat."

While she ate women washed the morning dishes and went about their tasks. She took care of her dishes before taking inventory of the bread she baked the day before and determined there was enough in stock for the day's meals.

"Isabel, would you mind if I worked in the garden this morning?"

The cook had overheard Glenna use the title and thought it best to do the same.

"My lady, you may spend your day as you wish. However, with so few, we do appreciate your help with the preparation of the evening meal."

What started out as a display of respect by a child had caused others to assume it as fact. Being addressed by her proper title was a little unnerving.

"Isabel, Glenna bestowed the title upon me. It's quite silly."

"Silly or not, others are assuming it to be true."

There was little use in arguing. She sighed.

"I'll return in time to help with preparations." Lady Averly nodded her head, left the kitchen, and went to the garden. Hardly knowing where to begin, she stared at the outline of burnt fence posts, the stone bench scarred with soot, and the chaotic debris throughout.

Bryce noticed Lady Averly standing on the edge of the garden as he led a horse out of the stable.

"My lady, did you need something?"

She looked toward the freckled-faced lad and smiled.

"I'm going to try to put the garden in order."

"Can I fetch a pitchfork for you?"

"Oh, Bryce, yes, that would be most helpful. Would you happen to know where I may find a pair of work gloves too?"

"I have a pair or two. They may be a bit large for your hands though."

He tied the horse to a post, disappeared into the stable, and returned moments later.

"Here's what I could find." Stabbing the pitchfork into the ground, he handed her the gloves and watched as she slipped them onto her dainty hands.

"They'll do fine. Thank you." She pulled the pitchfork from the ground.

"I give you credit for tackling such a job, my lady."

My goodness, even Bryce is calling me by my title.

"Thank you, Bryce."

The stableboy scampered off.

Lady Averly began to rake the debris into piles and carefully lift the charred lumber from the plants. Many of the new leaves were singed, but new growth appeared near the ground. She heard something rumbling behind her and turned to see Bryce with a wheelbarrow.

"All of the wagons are in use, my lady. I can empty this for you once it's filled. Just give a holler."

"Thank you." Lady Averly scooped up a raked pile and dumped it into the wheelbarrow.

With each pitchfork of darkness removed from the garden, established pathways were revealed. Much of what she was able to accomplish in the few hours could be credited to the stableboy's eagerness to empty the wheelbarrow as quickly as she filled it. Nagging blisters in the hollow between her thumb and index finger of each hand did not dissuade her. She considered them as a testament to her hard labor. She glanced at the sun's position in the sky. It was past midday. She took a moment to admire her progress.

Bryce lifted the handles of the wheelbarrow, ready to make another trip to empty it.

"Finished for today, my lady?"

She turned toward the stableboy.

"I believe I am."

"Just leave the pitchfork and gloves by the stable door. I'll put them away upon my return."

"Thank you for your help today."

"You're welcome, my lady." Bryce nodded as he set off to empty the load.

After following the stableboy's instructions, she made a mental note to locate a scrub brush and bucket. She would do her best to restore the true whiteness of the limestone bench.

*   *   *

Sir Garrick stood on top of a stack of seasoned lumber at the mill. He handed down a board to Lord Edwin.

"Is she truly a lady?"

Lord Edwin placed the board in the wagon.

"She neither denied nor confirmed the title, but simply stated the little girl bestowed it upon her."

The knight grabbed another board and passed it to his lord.

"Lady Averly, a pretty name for a pretty woman. She has a nice disposition as well."

"I agree." He placed the board on top of the rest. "That about does it for this load. Rand!"

The wolf scampered out of the woods and joined his master as the trio headed back to the castle. They crossed the drawbridge, reined the horse before the working men, and dismounted.

"My lord."

Lord Edwin turned around to see an elderly peasant man approaching.

"Yes."

The man nodded his head toward three men standing behind him.

"They heard they may find employment here."

Lord Edwin motioned for them to step forward as he crossed his arms over his chest and stood with his feet shoulder-width apart. The men looked healthy and strong.

"Please, tell me of your skills."

The tall, broad-shouldered man spoke.

"I'm a blacksmith, the other two are carpenters."

Rand sat next to his master, who patted his head.

"We're in need of both and have plenty of work for you at Tildenham. Since the talent of a blacksmith is greatly needed, perhaps the three of you may begin by reconstructing the shop." He pointed to the cleared space where the anvil, damaged forge, and a pile of tools lay on the ground. "We have an apprentice, Coleman, who did his best to repair the damaged chains of the drawbridge. I'd like you to verify his work and allow him to continue learning under your guidance."

"Yes, my lord. I'll teach him all I know. I've brought my own tools as well."

"Good. What remains of the blacksmith's tools shall be given to Coleman to use. Do you have families?"

"Yes, we hoped to send for them once we secured employment."

"Then the blacksmith shop needs a large loft as well."

"Thank you, my lord." The blacksmith nodded.

The three men wasted no time. They gathered their tools and went directly to the site to begin construction.

Lord Edwin turned toward the resonating hammers within the bailey in search of a few men to reassign to the blacksmith shop.

Recognizing the opportunity to have a moment of his lord's time, Sir Garrick approached.

"Since word has spread of our misfortune, I expect more freemen will arrive for employment."

"Let's hope so. We'll need field workers for plowing and planting soon." Lord Edwin saw Bryce heading toward the stable with an empty wheelbarrow.

"Bryce, please tell Lady Averly that we have three additional mouths to feed for the evening meal."

"Yes, my lord."

Lord Edwin turned back to his knight.

"Perhaps we should unload the wagon and get another load of lumber to ensure the men have ample supplies to keep working." He nodded his head toward the current construction.

"I agree, my lord."

Lord Edwin selected two sturdy men and instructed them to redirect their efforts to the blacksmith shop. The Lord of Tildenham and his knight unloaded the lumber and returned to the mill for more.

Chapter 24

LADY AVERLY ENTERED the kitchen and washed her hands in the tub of soapy water.

"Isabel, is there any salve?" She dried her hands with a linen from the shelf, went to the window, and broke off a leaf from the aloe plant.

"The basket of healing supplies and bandages are kept in a cupboard below the herbs." Curious, Isabel looked up from the contents of the large bowl she was stirring.

Lady Averly opened the double cupboard doors and saw a basket containing a small crock, bottled herbs and oils, a mortar and pestle, and bandages. Setting it on the table, she lifted each bottle and read its label before removing the mortar and pestle and squeezing the aloe leaf until its clear gooey liquid dropped into the vessel. She tossed the leaf into the slop bucket and wiped her finger on the linen before using the pestle to smooth the glob of aloe. After removing the oilcloth cover from the crock, she scooped out a fingertip full of salve and dropped it into the mortar. She mixed the two ingredients until they became smooth. Dipping the tip of the linen in a nearby pitcher of wine, she clenched her teeth as she pressed the damp cloth to each ruptured blister to clean them. Lady Averly applied the salve mixture and wrapped a strip of cloth around each hand. She was able to tie the bandage on her left hand but needed assistance for her right.

"Isabel, could you tie this for me?" She turned to the cook, who looked to the bandaged hands.

Isabel glanced at Lady Averly's face for her response as she tied the remaining bandage.

"My lady, what did you do?"

"A bit too much raking, I'm afraid. The gloves were a little too large for my hands." After the knot was tied, she ensured both bandages were secure. "Thank you."

"Ah, blisters. I dislike them. It's as if you aren't truly injured, but it hurts just the same."

Lady Averly chuckled.

"I agree, more of a nuisance than anything." She returned the items to the basket and put it away where it belonged. Knowing she would need to reapply the aloe salve, she spooned it into a bowl, covered it with linen, and set it on the windowsill before placing the mortar and pestle near the tub for washing.

Isabel added flour to the bowl.

"Did you make any progress in the garden?"

"Most of the debris has been removed. Bryce was kind enough to haul it away for me." She watched as Isabel resumed stirring. "Is there a stiff bristled brush that I may use to scrub the soot from the bench?"

"Yes, we have a few around here somewhere. From what I remember, its carvings are lovely."

"I failed to notice. The soot is so thick."

Bryce stepped into the kitchen.

"My lady, Lord Edwin wants me to tell you that there are three more men who will be eating with us tonight." The lad sniffed the contents of a crock containing jam and eyed the baskets of bread.

"Very well." Lady Averly watched as Isabel broke off a chunk of bread, spread it with jam, and handed it to the stableboy.

"Thank you kindly, Isabel." He bit into it with gusto.

Isabel wrapped her left arm around the bowl, lifted it from the table, and stirred the thick dough.

"We'll have enough food for three more mouths. I tend to overestimate the amount needed. It is difficult to determine the quantity hungry working men can eat."

The lad nodded his head and turned to leave but stopped as he heard Lady Averly ask a question.

"How's the construction coming along?"

The stableboy swallowed his mouthful before speaking.

"The blacksmith shop is coming along. He's getting his workshop organized so he can begin working soon. His residence may take a few days before it's completed."

Isabel paused in stirring and looked to the stableboy.

"We have a blacksmith?"

"As of today, we do. The other two men are carpenters and fast workers too." Bryce took another bite of bread before leaving the room.

Isabel turned to Lady Averly as she set the bowl upon the table.

"My lady, fancy that, we have a blacksmith. Maybe he can repair the hinges on the front door." Isabel grabbed another handful of flour from a crock and added it to the bowl.

*   *   *

The Lord of Tildenham and his knight sat with the newest members of the kingdom during the evening meal. Together the five men prioritized the repairs and construction. Lord Edwin's attention was drawn to the bandages upon Lady Averly's hands as she sat several plates across from him. He wondered if she had burned herself while preparing the meal, but his thoughts were distracted as he was drawn back into the conversation with the men.

One of the carpenters selected a piece of meat from the tray.

"My lord, construction of the blacksmith shop is going smoothly, a lot was done in one day."

"I agree. Let's hope the weather remains fair until it's finished, then our blacksmith can take up residence." Lord Edwin nodded toward the blacksmith. "For now, the three of you will sleep on pallets within the Great Hall. Once the village is rebuilt, there will be a residence for the each of you to live." He motioned toward the two carpenters.

It was a typical evening in Tildenham. The men continued their conversations over a tankard of ale or two. The women cleared the tables and tidied the kitchen before gathering around the fireplace to mend clothing or embroider.

Patrice sat on a bench in the corner of the room with children gathered upon the floor at her feet, anticipating the evening's enthralling tale. The storyteller noticed Lady Averly exiting the kitchen and motioned for a moment of her attention.

"My lady, Lord Edwin wants you to have this. He said it was for a very small dress?" She presented a lovely piece of royal blue fabric.

"Oh, it's lovely." Lady Averly accepted the scrap and looked toward Lord Edwin, who was deep in conversation. "Thank you, Patrice." She sat on a nearby bench, signaled for Glenna to come to her, and held the fabric for the child to see.

"It's a gift from Lord Edwin. It'll make a lovely dress for your doll."

Glenna traced her finger on the fabric's edge as she placed the doll in Lady Averly's lap, who glanced toward the men.

"Perhaps you should thank him."

Glenna looked at the group of men, skipped toward them, and stood behind Lord Edwin. She glanced at Lady Averly, who gave her a nod of encouragement. Glenna tapped him on the arm to get his attention.

Lord Edwin stopped talking and turned to see the little girl staring at him. She held her arms upward. He picked up the child, placing her in his lap.

"Thank you, Lord Edwin, for the beautiful fabric for my dolly's dress." She placed her arms around his neck and kissed him on the cheek.

"You're welcome, Glenna."

He placed her on the floor and watched the little girl skip to Lady Averly, who rewarded his kindness with a smile of appreciation.

Lady Averly watched as Glenna came toward her. The child could hardly contain her excitement.

"My lady, did you see, I gave Lord Edwin a big kiss for my dolly's new dress."

"Yes, I saw, but maybe you should have waited until his conversation with the men had finished."

"Oh, I don't think he minded. He liked my kiss."

Lady Averly suppressed a laugh as she picked up the doll from her lap.

"Have you given your doll a name?" She held the fabric over its body, taking measurements for the dress.

"I think her name should be Dolly."

Patrice began to tell a story. Her animated tale captivated the children and many adults as well.

"Glenna, why don't you take Dolly over to the storyteller and listen to the tale together."

Lady Averly gave Dolly to the little girl, who joined the other children on the floor. She glanced at Lord Edwin. He was staring at her. She smiled before borrowing a pair of scissors from a woman and cutting out the dress.

After placing another log on the fire, Bryce stood looking about the room. He wondered where he should sit. He was older than the children, who listened to the stories, but younger than the men at the table. He looked at a group of old peasant men with their murmured conversation between them.

Lord Edwin saw the stableboy standing alone.

"Bryce." He waved the lad toward him, making a space for him to sit on the bench. As the lad sat down, he patted his shoulder and handed him a full tankard.

Conversations quieted, stories were told, and a doll's dress began to take shape. Lady Averly laid the dress upon the bench, smoothing out the material. *Just attach the sleeves and hem the bottom. Maybe one of the women can embellish it with some embroidery.*

Another log was added to the fire as the last story came to an end. Candles were snuffed out as the children lay upon their pallets and closed their eyes. Only the golden glow of the fireplace illuminated the room. Lady Averly yawned, set the dress in one of the sewing baskets, and went to the staircase.

As she passed by his table, Lord Edwin rose and addressed the men.

"Excuse me for a moment."

The men smirked and raised an eyebrow or two as they watched him follow the beautiful lady.

"Lady Averly."

She reached for the banister, climbed the first step, and turned to face him.

"Even you are using my bestowed title now?"

"Yes, well, out of respect." He smirked as he leaned forward. "It also sets a good example for others." He reached for her hand lying on the banister. "Have you injured yourself?"

His touch was warm and caring as he turned her palm over in his hand and began to untie the bandage.

"It's nothing more than a blister. Too much raking in the garden with ill-fitting gloves, I presume."

He finished removing the bandage, but the darkened room made it difficult to examine her wound.

"I need more light." He nodded toward the glowing light of the kitchen and placed his hand on the small of her back as they crossed the Great Hall and entered.

Pulling out a stool from beneath the table, he motioned for her to sit before taking a taper from the mantel and touching it to a flame in the fireplace. Setting the candle between them, he pulled up another stool and sat before her.

She presented her hand.

"I applied salve and dressed my blisters earlier. They should be fine in a day or two."

"You're a healer?"

"Somewhat. I learned what I could from a knowledgeable apothecary."

He clasped her fingers, tilting her hand toward the light.

"Not bad, a little raw. Let me see the other." He removed the second bandage. In the candlelight, the area around the blister was red and swollen. "This one looks inflamed."

She leaned closer to examine it, nearly touching her forehead to his.

Even though she was unaware of her proximity, he took note of her closeness.

"It doesn't hurt but it's quite red." Lady Averly rose. She retrieved new bandages from the cupboard, the salve from the windowsill, and a pitcher of wine.

He watched as she dipped the edge of her overskirt in the wine and cringed as she washed the blisters. She applied salve and began to wrap her hands with a bandage.

"Here, let me." He tied each bandage securely, but gently. "You should keep them wrapped for tonight. Take off the bandages in the morning to air them out a bit. No working in the kitchen or the garden until they are healed."

Her mouth fell open.

"What am I to do with myself if I'm to avoid working in the garden and kitchen?"

"Well, perhaps you can sew clothing for the children. In truth, you should be doing more important tasks than cooking."

"What's more important than satisfying one's appetite? One must have food to live."

She has a point. He sighed.

"True, but others shall do it, not one as yourself, my lady."

"It's all I have ever done. I don't know how to be a lady."

Lord Edwin looked at her in earnest as he leaned toward her.

"You must tell me the truth. Are you of royal blood?"

She stared at the candlelight reflecting in the golden flecks of his hazel eyes. She had hoped to keep her title a secret. If she lied, he may someday discover the truth and never trust her word again. No longer able to withstand his stare, she looked to the fireplace and nodded her head slightly in confirmation.

He exhaled. *Royalty, from which kingdom? Was she abducted and later released, is she in hiding, or has she run away? It matters not, for I believe her admittance to being true.* He grinned.

"Well, as I recall, my mother would meet with the cook daily and plan the evening meal."

"But I'm not the Lady of Tildenham. I've no authority and Isabel may be offended if I were to tell her my preference or offer any guidance." She returned the salve to the windowsill.

"Many are filling roles within Tildenham that they haven't done before. You will do the same. I'll speak with Isabel to ensure her feelings won't be hurt." He stood and pushed his stool under the table. "And I'll see that you have properly fitting gloves for gardening." He picked up the candle and waited.

Lady Averly rose, returned her stool, and exited the kitchen with Lord Edwin following.

They crossed the Great Hall and ascended the staircase. He stopped before her bedchamber door and handed her the candle.

"I bid you sweet dreams and good night, my lady."

She opened her bedchamber door and looked over her shoulder.

"Good night, my lord."

Lord Edwin stood before the portal until he heard the click of the lock. His step felt lighter as he made his way back to the men at the table in the Great Hall. Even though they were quite tempted, they refrained from teasing their lord. In truth, they envied his pursuit of such a lovely woman.

Chapter 25

LADY AVERLY INHALED the aroma of freshly baked bread as she entered the kitchen.

"Good morning, Isabel."

The cook set aside an unbaked loaf to rise and covered it with a linen.

"Good morning, my lady. Lord Edwin said you wanted to plan the menu for the evening meal."

Lady Averly smiled meekly.

"He insisted I plan it. I hope you aren't offended." She removed the bandages from her hands and examined each blister. The redness and swelling had disappeared, but they oozed a clear liquid and were sore to the touch.

Isabel withdrew a ladle of porridge from a pot, dumped its contents in a wooden bowl, and inserted a spoon.

"Not at all, here." The cook set the bowl on the table before Lady Averly. "A change in menu will be to everyone's benefit."

They discussed various options while Lady Averly ate her breakfast. Isabel listened intently when Lady Averly described her favorite pastry. The cook was eager to make it and pulled the ingredients from the larder as Lady Averly stated them.

After eating the last spoonful of porridge, Lady Averly dropped her dirty dish and spoon in the washing water and offered to help with the baking. Isabel shooed her out of the kitchen and into the Great Hall. Picking up Dolly's dress from the basket, a needle and thread, and scissors, she went to her bedchamber and sat by the window to sew. By midday, she had finished the dress and a pair of matching slippers.

"I think Dolly will look lovely in this." She held the dress at arm's length, admiring her work. "Some embroidered flowers along the hem would be lovely. I'll ask one of the women to add them." Lady Averly set the dress and slippers on her bed and left the bedchamber in search of something else to occupy her time.

A tapping resonated from the Great Hall. Grasping the balcony railing, she peered down into the room. No one was in it. The tapping continued. She descended the stairs and walked toward the sound echoing from the hallway. The door was open, filling the walkway with light. Men had wedged the tilted door upward and held it against the Keep's wall. *Ah, the blacksmith is repairing the hinges.* Lady Averly walked to the end of the hallway, took her cloak from a hook on the wall, and wrapped it around her shoulders.

"My lady." The men greeted as she exited the Keep. She nodded and smiled.

"Gentlemen."

The pounding of hammers and sawing of boards echoed within the castle walls. She glanced toward the working men, noting the progress they had made. Pausing before the garden, there was new growth amongst the ashen soil as the spring sunshine encouraged plants to push their new leaves upward. A breeze blew a blonde lock of her hair across her eyes. She tucked it behind her ear and imagined the improvements she wished to make to the garden, but they would have to wait until her hands healed.

Something brushed against her leg. She looked down to see an orange tabby kitten with its fur matted and muddy. It reminded her of Harry.

"Well, who do you belong to?" She bent down and picked up the kitten. *Ah, I haven't spotted a single cat within the Keep. No wonder there were mice in the larder.*

Bryce stepped out of the stable.

"It's probably an orphan. Its mother may have been killed or run off during the attack."

She stroked the kitten's fur before looking to the stableboy.

"Since the duty of mouse catcher for the Keep seems to be vacant, I think he should assume the role."

"My lady, I suggest you ask Lord Edwin's permission. He isn't very fond of cats."

"Ah, he's so wee." She brushed her nose across the top of his head. *So, Lord Edwin is the reason we must dodge mice in the Keep.* "Nevertheless, I'll heed your advice." She held the kitten near her ear to listen to its purring. "Bryce, could you saddle my horse, please?"

"Yes, my lady."

Lady Averly returned to the Keep and went to the kitchen. She took a small bowl from the shelf, broke off a chunk of bread from a loaf on a table, and retrieved a pitcher of goat's milk from storage. She broke the bread into little pieces, placed them in the bowl, and poured enough milk over the bread until it was saturated. Setting the bowl on the floor, she pushed the kitten's nose into the soggy bread. It began to eat.

Isabel wiped her hands on her overskirt as she looked over Lady Averly's shoulder.

"What are you doing with that little thing?" The cook wrinkled her nose in disgust. *It probably has fleas.*

"It has a very important job now. It's our official mouse catcher."

"A big responsibility for one so small."

"Could you have someone put the kitten in my room once it has finished eating? I don't want it to get trampled with all of the activity in the kitchen." She headed for the doorway.

"Yes, my lady."

Before exiting, she stopped and turned back to the cook.

"Oh, please have someone bathe it first. I'm going for a ride and will return shortly."

The kitten sneezed after submerging its nose in the milk. Isabel chuckled.

"Yes, my lady."

*   *   *

Nelly was saddled and waiting when Lady Averly approached the stables. Bryce held the horse's bridle while the mare pawed her hoof impatiently on the ground.

"I think she is looking forward to the outing as well, my lady." He patted the horse's neck to calm her.

Lady Averly hoisted herself into the saddle and accepted the reins.

"Thank you, Bryce. I'll return shortly." She wove the reins carefully between her fingers.

"My lady, I believe Lord Edwin would prefer someone accompany you during your ride. Shall I find Sir Garrick?"

"It won't be necessary. I'll be fine."

Lady Averly trotted her horse out of the castle, through the rubble cluttered village, and into the woods. She followed the pathway to the mill and veered to the left in search of the clearing where the angel statue stood. Weaving her horse between the trees, she emerged from the woods and stared into the sullen face of the statue. From the vantage point atop her horse, she looked to the bench. It resembled the one in the garden. Lady Averly dismounted, tied the reins to a tree, and sat on the bench. Nelly lowered her head and nibbled on the spring grass.

Surrounded by the serenity of the forest, she exhaled and allowed her mind to wander. She thought of Mina and hoped she was well. She was thankful to have found Tildenham. Lord Edwin was kind. His attention toward her was unsettling. *I cannot deny my heart flutters at his touch, but it's also heavy with guilt knowing Father has committed my hand to another. Can I forget the past, move forward, and dare allow myself to fall in love with the Lord of Tildenham? I wish Mina was here offering her advice.* She grinned. *This is the first time a man has ever shown an interest in me, well, other than Sir Thomas.* Her lips curled into a sneer.

She looked to the face of the angel. Its calming expression conveyed hope. The detail of each feather in its wings, the roping around its waist, and the gentleness of its fingers on each hand were exquisite.

A chill ran up Lady Averly's spine. She pulled her cloak around her tightly as an uneasy feeling of being watched caused her to glance around the clearing. Except for Nelly, she was alone.

Nelly lifted her head, perked her ears, and looked behind her.

Rand stepped into the clearing, preceding his master who was upon Fulton. Lord Edwin dismounted.

"If I may make a small request." His irritation was obvious as he stood before her with fisted hands upon his hips. "With recent events, I would appreciate someone accompanying you outside the castle's walls."

"I fear little for my safety, my lord. With much of Tildenham in ruins, I doubt the barbarians will return." Her flippant comment caused him to narrow his eyes. She tried another approach as she looked to the blisters on her hands. "I have found little to occupy my time." She looked up to his eyes that glared down at her.

He ran his hand through his long brown hair, pulling it over his head and away from his face before sitting upon the bench next to her. *Mad? Angry?* He had difficulty deciding which emotion he was experiencing. Lord Edwin sighed.

"I was worried." He glanced at the angel before turning toward her.

Lady Averly was surprised by his admission. She stared at her hands in her lap as she fidgeted with the edge of her overskirt.

"I'm sorry to cause you such distress, my lord. It was inconsiderate of me to do so. I'm unaccustomed to anyone showing concern for my welfare."

Lord Edwin's face was stern as he stared into her eyes.

"My lady, when it comes to you, I'm very concerned." He broke the tension with a slight smile before looking down to her hands in her lap. "How are your blisters?"

Lady Averly shifted her knees toward him as she turned and presented both hands.

"They're healing nicely." She watched as his hands grasped her fingertips and he examined the wounds. She became acutely aware of his thumbs moving gently across her fingers before looking to his face.

"I agree. The air has done them good." He released her hands.

The silence seemed to stretch between them as if both searched for a topic of conversation.

Rand paced back and forth, causing Nelly to pull on her reins and sidestep as he drew near her.

Lady Averly stood.

"Perhaps we should return. I don't want to keep you from your duties."

Lord Edwin looked up to her sapphire blue eyes. He had enjoyed their time alone together even though it was only for a few moments. There was much he needed to accomplish before nightfall. He agreed with a nod of his head and stood.

"As you wish."

They climbed atop their horses with Rand leading the way back to the castle. As they crossed the drawbridge and rode into the bailey, a group of men stood before the blacksmith shop.

Lord Edwin noticed several men pulling on a rope woven through pulleys to raise a beam up the side of the building to the rooftop. He reined his horse, dismounted, and patted Fulton on the rear. The destrier headed for the stable. Lord Edwin looked to Lady Averly.

"Do take care."

"Yes, my lord." She urged Nelly forward.

After dropping off her horse at the stable, Lady Averly went to the kitchen.

"Oh, Isabel, whatever you're making, it smells wonderful." She stopped before a platter of her favorite pastries and inhaled. "Mmmmm..."

"Thank you, my lady. We should taste one to ensure its quality." Isabel raised her eyebrows and smiled.

Lady Averly giggled at the cook's devilish expression.

"Oh, yes. We want to ensure they taste as good as they smell."

Isabel selected a warm pastry and sliced it in half. She looked toward Lady Averly, who chose the smaller half and bit into the flaky crust. The jam filling painted the corners of her mouth.

"Mm...well done, Isabel, well done." Lady Averly licked the jam from her face.

The cook closed her eyes as she savored a mouthful of deliciousness.

"My lady, I like your recipe."

After placing the last bit of pastry into her mouth, Isabel licked her fingers clean and dried them on her overskirt.

"I had your little feline bathed and taken to your room. After filling his belly, he should be sleeping soundly."

"Thank you, Isabel. I think I'll see how he's doing."

*   *   *

"Who was that?" Lady Miriam glanced up from her embroidering as her husband entered the solar carrying an unopened missive.

"A messenger."

She tossed her sewing aside as she stood and snatched the missive from his hand. Ripping the wax seal open, Lady Miriam read it quickly before letting it fall to the floor and glaring at Lord Burton.

"Corn seed? They sent a missive requesting corn seed?"

"We have more than enough for Holbrook and can sell our excess."

"It's not enough to keep us solvent. Send Sir Thomas to search for Averly. If he finds her before Doran, then we won't have to pay the bounty." She crossed her arms over her chest, quite pleased with her suggestion.

"If he were to be alone with her, her virginity would surely be compromised. We must wait to hear from Doran and hope she is found alive."

*   *   *

The kitten raised his head and blinked its sleepy eyes as it looked toward the bedchamber door as it opened.

Lady Averly found the little feline curled upon her pillow.

"Did I wake you?" She sat upon the bed and stroked the top of the kitten's head. It stood up and stretched, arching its back.

She scooped the tiny kitten into her hands, held it close to her chest, and nuzzled the top of its velvet soft head. It began to purr. *I remember when Harry was this small.*

Curious, Lady Averly discovered the kitten was indeed male. She held him before her to look at his face. Even though she had yet to receive Lord Edwin's permission to keep the kitten, she couldn't squelch the urge to give him a name.

"You look like a Henry to me."

She picked up the top book from her nightstand. Even though she had read it before, she sat in the chair next to the window and placed Henry in her lap. The orange tabby snuggled against her and went to sleep as Lady Averly began to read.

Chapter 26

A BLOOD-CURDLING scream echoed from the bailey causing the hair on Lady Averly's arms to rise and dread to settle within her heart. She peered out the window to see the blacksmith emerge from his shop escorting a young man with his hand covering the side of his face. Blood trickled between his fingers. Lord Edwin hurried to the pair from across the bailey and spoke to the blacksmith, who nodded and guided the apprentice toward the Keep.

Lady Averly closed the book with a snap, tossed it onto the nightstand, and placed Henry upon the bed before quickening her steps toward the Great Hall.

The blacksmith and apprentice stepped into the room as she descended the staircase.

"My lady, the lad caught a bit of hot metal on his face. Thankfully it missed his eye. Lord Edwin asks that you see to it." The blacksmith encouraged the young man to sit on a nearby bench.

She sat on the bench and pulled the apprentice's hand away from his face. There were several lesions on his cheek and forehead. The skin was charred and hung loosely from his temple.

"Let me see what I can find to treat your injury." Lady Averly rose and hurried to the kitchen, trying to recall the burn remedy. She took the basket from under the cupboard and set the mortar and pestle on the table. Taking the cloth off the mortar, she discovered the remedy she had prepared for her blisters. *Not enough.* Breaking a leaf of aloe and sage from the plants, she placed them in the mortar and began crushing them. She opened the crock of salve and added it to the plants.

"Isabel, do we have an egg?"

Isabel reached in a basked and retrieved one.

"Here, my lady. I heard screaming. Is someone injured?"

"Yes, the blacksmith's apprentice." She cracked the egg and separated the whites, letting them drip into the bowl. She handed the shell with the yolk inside to the cook. "Scramble the yolk and add it to tonight's soup. I don't want to waste it."

"Yes, my lady."

Grabbing a clean wooden spoon from a crock on the table, Lady Averly whipped the burn remedy until it became slimy and smooth. The spoon stilled as she remembered another essential ingredient.

"Oh, honey! Isabel, is there any honey?"

"Yes, I'll get it." Isabel went to the storage room, returning quickly, and set it before her.

"Thank you." Lady Averly removed the oilcloth covering from the small crock, stirred the honey with its wand before drizzling the natural antibiotic into the bowl and mixing it well. She grabbed a linen from the shelf and dipped into a bucket of water before picking up the mortar, grabbing the basket, and returned to the Great Hall.

Setting the items on the table, Lady Averly sat next to the lad.

"This may sting, but we need to take some of the heat out of the burn." She applied the dampened linen to the injury and watched as the apprentice cringed.

The blacksmith cleared his throat.

"I can see he's in good hands." He patted the lad's shoulder. "If you don't mind, my lady, I'd like to return to my work."

"I believe we can handle things from here. Thank you for your escort." She smiled at the peasant as he nodded and left.

Returning her attention to her patient, she peeled the cloth away from the wound. It continued to bleed. She reapplied the linen to the injury, pressing gently. His uncovered eye stared at her as if asking for her assessment of his injury. She thought it best to break the silence between them and engage him in conversation.

"Your name?"

"Coleman, my lady."

"How old are you, Coleman?"

"Ten and six."

"So, you're responsible for repairing the drawbridge?"

"It was a temporary fix, my lady. The blacksmith and I were working to reinforce my repairs."

She lifted the edge of the linen. The bleeding had subsided.

"Have you eaten your midday meal?"

"Yes, my lady. It was brought to us so we could return to work quickly."

Lady Averly removed the damp cloth and examined the wound. The charred, dead skin would have to be removed. She retrieved a pair of sewing scissors from a basket on a bench near the fireplace and exhaled to calm herself as she sat.

"I have to cut away the dead skin. I'll be as gentle as possible. Keep your head still and avert your eyes toward the kitchen."

Coleman's eyes widened before he straightened his shoulders, exhaled, and stared at the doorway.

Lady Averly snipped the dead skin but paused as Colman jerked away slightly.

"If the skin is dead, then why do I feel pain, my lady."

"I apologize. Perhaps I cut a bit too closely." She continued to cut away as much of the dead skin as possible before exhaling. "There." A section of the wound needed stitching. She threaded a curved needle. "This may hurt, but the wound must be closed."

Coleman gripped the edge of the bench. With each stitch through his sensitive skin, he held his breath and clenched his teeth. With a snip of the thread, Lady Averly exhaled.

"There. Now, for my special burn remedy." She raised her eyebrows teasingly and smiled.

"Yes, my lady." Coleman grimaced, anticipating the pain.

She spread the green goopy mixture onto a bandage and applied it to the side of his face.

"Hold this in place, please."

Coleman put the palm of his hand on the bandage, pressing its coolness against his face. He watched as she tore a bandage into strips and secured the dressing as best she could.

"We must change and reapply the remedy several times a day."

"Thank you, my lady." The apprentice left the Great Hall and returned to work.

Isabel stilled her knife as Lady Averly entered carrying the healing supplies.

"How bad was he injured?"

"He has a burn on his face." She covered the remedy with a linen and set it next to the herbs before placing the basket back in the cupboard. Lady Averly went to the fireplace, dipped the edge of her overskirt into a pot of boiling water, and washed the scissors. After drying them, she sat on a stool and watched Isabel prepare some venison for cooking.

"I wish I could be of more help." She looked down at her hands, touching her blisters that had scabbed over, and was tempted to disobey her lord.

Isabel smiled.

"You helped by treating the lad's injuries."

Lady Averly sat for a moment wishing she could do more. Someone leaned over her to retrieve a knife. Another bumped into her as they hurried with a hot pot from the fireplace. Realizing she was a hindrance to the women, she left the kitchen, returned the scissors to the sewing basket, and went to her bedchamber to continue reading.

Before long, shadows stretched onto the page Lady Averly was reading. She set her book aside. Henry opened his eyes, stretched, and tucked his nose beneath his paw.

He went back to sleep. She stoked the fire in the fireplace, added a log, and lit a taper. Setting it on the nightstand, she returned to her chair and continued reading her book until the aroma of food drifted into her bedchamber and voices echoed from the Great Hall. She set the book aside, blew out the candle, and picked up the kitten.

"I bet you're getting hungry." She nuzzled the sleepy feline as she left her bedchamber and descended the staircase to the Great Hall.

She dodged servants bringing trays of food from the kitchen as she entered and fed Henry a bowl of bread, shaved tidbits of meat, and milk.

Everyone was seated as she joined the others and sat at the end of the bench. She listened to conversations as she sipped wine from a tankard and selected a choice cut of venison from a platter.

Henry meowed as he emerged from the kitchen. His full tummy swayed side to side with each step toward his mistress. Glenna watched as Lady Averly picked up the kitten and placed him in her lap.

Curious, Glenna went to Lady Averly's side.

"Is that your kitty?"

Lady Averly smiled and nodded her head.

"What's his name?"

"I've named him Henry."

"I think Henry is a good name." Glenna extended her index finger and petted the kitten on the head. "Can I play with him?"

"Are you finished with your meal?" She looked to the child's plate. There was food on it.

"Yes, I'm not very hungry."

"I can see that you aren't. Well, Henry is certain to have plenty of energy now that his tummy is full." Lady Averly held up the kitten, exposing his bulbous belly. Glenna giggled as she stroked its fullness.

Lady Averly placed the kitten in the little girl's arms and watched as she sat on a bench near the fireplace.

"I was able to locate a pair of smaller gloves for you."

Startled by his voice, Lady Averly looked across the table to where Lord Edwin had seated himself. His extended hand held a pair of brown leather gloves.

She grinned apprehensively as she accepted the kind gift and slipped them on her hands.

"They fit perfectly." Lady Averly rotated her hands, admiring the quality. "Thank you."

"You're welcome."

"Perhaps I can work in the garden tomorrow?" She displayed a devilish smirk as she removed the gloves and set them upon the table next to her plate.

Pleased by her enthusiasm, he was unsure how to reply. *Is she asking for my permission?* It was bold for him to do so, but he stated his heart's desire.

"Being the lady of the house, you may do as you wish."

Her smile faded.

"My lord, I'm not the lady of the house."

He rose from the bench and leaned toward her ear. His breath was warm upon her cheek as he spoke.

"Currently, you're the only lady residing within Tildenham. Perhaps someday you'll rightfully possess the title." He turned his head until his nose nearly touched her cheek and stared into her sapphire eyes, trying to determine if she entertained the possibility. She returned his stare, unsmiling. He grinned, lessening the tension he had created.

Lady Averly suspected his fondness for her but underestimated its depth.

Her unspoken reply accompanied by the look of confusion upon her face caused Lord Edwin to lean toward her and touch his cheek to hers as he whispered in her ear.

"I apologize for my bluntness. I've failed to take your feelings into consideration."

Lady Averly hoped their exchange could not be overheard by others.

"I must admit, I'm taken back, for I didn't know you felt so strongly."

With a nudge or two of an elbow, everyone's attention was drawn to the young couple. Sir Garrick tried to conceal his grin by taking a sip from his tankard. The residents of Tildenham held Lady Averly in the highest regards and welcomed the idea of her becoming their lady.

Glenna laughed, drawing the couple's attention.

The little girl dangled Dolly upside down. Its stringy rags of hair enticed the kitten to bat it away. Glenna noticed she was being watched.

"My lady, look, Henry likes to play." She giggled.

Lord Edwin scowled at the kitten.

Lady Averly smiled.

"I can see he does." Wishing to distance herself for a moment, Lady Averly remembered the small garment in her bedchamber. "If you will excuse me, my lord."

He stepped aside as she rose from her seat and watched as she ascended the staircase. He looked to Sir Garrick, who raised his tankard and winked.

Within moments, Lady Averly reappeared and went to Glenna.

"I was able to finish sewing this for you today. I think it would look lovely if one of the women would add some embroidered flowers to the bottom of the dress and slippers. Perhaps if you ask one of them nicely, they would sew them." She handed Glenna the new clothes for Dolly.

"For me! Oh, thank you, Lady Averly."

Henry's meow drew Lady Averly's attention.

"Would you like me to watch Henry, so you may play with Dolly?"

Glenna set the dress aside before picking up the kitten, kissing the top of his head, and handing him to Lady Averly, who turned toward Lord Edwin.

"I hope you don't mind. I found Henry near the stable. In truth, he found me." She nuzzled the kitten and stroked his fur. "He can catch mice in the kitchen and throughout the Keep."

Lord Edwin fisted his hands and placed them on his hips. He scowled as he remembered the day well. He was young, quite young when a large black cat jumped onto his back and dug in its claws, drawing blood. He detested cats.

"Henry?" He relented from exiling the feline to the stable. "If it pleases you, he may stay." His decision was rewarded with her smile.

"Thank you."

He failed, however, to restrain his true expectation of the feline.

"We'll see if he earns his keep."

*   *   *

Doran's horse crested the top of a hill. Lowell. Shadowed figures huddled for warmth around glowing campfires. Lightning flashed across the night sky illuminating the remnants of a wooden wall and the village in ruins. With the castle's windows blanketed in darkness, its lord was most likely dead. Taking refuge within it was unlikely. Doran would camp with the survivors and inquire about the barbarians and their direction of travel in the morning. *I doubt Lady Averly is amongst the survivors. If she had taken refuge within Lowell's walls, she's more than likely dead.* He would ask to confirm his assumption in the morning.

He reined his horse on the fringe of the village. Scavenging amongst the rubble, he made a lean-to from loose boards and broken fencing. After tying his horse to a fence post, he laid upon his horse blanket for some much-needed rest and hoped his crude shelter would protect him from the threatening dampness of the spring thunderstorm.

Chapter 27

THE RELENTLESS STORM disturbed Doran's sleep throughout the night. He woke with stiff muscles and aching joints as he stood from the hard ground, stretched his arms, and yawned. He was thankful to see the sun's rays break over the horizon, knowing they would warm the day and dry the dampness.

Doran untied his horse and walked through the remnants of the village. He questioned the survivors, receiving the answers he anticipated. The lord and lady had been murdered. His description of Lady Averly was met with blank stares and shoulder shrugs. The peasants indicated the attackers headed westward. He reined his horse toward Tildenham.

*   *   *

Henry poked his head out from beneath the covers. He touched his damp nose to Lady Averly's cheek, tickling it with his whiskers.

She cuddled the kitten, tucking him beneath her chin. Her thoughts drifted to Lord Edwin. She grinned. *He takes his responsibility as the Lord of Tildenham quite seriously and has a genuine concern for those who reside within his kingdom. He's a few years older than I am, tall, and quite handsome.* She smirked. *Yes, very handsome.* Her stomach fluttered. She kissed the top of Henry's head as she got out of bed, set him on her pillow as she donned Lord Edwin's robe, and left the bedchamber to use the garderobe. As she stepped into the hallway, she heard Lord Edwin's voice echoing from the Great Hall and paused to listen.

"Good. Then let's move onto the next and most important structure - the alewives' building." The lord's idea was met with cheers and laughter.

So typical.

After using the garderobe, Lady Averly opened the bedchamber door to see Isabel standing with a beautiful gown draped over her arm. She hesitated before stepping into the room.

"Good morning, Isabel."

"Good morning, my lady. Lord Edwin would like you to wear this today." The cook held the gown against her chest as she fanned out the skirt displaying its beauty. The delicate lavender bodice was accented with ivory lace, glass beading, and pearls. The sleeves were belled at the elbows with undersleeves extending to the wrist. The full skirt had several layers. It was the most beautiful dress Lady Averly had ever seen. Perhaps even more beautiful than any of the dresses Lady Miriam had worn. She touched the lace and looked to Isabel.

"Where did he find such a lovely garment?"

"I believe it belonged to one of his mother's ladies. It looks to be your size." Isabel brushed the skirt to flatten a wrinkle.

"Oh, Isabel, I cannot wear it."

Isabel lowered her arms.

"But my lady, you must. He'll be disappointed if you don't wear it."

Avoiding the astonished stare from the cook, Lady Averly inspected the healed blisters on her hands.

"I've never owned such a dress."

Isabel's mouth dropped open, for she was certain royal blood ran through Lady Averly's veins.

"Ever?"

Lady Averly let her hands fall to her sides as she looked to the cook's inquisitive face.

"Ever." She sat on the bed, picked up Henry, and set him in her lap.

"My goodness." Isabel sat in the chair. She wanted to know more of Lady Averly's past but thought it impolite to pry. "I must admit, you're a bit of a contradiction. Many believe you to be royalty, yet your proficiency in the kitchen is quite impressive, that of an accomplished peasant cook."

Lady Averly saw the earnestness on the cook's face. Whatever she divulged to Isabel may soon spread to everyone in Tildenham. She ignored the assumption.

"I'll take that as a compliment." She grinned.

Isabel stood, fluffed the dress, and held it up again.

"Nevertheless, I think we should humor Lord Edwin and have you ready yourself for the day."

Lady Averly leaned forward and touched the material. *Oh, I've dreamt of wearing such a dress.* She offered a compromise.

"It's lovely, but not something I should wear to work in the flower garden. Please have a bath drawn for me later this afternoon and I'll put in on for the evening meal."

Deflated, Isabel sat back down.

"Very well. Let me help you dress." She secretly planned to have Lady Averly looking so lovely that her lord's heart would be swept away by her beauty. "And pin your hair for your debut as the next Lady of Tildenham."

Lady Averly's mouth fell agape and her eyes narrowed in a subtle attempt for the cook to squelch her devilish plan.

"Isabel."

She scooted to the edge of the chair, nearly squealing with excitement.

"My lady, it's obvious that Lord Edwin is smitten with you."

Lady Averly's eyebrows rose.

"Obvious?"

"And he's so very handsome." Isabel watched Lady Averly's cheeks blush.

"Yes, he's quite handsome, but he possesses other amiable qualities as well. He's kind, thoughtful, and cares deeply for those who serve him." Lady Averly paused as Isabel began to smile. "What?"

"Never mind, my lady."

Even though Lady Averly kept her true feelings in check, Isabel understood what lay within her heart.

Lady Averly glanced at her peasant corset, shirt, and overskirt where they hung on a peg next to the armoire and the gloves upon her nightstand where she had placed them before retiring for the night.

"For now, I'll dress in my clothing, eat breakfast, and get some work done in the garden."

Isabel nodded before rising and going to the armoire. She hung the beautiful gown inside it and retrieved the garments from the pegs. She held up the overskirt and wrinkled her nose at the various grease spots and other stains.

"I think it's time to expand your everyday wardrobe. This one is getting a bit grimy."

"It will do for today." Lady Averly took off the robe and handed it to the cook as she accepted the skirt and put it on over the chemise. Isabel set the remaining items on the bed.

"Very well, my lady. I'll search for others to add to your wardrobe as well." Isabel hung up the robe and closed the armoire doors.

"Thank you, Isabel. Oh, and can you take Henry to the kitchen to be fed?"

"Certainly, my lady." Isabel picked up the kitten from the bed before leaving the bedchamber.

Lady Averly finished dressing, made her bed, and picked up the gloves Lord Edwin had given her. After eating, she gathered a pair of shears, a stiff bristled brush and filled a bucket with soapy water before going to the garden.

Anticipating her intent, Bryce retrieved the wheelbarrow and pitchfork for her to use.

"Here you go, my lady."

"Thank you, Bryce." She put on the gloves and began to work.

As she cleared another section of the garden, she noticed a series of three rose plants, evenly spaced, with sprouting leaves. *Red? Pink? I guess time will tell.*

The echo of hammering resonated within the bailey as construction continued. Bryce filled the wheelbarrow from the pile Lady Averly gathered and headed toward the gatehouse.

Lord Edwin emerged from the blacksmith shop carrying a bucket of nails and nearly bumped into Bryce, who avoided the collision.

"My lord."

"Bryce." He looked in the direction in which the stableboy came to see Lady Averly working in the garden. She was turned away from him. Setting the bucket on the ground, he tiptoed toward her. Smiling devilishly, he wrapped his arm around her waist and took the pitchfork from her hands as he twirled her to face him.

Lady Averly gasped and placed her hands upon his chest before scanning the bailey nervously to see who was watching them.

"My lord, you startled me."

"You didn't like the gown?" He raised his eyebrows upward teasingly.

"It's lovely. Thank you, but it's not the proper attire for working in the garden."

"Promise me you'll wear it tonight."

"I promise." She grinned.

He glanced down at her gloved hands.

"They fit nicely." He leaned closer and whispered. "Let's hope they protect you from any more blisters." He moved his hand from her lower back to the back of her head and kissed her forehead. Releasing her, he presented the pitchfork before her.

Momentarily dizzy, she grasped his arm as he held the pitchfork steadily.

Taking a few deep breaths, she smiled and accepted the tool.

"Yes, let's hope."

He nodded and left as Bryce returned for the next load.

Lady Averly continued to tidy the garden and often caught herself smiling as her thoughts wandered to Lord Edwin. She cleared the last of the debris before scouring the limestone bench until it was white once again. Bryce refilled the bucket from the well and rinsed the bench.

She dropped the brush inside the empty bucket.

"Well done, Bryce. Thank you."

"You're welcome, my lady."

"It would be nice to have the garden protected by a fence again."

"I agree, my lady." Bryce returned the wheelbarrow and pitchfork to the stable.

Lady Averly's dress was wet, her knees muddy, and her hair was damp with sweat as she went to the kitchen with the bucket in hand.

Her stomach grumbled, reminding her of the midday meal she had missed, as she watched Isabel drizzle warm honey over the tantalizing dessert. Her mouth watered at the thought of snatching one of the treats, but she settled for a wedge of cheese from the storage room after setting the bucket on the floor in its proper place.

Isabel finished the last sweet cake, placed it on a tray, and watched Lady Averly leave the room.

"I'll be there shortly, my lady."

Since her mouth was full of food, Lady Averly's reply was muffled.

Henry arched his back, stretched his legs, and extended his tiny toes as the door opened and his mistress entered. Still wishing to sleep, he stretched out on her pillow, shutting his eyes once again.

Lady Averly inserted her finger into the bathwater.

"Ah, nice and warm." She gladly rid herself of her dirty clothes and submerged her body in the tub. Picking up the linen that hung over the edge of the tub, she smelled several bars of soap from the basket on the chair before choosing the fragrance that appealed to her most.

Lady Averly dunked the cloth in water and slathered it with the soap. She looked down into the water at two dark circles.

"Oh, my knees."

The mud had soaked through both layers of skirting making oval marks upon them. She washed her face, upper body, and saved her knees for last. As was her habit, she dunked her head underwater to wet it thoroughly, used the soap to lather it, and ducked back under the water to rinse. She wrung most of the water from her long blonde locks, leaned back in the tub, and let her body relax while she listened to the crackling fire in the fireplace.

There was a knock on her bedchamber door.

"It's me, my lady."

"Come in, Isabel."

The cook noticed the damp blonde locks hanging over the tub as she entered.

"My lady, you already washed your hair?" Isabel set a small basket upon the bed.

"Sorry, I've always washed it myself."

"Well, at least I can towel it dry and comb out the tangles." Isabel took a linen from the chair, knelt on the floor, and squeezed the tresses to remove the excess water. She rubbed the towel over the top of Lady Averly's head until she was confident most of the water had been removed, then combed it free from tangles. Isabel held up the large linen. Lady Averly stepped out of the tub, folded it around her body, and stood before to the fireplace.

Opening the armoire, Isabel gathered the chemise in her hands. As the garment was placed over her head, Lady Averly pushed her arms through the sleeves letting the linen drop to the floor. She was layered in a dainty ivory blouse, an underskirt, a lavender overskirt, and bodice. The sleeves were tied at the top of each shoulder. She touched the beaded adornment on the bodice and ran the palms of her hands over the full skirt. She looked to Isabel for approval.

"Oh, you're stunning. We aren't done yet though. Sit and I'll pin your hair."

Isabel retrieved the basket and set it on the nightstand where she could reach it easily. Lady Averly sat erect in the chair. The cook twisted strands of hair and pinned curls in place with jeweled clips. When she was finished, she presented a matching pair of slippers. Lady Averly slipped them on and stood.

Isabel smiled and clasped her hands together as she scanned the woman who stood before her.

"My lady, you're breathtaking."

Lady Averly blushed as she ran her palms over the skirt.

"I've never worn such a dress. It's lovely."

"And so are you, my lady." Isabel gathered the soiled clothing. "Please come down at your leisure." Isabel curtsied and left the bedchamber, closing the door behind her.

Chapter 28

LADY AVERLY TRACED her index finger along the sleeve's detailed beading.

"Henry, can you believe its beauty? I feel like a queen in this dress."

Henry hopped off the bed, went to the door, and meowed.

"Yes, it's time for you to eat."

She scooped the kitten into her arms and stepped into the hallway. Her stomach fluttered as she paused to listen to the echoed conversations from the Great Hall. She exhaled and stroked Henry as she went to the top of the stairs. She hesitated as she saw everyone standing. The evening meal had yet to be served. *Are they waiting for me?* She searched the room until she saw the tall physique with mahogany hair. His back was toward her.

Isabel stood in the doorway of the kitchen wiping her hands on her overskirt, beaming with pride. She looked to her lord, anticipating his reaction.

As Lady Averly descended, the hum of conversation quieted with many looking toward the staircase. Sir Garrick saw the lovely lady entering the room.

"My lord, you may want to turn about and behold your future bride." He lifted his tankard toward the staircase.

Lord Edwin turned around to see Lady Averly descend the last few steps.

Glenna came forward as Lady Averly stood upon the Great Hall floor.

"My lady, you look so pretty." The little girl curtsied.

"Thank you, Glenna. Do you think you could take Henry to the kitchen, so he may eat his evening meal?"

"Yes, my lady."

Lady Averly placed the kitten within the little girl's hands and watched her scamper away.

Lord Edwin stared as he approached her. His devilish smile caused her to look down and brush an imaginary wrinkle from her skirt.

"Good evening." He clasped her hand and took a step backward to admire her in full.

"Good evening, my lord."

"Lovely." He stepped toward her, closing the gap between them.

She lifted the skirt to her side and let it fall in place.

"You are too kind, my lord, to allow me to wear such a lovely gown."

"It's yours to keep."

Lady Averly thought to refuse the gift but knew she would lose the argument.

"Thank you. It's truly beautiful."

"The one who wears it exceeds its beauty." He watched as she smiled and downcast her eyes to the floor. Her cheeks turned a rosy shade of pink.

With the understanding of her lord's intention, Isabel approached the couple.

"My lord, the staff thought it appropriate to set the High Table for this evening." She motioned toward the table upon the dais covered by a white tablecloth, lit candles, and greenery.

Lady Averly gasped at the implication.

"Isabel, how lovely, but I feel...."

Lord Edwin completed her objection.

"That she will accompany me for the evening's meal, on the dais."

"But my lord..." Lady Averly began.

Lord Edwin raised his voice for all to hear his proclamation.

"Everyone regards you as a proper lady, their lady, including me." He looked about the room to see he had captured everyone's attention. "I cannot think of a more kind and loving person in which to share my life." He knelt upon one knee as he continued to hold her hand within his. "Would you do me the honor of becoming my wife?"

Lady Averly's mouth fell open. Unaware she was holding her breath, she looked to the kind faces staring, awaiting her reply. Exhaling, she closed her mouth and looked into the hazel eyes of the man who knelt before her.

Lord Edwin's palms became damp. He wondered if his rapid heartbeat could be heard by everyone in the room. He displayed an encouraging smile with the hope of receiving an acceptance to his proposal.

Lady Averly traced his temple with her finger before brushing a wayward strand of hair to the side. She had grown to know him as one who rules with compassion and kindness, truly cares for all who live within Tildenham's land, and believed his heart to be true to only her. She put her betrothal behind her, assured she would remain safe within Tildenham for the remainder of her life. She searched her heart and smiled.

"Yes."

Lord Edwin grinned as he rose, drew her near, cupped her face within his hands, and kissed her passionately. Those within the Great Hall cheered while Rand circled the couple, trying to wedge in between them.

Sir Garrick called the wolf to his side allowing the newly engaged couple to celebrate their happiness.

Lord Edwin led his future bride to his mother's chair at the High Table. Once she was seated, he sat in his father's chair and everyone, including Sir Garrick, seated themselves at a table.

Lord Edwin reached for her hand and leaned toward her.

"We will have to wait to be wed. I must find a priest or friar to oversee the ceremony to make it proper."

Lady Averly nodded in understanding. Her thoughts drifted to what she would wear on her wedding day. She was thankful to have left behind Lady Miriam's hideously designed dress in a chest at Holbrook. Having to wait for a priest would give her enough time to design a gown of her own choosing.

She glanced around the room at the smiling faces. Everyone was happy. She was happy. With a sense of security, she was confident her past would remain in the past once she married and became the Lady of Tildenham. She looked to the portrait of Lady Mary and hoped to live up to the woman's fine reputation, improve the garden, and restore the interior of the Keep by replacing what had been destroyed. Additional staff and procuring an apothecary to ensure good health for all was also a priority. The efficiency of the kitchen and its staff would be directed through Isabel. Once the flowers were in bloom, she would fill the Keep with their beauty and fragrances. More than anything, she wanted to be a good wife to her future husband.

Lord Edwin reached for his tankard as he glanced toward his bride.

"You seem lost in thought."

She looked toward him and smiled.

"I was just imagining the future."

"And how do you see it?"

"I see it as a dream come true, where I will live a happy life with a wonderful husband."

A pounding on a table drew the couple's attention. They saw Sir Garrick standing. He lifted his tankard as the room quieted.

"My lord, and our soon to be lady, on behalf of all of us." He motioned with his tankard to those sitting at the long table. They stood before he continued. "We wish the two of you much happiness and a long life together." The knight raised his tankard toward the High Table.

"Hear! Hear!"

Everyone raised their drinks.

"Hear! Hear!"

Lord Edwin reached for his future bride's left hand, brought it to his lips, and kissed it gently before he stood.

"Thank you, everyone. With Lady Averly by my side and our continued effort to restore Tildenham to its full beauty, I foresee a bright future for us all."

Tankards were raised, followed with an astounding, "Huzzah!"

Lord Edwin resumed his seat. Lady Averly leaned toward him.

"I hope you don't mind, my lord, if I continue to work in the kitchen from time to time. It gives me pleasure to bake and provide food for all."

"My dear, you may do as you wish. However, a time may come when your responsibilities as the Lady of Tildenham may keep you from the kitchen." He raised his eyebrows up and down suggestively.

Understanding his insinuation, she smiled shyly, and her face reddened as she replied.

"There may be times when I keep you from your duties as well, my lord."

He laughed wholeheartedly.

"I can see we're going to get along quite well."

Lady Averly raised her eyebrows teasingly.

"I'm counting on it."

Lord Edwin lifted his tankard. Rand, sitting next to his master waiting patiently for a tidbit of meat, placed his paw upon Lord Edwin's lap. The Lord of Tildenham took a swig of ale as he absentmindedly gave a bit of venison from his plate to the wolf.

Isabel had been watching the couple at the High Table. She elbowed Patrice, who sat next to her.

"I think they make a grand couple."

The storyteller looked toward the pair.

"They appear quite comfortable with each other."

"Just think, after all we have endured, we'll be having a wedding. A joyous wedding." Isabel giggled. "We women will have to find time to sew a gown for the bride."

"I'm certain many will want to do so."

Merriment filled the room as the meal ended and the musicians began to play a lovely tune, for tonight a grand celebration was in order.

Lord Edwin looked to his future bride.

"Shall we dance?"

Lady Averly recalled her last attempt at twirling around the floor.

"I'll do my best."

He stood, pulled her chair away from the table, and held his open hand before her. She placed her dainty hand within his and stood.

Lord Edwin led her to the center of the room.

All eyes were on the handsome couple as they began to dance.

Sir Garrick drained his tankard dry, set it upon the table, and announced to the man across from him.

"I believe every man would appreciate the company of Lady Averly's beauty, at least for a spin or two around the room." He stood, walked to the dancing couple, and tapped Lord Edwin on the shoulder. The couple stopped dancing.

"My lord, if you would be so kind as to give me the honor of dancing with your future wife?"

Lord Edwin looked to Lady Averly, who seemed flattered at the request.

"She's an excellent dancer, so please take care not to smash her toes." He placed Lady Averly's hand within the knight's offered palm and returned to his chair.

Rand had remained beside his master's chair with his nose raised and sniffing toward the table top. Lord Edwin took a small slice of venison from the tray before a servant removed it from the High Table. He set it upon his plate and placed it on the floor for his pet.

He watched as each man took a turn spinning Lady Averly around the room. *I wonder if she's getting dizzy.* She smiled as each man stepped forward for their turn to twirl her about the room. The musicians continued to play until the last gentleman had taken his turn to dance with the future Lady of Tildenham. As the song ended, she curtsied, and the elderly man bowed before escorting her to the High Table.

Isabel approached the couple.

"My lord, I believe us women would like an opportunity to dance with you as well." She winked at Lady Averly, who nodded as she snickered.

Lord Edwin glanced at Lady Averly before replying.

"And I would like the opportunity to dance with each of you as well." He nodded to the musicians to play another tune, dismissed himself from the High Table, and taking Isabel's hand, led her to the dance floor. He took turns twirling the women about the room until he thought he had danced with them all, but the musicians continued to play. A tap on his thigh drew his attention. He looked down into the chestnut eyes of Glenna.

"I believe it's my turn, my lord." She curtsied before him, causing him to smile.

"Very well." He scooped Glenna up into his arms and began to dance. He looked over his shoulder as he twirled past his bride.

"You have a rival, my lady."

Lady Averly chuckled.

"I believe so." She reached down and stroked the top of Rand's head. With a full stomach, the wolf had little desire to do anything other than sleep. Lady Averly had grown comfortable with the large canine by her side. She placed her right hand over her mouth to camouflage a yawn.

The tune ended. Lord Edwin set Glenna on the floor and bowed. The little girl curtsied.

"Thank you, my lord. That was fun."

"You're welcome, Glenna." As the little girl skipped away, Lord Edwin looked toward the High Table and caught Lady Averly in mid-yawn. The musicians began a lively tune. Many took to the floor to dance.

Lady Averly thought her future husband was returning to his seat, but he leaned close to her ear and whispered.

"Come, I want to show you something." He pulled out her chair and helped her to stand.

They ascended the staircase and walked down the hallway. He opened the door to his bedchamber and stepped inside.

An uneasy feeling warned Lady Averly to remain at the threshold. She watched as he took a taper from the mantel and set it aflame from the fire in the fireplace.

He turned to see her standing in the hallway nervously fidgeting with her hands and a hesitant expression upon her face.

"I promise to refrain from compromising your maidenhood. After we are wed, I guarantee my promise will be broken." With a devilish grin and a wink of his eye, he motioned for her to come into the bedchamber.

Stepping forward, she smiled meekly and toured about the room, searching her mind for another topic of conversation.

The bed was exquisite. Its four carved posts and tall headboard with royal blue curtains could be drawn to keep those who slept within warm and protected from any draft. There was a nightstand with small candelabras on each side of the bed. A large armoire stood against one wall, a table with two chairs was next to a window, and two high back chairs with a small table between seemed quite inviting in front of the fireplace. A plush rug covered most of the stone floor. A gentleman's portrait hung over the fireplace. She assumed it was Lord Edwin's father. The family crest was decoratively carved into the edge of the mantel.

"The room is quite beautiful, my lord."

"Come with me." Lord Edwin led the way through an archway to the left of the fireplace.

She followed him into a smaller chamber.

"This is the solar." He paused momentarily, holding the lit taper aloft before continuing through the next doorway. "This will be your bedchamber."

She looked about the solar quickly and saw several chairs, a desk, fireplace, and a small table with a chessboard upon it. Discovering herself alone in the small room, she followed the echo of his voice into the next room.

"This was my mother's bedchamber. It shall be yours once we are wed." He turned to see her standing in the doorway.

With her mouth agape, she walked around the bedchamber. Even in the dim light of the single taper, the elegance of the room was apparent. The bed was a replica of Lord Edwin's bed except for the color of the drapes appeared to be a lighter shade. The room was heated by a large fireplace. She was drawn toward the window seat. She looked through the glass panes into the darkness of the night and wondered of its view.

"My mother spent many hours sitting there while she embroidered."

She turned toward him.

"My lord, I don't know what to say." Her voice began to crack. "I don't know what I've done to have such fineries." A tear spilled onto her cheek.

Lord Edwin watched as it cascaded down her face. Uncertain as to why she was crying, he stepped before her and placed his hand upon her arm.

"I thought you would be pleased."

"I am."

"Then why the tears?"

"I'm not quite sure. Perhaps I'm overwhelmed."

He had often wondered about her life before coming to Tildenham. The fragments she revealed were puzzling, but he assumed she would share the details when she was ready.

"In truth, Averly, you deserve more than I can give."

They stood in silence for a moment as she wiped away her tears and he ran his hand up and down her arm before clasping her hand within his, bringing it to his lips, and kissing it gently.

"It's been a life-changing day. Perhaps you're tired." He led her through the bedchamber door, into the hallway, and stopped before her bedchamber. The door was open. He wrapped his arm around her waist, pulled her gently toward him, and kissed her forehead.

"Sleep well."

"Good night." Lady Averly stepped into the room, closed the portal, and listened to his retreating footsteps. She smiled, spread her arms wide, and twirled around the room until she fell upon her bed nearly falling on to Henry.

Chapter 29

THE RAYS OF the morning sun reached skyward, turning night into day. After an evening filled with celebration, dancing, and drink, the residents of Tildenham rose lethargically from their beds to meet the demands of their responsibilities.

Lord Edwin was in a splendid mood. His knight accompanied him through the bailey to the mill.

Sir Garrick cringed as each hammer struck a nail.

"Oh, my head. I don't recall drinking that much, but then again, I lost count."

Ignoring his knight's complaints, Lord Edwin scanned each new building they passed. With village construction beginning in the next day or two, an inventory of the lumber was necessary. They veered their horses onto the worn pathway leading to the mill. Lord Edwin spotted a few people walking on the road toward the gatehouse.

"It looks as if the word is spreading." He nodded his head in the direction of the new arrivals.

Sir Garrick turned his head to see the people who carried piglets, baskets of chickens and led tethered cows and packed horses.

"I hope they're field workers. We need to begin tilling the soil and planting crops soon."

"Was all of the seed destroyed during the attack?"

"It's doubtful any remains. I'll investigate upon our return, my lord."

"I think it's safe to assume that much of what was in storage will need to be replenished. We can confer with the planters, make a list of what is needed, and within the next few days, one of us will accompany a wagon to purchase this year's seed."

"Very well, my lord."

*   *   *

"Good morning, everyone." Lady Averly entered the kitchen dressed in peasant clothing. She carried Henry within her arms.

Isabel and the women left their duties to gather around Lady Averly and offer their congratulations, suggestions, and advice.

"A dress, we must make you a dress."

"The sewing room has bolts of materials."

"Oh, what color, my lady, what color?"

"White!"

"No, ivory!"

"I've always been partial to pastel pink. I think you should wear that color, my lady."

Isabel interrupted.

"Ladies, I believe she will take your advice into consideration, but will ultimately choose the color of her dress herself." Isabel turned toward Lady Averly. "My lady, I would be happy to show you to the sewing chamber once I set the bread to rise. Everyone else, back to work."

The women returned to their duties while continuing to chatter about the wedding and ideas for the dress. Lady Averly giggled at their merriment. She fed Henry before sitting for her morning meal and watching the women go about their tasks.

Isabel set the last loaf near the warmth of the stone baking oven.

"There, finished." She wiped her hands on her overskirt and looked at Lady Averly. "Come with me, my lady."

Lady Averly downed the last bite of porridge before placing her bowl and spoon in the bucket for washing. She followed the cook, who led the way through the Great Hall and up the staircase at a quick pace.

Isabel tilted her head to look over her shoulder.

"Once the barbarians discovered there was nothing more in this chamber than sewing supplies, they left the room unscathed." She stopped before a door a few down from Lady Averly's bedchamber, pushed it open, and allowed her lady to enter first.

"Oh my." Lady Averly turned in a circle to view the room in its entirety. The well-lit chamber contained bolts of various materials on shelves, baskets heaping with thread, and countless other supplies. A large rectangle table with benches on its longest sides was in the center of the room. Windows stretched across the far wall to allow sunlight into the room for sewing.

Isabel was pleased by her lady's reaction.

"With so much to choose from, I'm confident you'll find the right material for your gown, my lady." She noticed Lady Averly was once again wearing peasant attire. "Didn't you like the gowns I hung in the armoire?"

Lady Averly realized the cook was staring at her chosen wardrobe.

"I do like them, but with so much to do throughout the day, I didn't want it to get soiled. I promise I'll dress properly for this evening's meal."

Isabel nodded her head approvingly.

Lady Averly went to the wall of shelves and pulled a few bolts of material to view them in the daylight. She searched for a color to represent the purity and innocence of a traditional wedding dress. Pulling an ivory silk, she ran her hand across the softness of the material, looked to Isabel, and smiled.

"I like this one."

"An excellent choice, my lady."

Lady Averly continued to a basket filled with lace and selected a delicate pattern.

"And this lace."

"Lovely, with perhaps beading and pearls too." Isabel displayed two wooden boxes before Lady Averly, who peeked inside.

"That would be nice, but not too many."

The cook returned the boxes to the shelf and sighed.

"I'll leave you to finalize your choices, my lady. Perhaps you should consider the design. I believe there are paper and ink within the drawer of the table." Isabel made her way to the door.

"Very well, thank you." Lady Averly watched the cook leave before setting the ivory bolt of material on the center work table. She added the lace and found the beading and pearls for embellishments. She was drawn to a beautiful, almost transparent ivory sheer and wondered if her blouse could be made of such a material. She selected a fine muslin for a new chemise.

Lady Averly tried to imagine a style of dress she preferred. Much of the design would be determined by the length of time allotted to sew the garment. Unable to know the length of time it would take before a man of the cloth could be located to perform the ceremony, she decided a simple design would be best. Additional details to the garment could be added if time permitted. She was eager to begin sketching her dress and to decide on a design.

"Oh, the garden will have to be put off until tomorrow."

Opening the drawer within the side of the table, she discovered a piece of handmade paper, ink, and pen. Sitting on a bench, she tried to imagine her wedding dress. Her mind drifted to the hideous wedding dress designed by Lady Miriam. She shuttered, hoping it would remain in the trunk at Holbrook forever. *I need a dress, a dress that represents my new life, filled with happiness with my future husband.* The mere thought of Lord Edwin caused a flutter in her stomach and a grin to appear on her face.

Henry's high-pitched cries echoed in the hallway.

She went to the door, opened it, and called for the kitten. He came bounding into the room and rubbed against his mistress' leg. She scooped him up in her arms, snuggled him closely, and shut the chamber door.

Henry lifted his chin as she rubbed the tips of her fingers up and down the soft fur of his neck while she returned to her seat. Placing him in her lap, she continued to sketch. Henry curled into a ball and nestled into the warmness of her lap as he closed his eyes and lowered his head to her thigh.

Lady Averly tried to sketch a dress. She held the paper up and extended her arm, holding it at a distance, wrinkled her nose, and drew another design. She had nearly drawn a dozen or more sketches when Isabel stepped into the sewing room carrying her lady's midday meal.

"Oh, I see you found the materials for sketching. How are your ideas coming along?" She set the tray of food next to Lady Averly and peeked over her shoulder at the drawings.

Lady Averly glanced at the tray of food before laying out the sketches.

"I'm trying to combine this bodice," she pointed to it, "this sleeve, and this skirt into one drawing to see how they look together."

Isabel examined each sketch and tried to imagine the three parts as one dress.

"It's a simple design, elegant too, but if you still aren't pleased with it, perhaps the women may be able to suggest changes until you can finalize the dress. We can begin cutting and sewing later this afternoon."

"I would appreciate their opinion and yours as well, Isabel. Thank you for the suggestion."

"You're welcome, my lady. I hope you enjoy your meal." The cook returned to the kitchen.

Henry's nose twitched as he awoke from his nap. He lifted his head from Lady Averly's lap and sniffed the tantalizing aroma. He arched his back as he stood and stretched, looked to the edge of the table, and blinked his eyes several times until he became fully awake.

Lady Averly took a bit of meat from the tray, set the sleepy kitten upon the floor, and held the tidbit in front of his mouth. Henry sniffed it once before eating it ravenously. He growled as he ate, as if someone may try to steal his treat. As he swallowed, he looked toward his mistress for more. She tossed him another bite and continued to sketch while she ate her meal.

*   *   *

Word spread to nearby kingdoms that freemen were needed at Tildenham. Lord Edwin stood on the edge of the drawbridge overlooking the village and observed peasants walking on the road toward the castle. He turned to the two carpenters who stood behind him.

"It's time to begin construction of the village."

One of the carpenters glanced over his shoulder to the nearly completed alewives building.

"If you don't mind, my lord, I would like to see the alewives building to completion. It should be done by nightfall."

"Very well." Lord Edwin looked to the other carpenter. "Take a crew of men and begin clearing an area large enough for three dwellings."

"Yes, my lord."

Lord Edwin looked to the pile of salvaged objects at the end of the village. He would ration each peasant's household a pot and lid. Not only could it be used for cooking, but during the colder months, it could be filled with embers from a fire for warmth. He looked to the distant fields. The peasants could lease a parcel of land to grow their crops, give him a portion of their produce as payment for rent, and sell or trade the excess. As they obtained wealth, they could add a second room onto the simple residence he was providing for them. Some of the widowed women would live and work in the Keep. He was determined to find a place and purpose for everyone.

*   *   *

"Oh, my lady, this material is exquisite."

"Please hold still, my lady, while I pin this in place."

"The design is lovely."

Stripped down to her chemise, Lady Averly stood like a statue. With some suggested alterations from the women, the material had been cut to the agreed upon design and pinned for sewing. Pleats were basted, and the skirt sized to her waist.

Henry discovered a comfortable basket filled with scraps of material, lay down, and went to sleep.

An elderly woman smiled as she measured the length of her lady's arm.

"Oh, this is going to be such a lovely dress."

The women's happiness was contagious. Lady Averly's cheeks ached from the incessant grin upon her face.

With limited time before serving the evening meal, the women worked quickly and efficiently. Lady Averly was directed to turn in a circle forward and backward. Her arms lifted for a measurement and then lowered like a bird flapping its wings. As the sun set and the room darkened, Isabel took charge.

"It's time we tend to the evening meal."

The women set aside their work and began to exit.

"Thank you, everyone." Lady Averly touched the bodice, which lay in several pieces on the table.

Isabel returned a needle to a pin cushion.

"My lady, I'll help you dress once I see to the evening meal preparations."

"Thank you, Isabel." Lady Averly watched the cook exit before she picked up her discarded clothing, Henry, and tiptoed to her bedchamber, hoping to remain unseen.

Once safely in her room, she laid her dress upon the back of the chair and placed Henry on the bed. Opening the armoire, she looked through the wardrobe to select a dress. There were six dresses, all equal in quality and beauty.

Isabel knocked on the bedchamber door.

"My lady?"

"Come in, Isabel."

Isabel stood behind Lady Averly and watched her shuffle through her options.

Lady Averly looked over her shoulder at the cook.

"They're so beautiful. It's difficult to choose."

Isabel watched her future mistress touch the sleeve of a lovely golden dress trimmed with cranberry accents.

"I was given permission to search his mother's trunk. That dress was her favorite."

"Do you think Lord Edwin will mind if I wear it?"

"I think he will be pleased."

"Let's hope so." She pulled it from the armoire and held it aloft to admire its beauty in full.

Chapter 30

WITH A SENSE of pride in the progress made for the day, Lord Edwin went to the Keep with ample time to bathe for the evening meal. He had extended an invitation to the newcomers and hoped to learn more of their origin, travels, and skills after they had eaten.

He dressed in a blue tunic trimmed in silver, opened his bedchamber door, and stepped into the hallway. Hearing Lady Averly's bedchamber door open, he paused as she emerged from her bedchamber.

Unaware of being watched, Lady Averly left her door ajar so Henry could join her when he woke from his nap. She brushed her skirt with the palm of her hand to straighten a wrinkle before looking up into her future husband's eyes and smiling shyly.

Lord Edwin scanned her gown, looked to her face, and smiled.

"My dear, you're breathtaking." He crossed the hallway, took her hand, and kissed it.

"My lord, you look quite handsome as well." She gazed into his eyes.

He glanced down the hallway in each direction confirming they were alone before taking a step closer. Even though he could hear voices echoing from the Great Hall, he bent his head toward her lips, paused, and looked into her sapphire eyes for a sign of approval. She had not flinched or pulled away. He bent lower until his lips touched hers, closed his eyes, and felt the gentle touch of her fingertips on the side of his face. As he deepened his kiss, he wrapped his arm around her waist and pulled her toward him.

Lord Edwin opened his eyes as he heard footsteps on the staircase. With an abrupt end to their kiss, he looked in the direction of footsteps to see Isabel. He removed his hand from her waist and took a step backward, furthering the distance between them.

Isabel slowed her pace as she realized she interrupted a moment of intimacy between the couple. She watched as Lady Averly turned away to wipe the back of her hand over her mouth. Lady Averly entwined her fingers together, faced Isabel, and rolled her lips inward before forcing a smile.

Isabel tried to pretend as if she had not intruded upon the couple.

"I'm sorry, my lady. I thought something was keeping you from joining us below." *Apparently, the Lord of Tildenham is the reason for your delay.* "The meal is ready." She curtsied.

Lady Averly nodded to the cook.

"Thank you, Isabel. We'll be right down."

The cook nodded her head and left.

Lady Averly glanced down to her hands before looking up into her future husband's eyes. He was staring at her.

Lord Edwin unlaced her fingers and held both of her hands within his palms.

"If it was possible to wed you this very second, I wouldn't hesitate to do so." He took her left hand, placed it within the fold of his right arm, and covered it with his other hand.

Lady Averly's heart skipped a beat.

"It's my fondest wish as well."

Henry emerged from the bedchamber and raced toward the Great Hall.

All heads turned toward their Lord and soon to be Lady of Tildenham as they descended the staircase and took their rightful place at the High Table. Sir Garrick sat to the right of his lord.

Lord Edwin noticed the vacant place to Lady Averly's right.

"Has Isabel continued to help you dress and see to your needs?"

"Yes."

"Then perhaps we should promote her to your lady in waiting?"

Lady Averly thought of Mina. She would have been her first choice, but Isabel could do the job just the same.

"I think that's an excellent idea." Lady Averly looked toward the cook who sat at a table with the kitchen staff eating her meal. "I'll discuss it with her tomorrow."

Lord Edwin nodded his head in agreement. He scanned the Great Hall. The ambiance of the dancing candlelight, the warmth from the fireplace, and the growing population of Tildenham filled the room with comfort, security, and merriment. He was pleased to see the use of two tables to seat everyone for the evening meal. He reached beneath the table and placed his hand upon his bride's hand as if to say all was well. She grinned before looking about the room at those in attendance.

Rand trotted into the room from the kitchen and took his usual place at his master's side. He placed his nose beneath his master's arm and gave it a nudge.

Lord Edwin looked down at his pet.

"I have a feeling you've already enjoyed a meal in the kitchen." He stroked the top of the wolf's head. "Still hungry?"

Rand perked his ears and tilted his head to the side as he looked up at his master.

Lord Edwin selected a bone dripping with shards of meat from the platter. He held it before Rand, who took the treat within his mouth, went to the back of his master's chair, and lay down.

When Lord Edwin finished his meal, he squeezed Lady Averly's hand before leaving the High Table to talk with the new arrivals to Tildenham.

After washing down her last bite of pastry with wine, Lady Averly joined the women by the fire. With Dolly in hand, Glenna climbed onto her lap.

"Where's Henry?" The little girl straightened Dolly's dress.

"He's around here somewhere. Maybe he is eating in the kitchen." Lady Averly pulled Glenna's sun-streaked blonde hair away from her face, finger brushed it smooth, and braided it while the little girl continued to play with her doll. Lady Averly glanced to her future husband.

Lord Edwin sat across from a man and his wife, deep in conversation. They looked tired, weathered by the sun, and their clothing was tattered and dirty.

"We came from Lowell, my lord. Not much of it remains. When we heard of your need for field workers, we gathered what little we had and began walking." The man took a deep breath and went on to explain. "It was horrible. They attacked suddenly. We were lucky to escape with our lives." The man looked to his wife, who wiped a tear from her cheek. He placed his hand upon her arm and gave it a gentle squeeze.

Lord Edwin nodded toward the people sitting at the next table.

"Only a few of our citizens survived the attack on Tildenham. From your description, the attacks sound similar, probably the same group of men. As they continue to wreak havoc on our land, I pray for our lords to combine their forces and stop this madness. For without a garrison, Tildenham is of little assistance." Lord Edwin looked toward Lady Averly. She was staring at him. He smiled, tipped his head in her direction, and returned his attention to the conversation at hand.

The coupled looked back to their lord. The man nodded as he spoke in earnest.

"My lord, we thank you kindly for allowing us to settle in Tildenham. We're farmers by trade and hard workers too. We'll do our best to ensure a successful harvest."

"Good. As you can see, we are constructing the village as quickly as possible. Until a residence is assigned to you, you will be residing within the Keep."

The couple's eyes widened.

"Thank you, my lord."

Sir Garrick approached Lord Edwin and leaned close to his ear.

"My lord, a word with you if I may."

Lord Edwin rose from the bench.

"Excuse me." He followed his knight to a quiet corner of the room.

Sir Garrick turned to face his lord.

"I spoke with the two men at the end of the table. They're from Heywood and described an attack much like what Tildenham experienced."

"The couple from Lowell said the same." Lord Edwin looked to the new faces within the Great Hall. "I believe the barbarians won't return to Tildenham, however, we may be called upon by Baron Vinson to aid in the fight."

"Unfortunately, only two of our garrison remains, and one happens to be its lord."

"We need to get word to the baron. We also need to purchase seed for the fields. I doubt if our new citizens have brought their own seed stock. Both matters need to be addressed immediately, yet we can't leave these people defenseless." Lord Edwin sighed.

"I'll go with a few men and a wagon to the nearest market. We can purchase the needed seed. I can carry a missive from your hand, find a messenger to take it to the baron, and protect the seed during its return."

Lord Edwin nodded his head in agreement.

"We've little choice. While you're away, I'll assign the fields. They can begin plowing and plant the seed upon your return. Those not working the fields can continue building the village."

The women finished clearing the tables. The musicians tuned their instruments.

Lord Edwin grinned as he patted his knight on the shoulder.

"We'll meet with the field workers tomorrow morning and decide the necessary seed before you go. For now, I wish to dance with my future wife." He crossed the room, stood beside his wife, and leaned close to her ear.

"My lady, would you care to dance?"

The flickering candlelight reflected in her future husband's hazel eyes as Lady Averly looked toward him and smiled.

"I would love to. Glenna, could you sit in my seat and keep it warm until I return?"

"Yes, my lady." Glenna hopped to the floor. Once Lady Averly stepped away, the little girl plopped herself onto the bench as the couple took to the floor.

Henry appeared in the kitchen doorway with a mouse hanging limply from his mouth. He meowed, drawing Glenna's attention. As she went to him, he dropped the dead mouse on the stone floor.

"Good boy, Henry." She picked up the kitten before lifting the mouse by the tail and tossing it into the fireplace. Snuggling Henry, she returned to her seat and placed him in her lap.

Many watched the young couple twirl about the floor.

"You look happy, my dear." Lord Edwin increased the pressure of his hand on the small of her back drawing her near.

"I am."

"Good. I hope to keep you that way forever."

Chapter 31

THE MORNING BROUGHT to light the priorities of the day. Lord Edwin, Sir Garrick, and several peasant men shared a table at breakfast. They discussed which crops to plant and the amount of seed needed. With the meeting adjourned, Sir Garrick selected two sturdy men to accompany him for the journey.

Lord Edwin went to his bedchamber, entered the treasury chamber, and filled a small wooden chest half full of coins. He estimated the value and added a few more coins before closing the lid. He removed the key tethered to the handle and locked the chest. He went to the solar and sat at his father's desk. Quickly jotting down a missive on paper, he returned the quill to the holder, and reread his message to the baron. His request was simple. He needed men to rebuild the garrison. He wrote a second missive asking for the services of a man of the cloth. After folding the missives, he lit a red wax candle, dripped the wax onto the folded edges, and pressed his ring into the warm puddles of wax to seal them securely. With the missives, chest, and key in hand, he left the Keep and joined the men at the stable.

Bryce ensured the wagon's wheels were in good condition before hitching up a pair of horses. He saddled the knight's warhorse, led it out of the stable, and waited for its rider.

Women carried satchels of food and several flasks of wine. They placed them in the back of the wagon before returning to the kitchen.

Lord Edwin handed the missives to his knight, who tucked the correspondence inside his tunic. He presented the chest and key.

"I believe this will cover any expense you may incur."

Sir Garrick dropped the key into his belt bag.

"I'll do my best to negotiate a good price for the seed and see that your requests are entrusted into dependable hands." He set the box of coins beneath the seat where the two men sat with the reins of the horses in hand and covered it with a large oilcloth that would be used to protect the purchased seed from damp weather.

Lord Edwin grasped his knight's forearm.

"Safe journey."

"I'll return as soon as possible, my lord."

With the wagon loaded, Bryce released the bridle as Sir Garrick climbed atop his warhorse.

Rand sat next to his master and looked up toward him.

"We'll go hunting later." Lord Edwin patted the wolf's head and stood silently, watching his knight precede the wagon toward the gatehouse and exit the castle.

*   *   *

Even though there was plenty of work to do in the kitchen, Isabel allowed a few of the women to go to the sewing chamber to work on the wedding dress.

Lady Averly stood in her chemise and wedding skirt. She felt the material between her fingers and tried to stand still while the hem was pinned in place.

After straightening the skirt and inserting a pin, a young peasant woman, Sarah, looked up to her lady. The twinkle in her brown eyes conveyed her excitement.

"Oh, I hope the wedding is soon."

An elderly woman adding beading to the bodice stilled her needle.

"At least in my lifetime."

Some of the women chuckled. Lady Averly smiled sweetly.

"I've been told we'll be wed once a man of the cloth arrives. I look forward to the day."

Sarah placed another pin in the hem and looked up.

"As we all do, my lady."

Lady Averly looked across the room at the bolts of cloth on the shelves. She searched for an appropriate shade of green or brown for a new dress for Glenna. *A simple design and a little oversized to allow for future growth.* Feeling Sarah's palm press upon her thigh, she rotated so the last section of the hem could be pinned.

The chamber door opened and a woman from the kitchen stepped into the room.

"My lady, Isabel says she needs everyone in the kitchen."

The women set aside their sewing and began to file out of the room. Sarah selected another pin from the cushion upon her wrist and wove it in the material of the skirt.

"Oh, I'm nearly finished pinning the hem."

Lady Averly glanced down at the unpinned section before addressing the woman in the doorway.

"Please tell Isabel that I'm retaining Sarah for a few more minutes. She will be there shortly."

"Yes, my lady." The woman closed the door, leaving her lady and Sarah to finish.

In very little time, the hem was pinned, and Sarah joined the others in the kitchen. Lady Averly dressed in her peasant clothing, selected the material for Glenna's dress, and began cutting it to size.

*   *   *

Doran reined his horse to the side of the road as a wagon driven by two men and another on horseback approached him. Spying the length of the sword and saddle upon the war horse, he assumed the gentleman to be a knight.

Halting his horse before the stranger, Sir Garrick took note of the man's fine horse, sword, and multiple dirks upon his belt. *Not a knight but looks as if he could defend himself in a battle.*

"Good day."

"Good day, sir." Doran nodded his head in acknowledgment.

"Where are you headed?"

"Tildenham."

A Freelancer? Sir Garrick moved the reins to his left hand, freeing his right to grab his sword if necessary.

"May I inquire as to why you will be visiting the kingdom?"

"I've been ordered by Baron Vinson to track the barbarians and discover where they have set up camp."

"The Lord of Tildenham, Lord Edwin, can give you the information you seek. You may tell him that you met Sir Garrick on your journey."

"Thank you and good day, Sir Garrick." Doran nodded his head and urged his horse forward.

"And to you." Sir Garrick pressed his heels to his horse's sides and joined the wagon that had continued without him.

Doran looked over his shoulder at the knight. He assumed Sir Garrick's mission was important. As the road crossed a stream, Doran allowed his horse to rest while he ate some dried venison. After a cold drink from the stream, he climbed atop his horse and continued down the road.

After riding for several hours, Doran and his horse emerged from a forest in the late afternoon to see the kingdom of Tildenham in the distance. He saw the ashen scars on the ground where buildings once stood and a charred pile of cleared debris to one side of the village. He assumed the kingdom would be in shambles but was surprised to find he was wrong.

Doran observed men working on a small one-room residence, the fifth he counted in a row of newly constructed dwellings as he rode toward the gatehouse. Once over the drawbridge and into the bailey, he reined his horse at the stable.

Bryce came forward and took the horse by the bridle.

"Good day."

Doran dismounted.

"Good day. I would like to speak to the Lord of Tildenham."

"Lord Edwin is out and about now. If you would like to wait in the Great Hall, I'll go fetch him." Bryce pointed toward the Keep. An unexpected guest was seldom welcome. It was best to give Lord Edwin time to prepare for a visitor, even if he had little knowledge of the topic of discussion.

"Thank you kindly." Doran turned and walked in the direction indicated.

Bryce led the man's horse into a stall, gave it oats and water, and ran to fetch Lord Edwin, assuming he was somewhere in the village.

*   *   *

Doran stepped from the hallway into the Great Hall. There was something odd about Tildenham, but he had yet to pinpoint what it was.

Sarah nodded to the stranger as she passed by him on her way to the kitchen.

"Isabel, there's a man in the Great Hall."

Isabel looked up from the pot she was stirring.

"Who is he?"

Sarah shrugged her shoulders.

"He's pretty dusty. Must have traveled for days."

Isabel grabbed a tankard, filled it with ale, and handed Sarah the spoon.

"Stir the pot until I return." The cook left the kitchen, stepped into the Great Hall, and forced a smile upon her face as the stranger turned to face her.

"Good day, welcome to Tildenham. It looks as if you've been on the road for days. Here's a tankard of ale to quench your thirst." Isabel set the mug upon a table.

"Thank you. I'm here to see your lord. The stableboy went to fetch him."

"Very well. Please seat yourself until Lord Edwin arrives." Isabel curtsied and returned to the kitchen.

Doran sat on a bench. He stretched out his legs, crossing them at his ankles, and leaned back against the table while he examined the architectural features of the impressive room, drank the cool ale, and waited. He had nearly emptied the tankard when he heard footsteps in the hallway and watched as a young man and a gray wolf stepped into the room.

Lord Edwin approached the man who remained seated and stood with his fisted hands upon his hips.

"You wished to see me?"

Doran's eyebrows rose in disbelief. *Lord Edwin?* He stood quickly.

"Excuse me, my lord. I was expecting someone much older." He extended his hand, which was clasped by the young lord. Doran glanced at the wolf as it stepped forward and sniffed his boots. *Such an unusual companion.*

"I'm Lord Edwin. My father was killed during the attack."

Rand sat next to his master's feet. His piercing yellow eyes stared at the stranger.

"My condolences, my lord. My name is Doran. I've been sent by Baron Vinson to track the barbarians."

"Following the trail of destruction, so to speak. I wish we could aid the baron. However, my knight and I are the only surviving members of the garrison. From what others have told me, the barbarians traveled westward toward Morton."

Lord Edwin patted the top of Rand's head.

"If I may request a place to rest my head for the evening and a meal, I'll continue my journey in the morning."

"Certainly. Let me speak with Isabel. She will see to your accommodations."

"Thank you, my lord."

Rand remained frozen in place as his master left the room. His unblinking yellow eyes watched the stranger's every move.

Lord Edwin stepped into the kitchen.

"Isabel."

Isabel turned to see her lord in the doorway.

"Yes, my lord."

"Our guest will need a bedchamber. Could you see to his needs?"

"Yes, my lord."

Lord Edwin passed through the Great Hall, nodded to his guest, and slapped his thigh. Rand sprang to his feet and followed his master as they returned to work.

Alone in the room, Doran drained his tankard dry, set it on the table, and turned toward the sound of footsteps to see the same woman who had brought him the ale.

"Lord Edwin says you'll be staying the night."

"Yes, if it won't be too much trouble."

"Not at all. Follow me." Isabel ascended the staircase, walked down the hallway, and stopped before a bedchamber door and pointed to the door at the end of the hallway.

"The garderobe is there." She opened the bedchamber door for him to enter. "It's small but will fit your needs for tonight."

Doran stepped into the room. There was a cot, a candle on a nightstand, and a chair.

"It's perfect."

Isabel stood in the doorway.

"Shall I alert you when the evening meal is served?"

"No, thank you. I'd prefer a meal brought and left on the chair if I'm asleep."

Isabel thought the request was odd.

"Very well." She returned to the kitchen.

Doran shut the door. He sat on the bed, slipped off his boots and weapons, and lay upon the cot. Within minutes, he was asleep.

*　　　　　*　　　　　*

A dainty knock sounded upon the sewing chamber door. Lady Averly looked up from her stitching.

"Come in."

Glenna entered, carrying Henry in one hand and Dolly in the other.

"Lady Averly, guess what I did."

"What did you do?"

"I helped Isabel in the kitchen. I put the cut vegetables into a bowl."

"Well done."

"She said it would be all right to come and visit you. I brought Henry too."

Lady Averly smiled as she pulled the needle through the material. *Not that I mind. Isabel more than likely needed the little one out from under her feet.*

"What are you making?" Glenna kissed the top of Henry's head before setting him on the floor.

"I'm making a dress for you." Lady Averly watched as the child's mouth fall open before smiling.

"For me?"

"Yes. I thought you might like a new dress."

"Oh, thank you, my lady." Glenna sat on the bench scooting close enough to Lady Averly to touch the fabric of the dress.

"You're welcome. Do you like the color?

"Oh, yes."

"It will take me a few days to finish it." She set the dress aside. "But for now, I think our evening meal is close to being ready. Let's go join the others." She stood, pausing momentarily as she realized she had yet to dress properly for the meal. *This dress will just have to do for tonight.*

They left the sewing chamber hand in hand with Henry following and descended the staircase into the Great Hall.

Lord Edwin awaited his future bride on the dais. He turned to see Lady Averly walking toward him and pulled her chair out from the High Table.

"I sent a missive with Sir Garrick requesting a man of the cloth." He pushed her chair inward as she sat, took his place in his chair, and looked to her as he lifted his tankard. "I hope to have one in residence in less than a fortnight."

"A fortnight isn't so very long to wait." She smiled, confident her wedding dress would be finished for the ceremony.

"With putting Tildenham in order, the days should go by quickly."

Rand took his usual place by his master.

Lord Edwin scanned the Great Hall for the man he had spoken to earlier in the day.

Her future husband's silence drew Lady Averly attention.

"Is something amiss?"

Rand placed his paw on his master's lap.

Lord Edwin patted the wolf's head.

"No, I was looking for someone who asked for a night's stay. Perhaps he chose not to join us for the evening meal."

Being ignored, the wolf tapped his paw on his master's lap.

The Lord of Tildenham tore a piece of meat from a bone and tossed it to the wolf. Rand caught it within his jowls and swallowed it whole.

Lord Edwin lifted Lady Averly's hand to his lips and placed a kiss upon it. He grinned as he returned her hand to the table top.

She smiled at him before taking a bite of bread and looking at those in the room. She looked forward to fulfilling her duties as the Lady of Tildenham, living in a kingdom with people who appreciated her efforts, and sharing her life with a husband she loved.

Chapter 32

DORAN WOKE AT first morning's light to find a tray of food sitting on the chair next to his bed. After dressing and using the garderobe, he ate the stale food and washed it down with the tankard of tepid ale before donning his weapons and leaving the chamber. As he descended the staircase into the Great Hall, he saw Isabel setting a breakfast tray on the table.

"Thank you, Isabel, for your hospitality."

The cook looked at the guest.

"You're welcome."

"Where may I find Lord Edwin?"

"I'm here." Lord Edwin descended the staircase. Hearing his master's voice, Rand trotted out of the kitchen and greeted him at the base of the staircase.

Doran turned to see the young lord followed by a beautiful lady with golden blonde hair.

Lord Edwin noticed Doran's attention focused on Lady Averly. He turned, lifted her hand as if to help her descend the last step, and presented her.

"Let me introduce you. Lady Averly, my soon to be wife."

The smile from Doran's face faded.

"Did you say Lady Averly?"

"Yes. Why?"

Doran took the missive from an inside pocket of his tunic. He looked to the stunning young woman as he handed it to Lord Edwin, who stepped away to read it.

"I assumed our paths would never cross, Lady Averly."

Her heart began to sink within her chest and beat rapidly. She looked toward Lord Edwin's back. His continued to read as she went to his side and placed her hand upon his forearm.

"What did he give you?" She peered at the letter, recognizing her father's handwriting.

"It appears to be a decree stating you're committed to another. You're to go with Doran." He looked up from the missive and searched her eyes for the truth. "Are you betrothed to another?"

She wanted to lie, to stay within Tildenham, as his wife. Her heart ached. She found it difficult to breathe, but his questioning stare forced her to speak.

"I ran away because I didn't want to marry someone I didn't know or love." She took a deep breath and exhaled. "I'm being exchanged for the largest dowry they could obtain. I'm truly sorry."

Lord Edwin tossed the missive on a nearby table, clasped her hand, and led her to the side of the room for privacy.

"Do you care for me? Love me at all?" He prayed she would reveal her true feelings.

Unable to hold her love for him within her heart any longer, it welled as tears.

"With all of my soul, my every being."

"Then if I strike this man down, no one will know you're here." He secretly wished Sir Garrick was available for advice or at least provided an extra sword for support.

"Won't someone wonder why he's missing? Wouldn't they follow his travels and eventually come to Tildenham?" She looked to the balcony, to the chamber containing the wedding dress she would never wear. Unable to contain her disappointment, Lady Averly closed her eyes, spilling tears upon her cheeks before meeting Lord Edwin's inquisitive stare.

"I wish to stay and forever be your wife, but I'll not put your life in danger to do so."

"We can run away together."

"You have a responsibility here, to your people."

Lord Edwin drew her into his embrace as she began to cry in earnest. She wrapped her arms around his waist while trying to find the strength to let go.

He kissed the top of her head and inhaled the fragrant scent of her golden locks.

"You know I love you."

She nodded her head before looking up into his eyes.

"As I do you."

Rand tried to wedge himself between the couple.

Lord Edwin cradled her face within his hands, brushing the tears away with his thumbs. He cast to memory her sapphire eyes as he leaned forward and placed a kiss on her lips. As he released her, she curled her arms around his neck and embraced him one last time.

Glenna looked up from her breakfast. She stared at her lord and lady, sensing there was something terribly wrong. Henry, sitting in her lap, poked his head above the edge of the table to see what was on her plate.

Word spread within the Keep. The women in the kitchen came to the doorway and stood. Their sullen faces watched as their lord and lady's fate unfolded.

Doran sighed as he looked to the young couple.

"I'll see to the horses." He left the Great Hall.

Isabel sighed. *This isn't right.* She turned to the kitchen staff.

"We better see to their food for the journey."

Lady Averly felt a tug on her dress. She looked down to see Glenna standing next to her with Dolly tucked under her arm and holding Henry next to her chest. Her precious face masked with concern.

"My lady, why are you crying?"

Lady Averly dried her tears as she knelt before the child and tried to smile.

"I must go away."

"Why?"

"Because I must."

"Will you come back?"

Lady Averly sighed as she built the courage to say what must be said. She traced Glenna's hairline with her finger and brushed her blonde hair from her shoulders.

"Perhaps for a visit, someday."

"No, I want you to stay. Don't go." Dolly dropped to the floor as Glenna threw her arms around her mistress' neck and began to cry. Lady Averly embraced the little girl tenderly, trying to control the sorrowful torment with her heart.

Henry squirmed between them.

Lady Averly petted the tiny kitten's head.

"My departure will be eased knowing you'll take good care of Henry." She kissed the top of the kitten's head and the little girl's cheek. "Since he's so very little, you'll need to watch him closely until he gets bigger. Can you promise to watch over him for me?"

"I promise. But Lady Averly, I don't want you to leave." Glenna's bottom lip quivered as tears spilled onto her cheeks.

Lady Averly picked up Dolly and straightened her dress before handing it to Glenna, hoping to calm her. She brushed away the child's tears with her fingers.

"It is my wish as well, but I must." She placed the palm of her hand on the child's cheek as she stood.

"No!" Glenna threw her arm around Lady Averly's legs.

Isabel emerged from the kitchen.

"Let me take her, my lady." She picked up the distraught child and placed Glenna upon her hip. Unable to keep her emotions in check, Isabel's voice quivered.

"May I reiterate Glenna's sentiments, my lady? We wish you to stay." She nodded her head toward the kitchen doorway. Many of the staff nodded their heads and smiled meekly.

A pair of women squeezed through the crowded doorway holding several leather bags of provisions for the trip. They nodded to the couple as they passed by them on their way to the stable.

Lady Averly tried to compose herself. After all, those of royal blood must act in a dignified manner while among others.

"You've been so very kind. Thank you, Isabel, for everything you have done for me." She reached out and touched the cook's forearm.

"You're welcome, my lady. I'll send someone to your bedchamber and gather your belongings." Isabel nodded to two women in the doorway who crossed the room and ascended the staircase to gather their lady's items. She looked to Lord Edwin. His eyes were downcast to the stone floor as he ran his hand through his mahogany hair, pulling it away from his face. Her lord was clearly shaken by the turn of events.

Isabel patted Glenna's back as she continued to cry. She headed toward the kitchen.

"Let's get Henry something to eat."

Glenna looked over the cook's shoulder to Lady Averly.

"But I don't want her to go!" the child's voice echoed from the kitchen.

Doran stepped into the Great Hall. All heads turned toward the man who had disrupted the happiness of the kingdom.

"The horses are ready." His face was stern.

Lord Edwin's chest tightened as he scrutinized the man from head to toe. An ill feeling settled within his stomach. Dare he entrusts the care of the woman he loves to him? He knew nothing of Doran's character. He stepped to Lady Averly's side.

"Other than Isabel, I need you to choose one of the women to accompany you during the journey, for your safety, that is."

Looking at the kitchen doorway, Lady Averly spotted a familiar face.

"Sarah."

He turned toward the kitchen.

"Sarah, you'll accompany Lady Averly. Gather your things."

"Yes, my lord." Sarah hurried to her chamber.

He turned to Doran.

"If you would be so kind as to inform our stableboy to saddle a horse for Sarah?"

Doran nodded and left the room with Rand following.

The Lord of Tildenham reached for Lady Averly's hand and tucked it into the crook of his arm. He placed his left hand over hers, entwining their fingers together.

Lady Averly looked to the strong hand donned with the signet ring as they strolled out of the Keep. It was as if he was trying to give her the strength she needed to leave him and face whatever may come.

The women descended the staircase, each carrying an armful of clothing and placed them on a table as Isabel emerged from the kitchen with a folded oilcloth.

One of the women pulled Lady Averly's cloak from the jumbled pile. She put the dirk that was hanging in the armoire into its pocket.

"Isabel, we gathered everything we could find." She set the cloak upon a bench.

"Good, if we can manage to do so, I believe Lord Edwin would want her to take a gown or two." Isabel unfolded the oilcloth upon the table. The three women worked quickly, laying each item flat upon the cloth. They folded in the sides, rolled it tightly, and tied it securely with twine. The women picked up each end of the bundle and carried it to the stable. Isabel snatched the cloak from the bench and followed.

Bryce attached the bundle of clothing behind the saddle onto Nelly's rump. He looked toward the Keep and saw Sarah with her satchel in hand. The stableboy strapped her bag to the saddle before offering a hand to boost her onto her horse.

Wanting to delay her departure, Lord Edwin paused before his mother's flower garden. He raised Lady Averly's dainty fingers toward his mouth and kissed them.

Lady Averly looked toward the buds on the roses.

"I wish the roses were in bloom. I would have liked to have witnessed their color and beauty."

Doran's impatience grew as he circled his horse back to the stable. He urged his horse toward the couple.

He despised tearful farewells. He would ensure Baron Vinson remained ignorant of this out of the way venture by pushing the horses to near exhaustion each day in order to make up for the lost time. Doran glared at the couple.

Lord Edwin glanced over his shoulder to see Doran's intolerant stare.

"Are you certain I can't run him through?" he smirked.

Lady Averly glanced at the sour expression upon Doran's face.

"I'm tempted to let you do so."

After a moment of silence, Lord Edwin sighed.

"Perhaps our paths shall cross again."

"Unfortunately, I'll be married to another."

"Then I can run your husband through." He chuckled.

She displayed a sideways grin.

Lord Edwin released her hand and wrapped his arms around her waist. A tear escaped the corner of her eye and rolled down her cheek as their lips met in a final farewell.

"I love you." He whispered, before kissing her forehead.

"And I love you."

He ran his hands down her arms and exhaled. Placing a firm hand behind the small of her back, he stepped aside as she approached Nelly.

Isabel held the cloak open for Lady Averly to place upon her shoulders.

"Good-bye, my lady."

"Good-bye, Isabel. Do take care." She stepped into the garment and secured the clasp beneath her chin.

Bryce held Nelly's bridle. His chin quivered as he averted his eyes to hide his tears.

"My lady, I wish you a safe journey."

"Thank you, Bryce." Lady Averly turned toward Lord Edwin. She knew she belonged within his arms, as his wife. She looked toward his face and tried to smile.

He sighed as he forced a grin upon his face. Lord Edwin cupped his hands, leaned forward, and helped her onto her horse.

Bryce released Nelly's bridle and returned to the stable.

Lady Averly stared down at Lord Edwin, casting the features of his face to memory.

"Good-bye." She urged Nelly forward.

Rand went to his master's side and sat. Lord Edwin stared at the woman he loved until she disappeared from his sight.

Chapter 33

ONCE THE TRIO was over the drawbridge, Lady Averly looked to the vast forest.

"I'd like to make one stop before we take to the road."

Doran looked over his shoulder at the two women following him on horseback and scowled but relented.

"Very well."

As they rode through the village, Lady Averly veered from the pathway toward the mill with Doran and Sarah following.

"I'll only be a few moments." Guiding her horse through the woods, she came to the clearing where she had first met Lord Edwin, dismounted, and walked toward the bench. Wildflowers were beginning to bloom around the base of the statue, dotting the ground with yellow, white, and blue.

Unwilling to let the woman out of his sight, Doran followed, reining his horse at the edge of the clearing while Sarah remained on the pathway and waited.

Lady Averly sat on the bench and stared at the angel. The memory of the day they first met flashed within her mind.

Why must it be this way? Tears welled within her eyes. She bowed her head, allowing them to fall into her lap. *Why am I forced to wed another when I love him so?*

A female voice whispered.

"My dearest, all is as it should be."

The hair on the nap of Lady Averly's neck rose. Keeping her head downcast as to not alert Doran, she looked toward the statue to see a woman standing beside it. Her face was kind, dark hair pinned neatly in place, and blue dress with its full skirt donned with intricate black beading. Lady Averly glanced toward Doran. He seemed ignorant of the woman's presence.

The woman smiled.

"Have faith. All is as it should be."

Lady Averly recalled the portrait over the Great Hall fireplace.

Lady Mary?

The woman nodded before dissipating into a white mist and vanishing.

Lady Averly wished she could be optimistic about the future. Returning to a life of verbal abuse by her stepmother, mocking by her half-brother, and marrying a stranger gave her little hope for a life filled with happiness. The only positive aspect of her dire situation was seeing Mina and once married, she would live in a kingdom far away from her family.

She looked to the calm, solemn face of the angel, exhaled in defeat, and rose. She climbed atop Nelly. Doran turned his horse around. She followed obediently.

*   *   *

Lord Edwin enclosed himself in the solitude of his solar. Rand sat patiently next to his chair with his head upon his master's lap and would tilt his head occasionally to look at his master's face.

The Lord of Tildenham was tired of everyone's empathetic stares and comments. He slouched in his chair, staring at the open missive on the top of his desk. With thoughts absent from his mind, he placed his hand upon Rand's head and petted it. A knock at the door caused him to look toward it.

"Come in."

Isabel opened the door and stepped into the room.

"Is there anything you need, my lord, possibly a stout ale?"

"The return of my bride." He muttered to himself.

Overhearing his comment, she smiled slightly.

"We all wish that, my lord. Can't you undo the betrothal and get her back?"

"It's highly unlikely. Unless her betrothed should die before they wed, the contract is binding." He lifted the missive and examined the signature. "I don't even know the kingdom in which she returned. The signature is indecipherable."

Isabel glanced at her lord. His sullen mood affected everyone in the kingdom. Even though his heart needed time to heal, she wanted to raise his spirits.

"Well, I'll fetch you a mug of ale. Better yet, a full pitcher and something to eat too." She left the solar, closing the door behind her.

Lord Edwin stared at the closed door. He exhaled and sank a little deeper in his chair. *I'm not sure getting drunk will help matters much. And I can't stay here all day. There's a kingdom to be rebuilt.* He sat up in his chair, and ran his hand through his hair, pulling it away from his eyes. He took a deep breath to pull himself together before he stood and left the solar with Rand following. He met Isabel in the Great Hall. She carried a pitcher of ale, a tankard, and tray of food as promised.

"My lord?" She stopped before him.

He accepted the pitcher and mug from her hand, poured the ale into the vessel, and drank its contents.

"Thank you, Isabel."

The cook accepted both items as her lord handed them to her.

"You're welcome, my lord." She stood transfixed as she watched Lord Edwin and his wolf leave the Great Hall and exit the Keep. "I guess I should have offered the drink sooner."

Pounding hammers became silent as the men in the bailey paused to watch their lord walk toward the stable with commanding strides.

Lord Edwin stopped before his mother's flower garden while Rand sniffed the ground, attempting to follow an unfamiliar scent. The limestone bench was white once again. The plants flourished with their full green leaves and buds ready to burst open.

Bryce saw his lord and joined him.

"Lady Averly did a fine job of tidying the garden."

Lord Edwin looked to the stableboy.

"Yes, she did."

"She said it would be nice if the fence was rebuilt to protect the plants." He grinned.

Lord Edwin nodded.

"I agree." He turned toward a building under construction and signaled for an elderly man to come forward.

"Yes, my lord."

"I know this may sound like a frivolous request, but it's important to me to fulfill the wish of Lady Averly and build a fence around the flower garden."

"Yes, my lord."

"If need be, have someone help you."

"Yes, my lord."

Lord Edwin patted the man on the shoulder before walking with Bryce to the stable.

"My lord, would you like me to saddle Fulton?"

"Yes, I need to clear my head and thought a ride would do me some good."

"Very well, my lord." Bryce retrieved the blanket and saddle as he watched his lord grab a bridle from a peg and step into his destrier's stall. Bryce threw the blanket over Fulton's back and straightened the wrinkles while Lord Edwin placed the bit in the stallion's mouth and put the bridle over his ears. With the two of them working together, Fulton was saddled and led from the stable in record time. The Lord of Tildenham climbed atop his war horse and headed toward the gatehouse. Rand peeked around the side of the stable and darted after his master.

Lord Edwin rode through the village. He nodded to families who had taken residence within the newly constructed dwellings. All was progressing as planned. The final wall was erected to complete the sides of another building and workers plowed the field. He reined Fulton at the mill and watched men load lumber into the back of a wagon. All was going as planned, except for the desire that lay deep within his heart.

A resonant throaty growl warned of danger. Lord Edwin turned to see Rand tiptoe into the fringe of the woods and disappear amongst the spring foliage. He reined his horse, encouraged Fulton forward, and listened to the fading steps of the wolf. Anticipating the sound of a vicious encounter with another animal, he heard only silence. *A poacher?* He dismounted, tied Fulton's reins to a sapling trunk, and entered the woods, pulling his sword from its sheath as he tiptoed forward. Suppressing the urge to call Rand in fear the intruder would flee, Lord Edwin pushed aside a low branch and stepped into the clearing where the angel statue stood. Rand backed away from the bench and looked at his master while his tail wagged back and forth.

"What are you doing?" Lord Edwin returned his sword to its sheath.

Rand looked as if he was smiling. His mouth hung open with his tongue hanging to the right. He turned his head toward the bench, to his master, and crouched low to the ground with his bottom in the air, challenging his lord.

"Oh, you're in the mood to play." Lord Edwin bent down to the wolf's level with his arms in a wide arc. He took a step forward, stomping his foot.

Rand hopped on his front paws from side to side as his master approached. He knew Lord Edwin would draw his attention with one hand while touching his head with the other. As the wolf felt a touch on one side of his head, he tried to nip at his master's hand but missed.

Their antics resulted in the pair falling to the ground and tumbling as they wrestled. Lord Edwin laughed as he laid still, his chest heaving, and tried to catch his breath. He watched a bird fly over the clearing and noticed the sky had turned to dusk.

"You've worn me out, Rand." Lord Edwin rolled onto his stomach.

Rand sprang to his feet. He pranced back and forth, teasing his master with the hope of continuing their play as he watched him stand.

"No, it's time for us to return." Lord Edwin slapped the side of his thigh, signaling Rand to follow as he left the clearing and went to his horse.

The wolf watched his master leave before going to the bench and sitting before the woman who reappeared.

"*Good boy. It's nice to see him laugh.*" Lady Mary patted Rand's head.

"Rand!"

The wolf ran toward his master's call.

They arrived in time for the evening meal. Lord Edwin preferred to have a tray of food sent to the solar where he could eat alone but joined the others at the table. He averted his eyes away from the solitary place setting and vacant chair at the High Table.

After Glenna finished eating, she wandered toward her lord with Dolly in one hand and Henry following closely at her heels. She squeezed between Lord Edwin and the man next to him and sat on the bench.

"I miss Lady Averly."

Lord Edwin set down his tankard and looked at the little girl. He touched Dolly's hair, recalling the day Lady Averly found it in the mud.

"As do I."

"Can't you go and get her and make her come back?"

"It isn't that simple."

Henry meowed. Glenna reached under the table, picked up the kitten, and placed him in her lap.

"Where did Lady Averly go?"

"I don't know. Wherever she is, we must pray for her happiness."

"I'm doing a good job taking care of Henry, don't you think?" Her askance brown eyes looked toward her lord.

Lord Edwin touched the top of Henry's head and stroked it with his index finger as he recalled Lady Averly's fondness for the feline.

"I think you're doing an excellent job."

*   *   *

The moonless night made it too dangerous to travel, especially with the women in tow. Doran looked over his shoulder.

"We'll camp here for the night." He directed his horse off the road and into a cluster of trees.

Lady Averly sighed with relief. Her bottom ached from the rigorous pace of their travel. With little to occupy her mind, she thought of Lord Edwin often and wondered how he was coping with their permanent separation. She reined the horse to follow Doran. Sarah followed.

After dismounting, Doran led the horses to a tree where he secured their reins. He removed the saddles and blankets and placed them in a small clearing where he would build a fire in the center for warmth.

While Doran gathered wood, the women sat next to their saddles, pulling the horse blankets around their shoulders. Lady Averly untied the satchel of food, opened it, and inspected what was inside.

Realizing each person was given provisions; Sarah retrieved her satchel, flask of wine, and took a long drink. The lack of conversation from Lady Averly was unnerving but understandable.

"Are you well, my lady?"

"Yes, Sarah. It's been a long day."

With the fire ablaze and her aching body requiring a good night's rest, Lady Averly propped her head against her saddle and snuggled beneath her blanket as she lay upon the ground. She watched the twinkling sparks from the fire rise toward the ebony blue sky. Thoughts of Lord Edwin, Glenna, and Henry crossed her mind, causing tears to spill from her eyes. She recalled the angel in the woods and Lady Mary. *Is everything as it should be? Perhaps it was until he came to Tildenham.* She stared at Doran as he lowered himself to the ground to sleep. She watched the flickering flames of the campfire before closing her eyes and falling asleep.

Chapter 34

LADY AVERLY'S BODY rocked back and forth. She opened her eyes to see Doran crouched next to her. She blinked her eyes to clear the fogginess and looked to the pink sky in the east. The birds chirped like nature's alarm clock, announcing the new day. She shivered, pulling the blanket over her shoulder as she lay on her side and glanced at the campfire with its embers covered by white ash.

Doran stood.

"We must be on our way." He turned to Sarah and shook her awake.

Lady Averly let her horse blanket fall onto her saddle as she rose and stretched. Her neck ached, her back was stiff, and her right hip seemed bruised. When she looked to the ground for a rock or root, there was none. Finding the nearest bush to relieve herself, she lifted her cloak and skirt and felt something deep within her pocket. *My dirk.* She strapped it to her calf.

Sarah curtsied as Lady Averly returned to the campsite.

"Good morning, my lady."

"Good morning, Sarah."

Doran saddled the horses while they waited for Sarah, who disappeared behind a bush.

Lady Averly pulled a wedge of cheese from her satchel, held it in her mouth, and climbed astride her horse as Sarah joined them. The women reined their mares and followed Doran to the road, resuming their wicked pace.

Sarah reined her horse near Nelly, so she may speak quietly.

"My lady, where are we headed?"

Lady Averly glanced toward Doran, who rode ahead of her.

"Holbrook."

"How much farther must we ride?"

"A day or two? I honestly don't know."

*   *   *

Rand wedged his nose under his master's hand and lifted it upward to wake him. Groaning, Lord Edwin rolled onto his side and shielded his eyes from the bright morning sunlight radiating through his bedchamber window. He opened his eyes a mere crack to see his pet staring him in the face and closed them again.

Rand nudged his master's hand again.

"Go away." Lord Edwin rolled onto his back and placed his arm over his face, casting his eyes into darkness once again. His head throbbed like it had been kicked by a horse. He assumed his consumption of the bottomless pitcher of ale Isabel kept placing before him was the cause. He prayed she had a remedy for the pounding ache within his head.

Losing his patience, Rand jumped on the bed, lay on his master's chest, and licked his face.

"All right, I'm awake." Lord Edwin tried to push his pet away. The persistent wolf dodged his master's attempt. Rand pranced as he jumped from one side of his master's body to the other until he miscalculated and fell off the bed.

"Serves you right." Lord Edwin tossed the covers aside, sat on the edge of the bed, and cradled his head in his hands as he leaned his elbows upon his thighs. After the room stopped spinning, he stood, put on a pair of breeches, and pulled a tunic over his head before heading toward the kitchen with Rand leading the way.

*　　　　*　　　　*

Unwilling to spend another night on the road and spare any more time away from his assignment, Doran pushed the horses to near exhaustion as they continued to travel through the day and into the middle of the night. They rode through the slumbering village of Holbrook in the wee hours of the morning, the guard allowing them to pass over the drawbridge and enter the castle. Reining their horses at the stable, Doran dismounted and banged his fist upon the stable door, rousing the stableboy.

Sleepy-eyed Emmet climbed down from the loft, opened the door, and recognized Nelly. He looked lethargically to the person who sat atop the mare. His eyes widened as he became fully awake.

"Lady Averly!" He took the reins of Doran's horse and grasped Nelly's bridle.

Lady Averly dismounted, as did Sarah.

"Hello, Emmet. It's good to see you again." She turned toward the Keep. Her knees locked.

Doran stepped beside her and motioned toward the door with the palm of his hand.

"My lady, shall we go inside?" He had gone out of his way to bring her this far. He was determined to collect his reward, rest briefly, and be on his way at first morning's light.

She glared at Doran, curling her lip in disgust. *Lady Miriam must be paying him a great amount.* She sighed.

Sarah joined Lady Averly.

"I'm right beside you, my lady."

Lady Averly took a deep breath and walked toward the Keep with Doran following closely behind.

*   *   *

Women's screams and children's cries echoed throughout the village of Morton. Thatched rooftops sent flames, sparks, and smoke high into the night sky. The castle gates were breached, and chaos erupted within its walls. The barbarians slaughtered everyone they encountered, leaving dead bodies scattered like leaves upon the grass.

*   *   *

Lady Averly entered the hallway. Even though the evening meal had finished long ago, she could hear the echoing conversations of lingering guests. She hoped to go directly to the kitchen unnoticed. Heaven forbid Lady Miriam was still awake at this hour and subject her to any public humiliation after the long day's ride.

Stepping into the Great Hall, she refused to make eye contact with anyone sitting at the High Table. She turned toward the kitchen and had nearly made it to the

313

doorway when she heard the screeching voice of her stepmother.

"Averly! Come here at once!"

Lord Burton leaned his head against the back of his chair and closed his eyes, pretending to be asleep.

A dreadful shiver ran up her spine as Lady Averly froze in place, abruptly causing Sarah to bump into her back and force her to take a step forward.

The few who remained within the Great Hall stopped their conversations and stared at Lady Averly with their mouths agape. She turned ever so slowly to face her stepmother. Her father appeared to be sleeping. An obese man sat in Sir Thomas's place. Scraps of food clung to his scraggly graying beard. Pockmarks dotted his face. He looked to be as old as her father, if not older and stared at her intently with his bloodshot blue eyes. She prayed he was not her betrothed.

Shuffling footsteps caused Lady Averly to glance over her shoulder to see Mina and other members of the kitchen staff standing in the doorway. She nodded her head for Sarah to join the women before looking back to the High Table, lowering her chin, and narrowing her eyes at the person responsible for making her life unbearable. She clenched her teeth until they nearly cracked.

"Yes, my lady." Lady Averly walked toward the High Table.

Lady Miriam snarled as she stood and leaned with both hands upon the High Table.

"Where have you been?"

Doran found a vacant seat at a nearby table, grabbed an empty mug and pitcher of ale, and poured himself a drink.

Lady Averly ensured her retort was heard by everyone in the room.

"On holiday!"

Many in attendance smiled and a few chuckled. Lady Miriam scowled.

"Well, your holiday is over. Go to your bedchamber."

"Gladly." Lady Averly turned abruptly and left the Great Hall. She stomped up the staircase and entered her small chamber as tears threatened to spill from her eyes. Leaving the door open to allow the light from the hallway candelabra to shine into the dark room, she took off her cloak and dirk and tossed it on the end of the bed before sitting upon it, covering her face with her hands, and allowing her tears to fall.

"My lady, I'm relieved to see you."

Lady Averly looked toward the shadowed figure standing in the doorway. It was Mina, carrying a tray of food and a lit candle. Sarah stood behind her. Lady Averly took a deep breath and exhaled.

"Oh, Mina, I've missed you so." She brushed away her tears as she stood.

Mina set the tray of food and taper on the table. She put her arms around her friend and squeezed gently before releasing her.

"Where have you been?" They sat on the bed.

Sarah stepped into the tiny room and looked about.

Lady Averly smiled as she brushed away another tear.

"After riding Nelly through the storm for what seemed like days, the Lord of Tildenham found me while he was hunting. He mistook me as one of the villagers. When I became ill, he ensured I was attended, sometimes by himself. We were to be wed, but then Doran discovered where I was hiding."

"A lord, wed a lord?"

Lady Averly smiled.

"Yes. It was quite unexpected. I fell in love with him and he with me." Her smile faded. "But now that I've returned, Lady Miriam will ensure I marry another. I've been sold like a piglet at a market to the highest bidder. God help me. Is my betrothed the man sitting next to Father? What if he is abusive?"

Mina reassured her lady and friend.

"Calm yourself. He is a guest."

Lady Averly exhaled as if a weight had been lifted from her shoulders.

"Thank goodness."

"Here, I brought you something to eat." Mina rose and pushed the table toward the bed.

"Thank you." Lady Averly motioned to the chair across the table. "Sarah, take off your cloak and sit, please. We can tell Mina all about..."

A shadow in the doorway blocked the hallway candelabra light.

"I'm sorry. That little tale will have to wait until another time." Lady Miriam stepped into the chamber. Mina curtsied and left the room. Sarah froze with a bit of bread held before her mouth.

Lady Miriam glared at the seated stranger.

"You, out."

Sarah popped the bread in her mouth, grabbed her cloak, and left the room.

Lady Miriam crossed her arms over her chest and pursed her lips.

"I don't know where you've been and only God knows what you've done, but you'll remain in this room until your betrothed arrives and takes you as his wife." Lady Miriam took her stepdaughter's dirk from the bed, exited the room, and shut the door.

Lady Averly stared at the door as the lock clicked. She wondered if anyone in the Keep, perhaps one of the cleaning women, may have a duplicate or a master key.

Lady Miriam stood on the other side of the portal, dropped the key into her bodice, and made her way to the Great Hall. She returned to her place next to her husband at the High Table, leaned toward him and whispered.

"She won't be going anywhere soon, my dear."

Lord Burton finished drinking the last of his wine. He set the tankard upon the table.

"What have you done to ensure she will remain in Holbrook?"

"Since she's so hell-bent on fleeing, she'll remain locked in her chamber until she is wed." Lady Miriam smiled with confidence. "We must return the signed contract and set a date immediately."

"Very well." Lord Burton rose from his chair and headed toward his bedchamber to retire for the night.

Chapter 35

AFTER SLEEPING FOR only a few hours, Lord Burton was awakened by a servant. He looked to his bedchamber window. The sun had yet to rise. He slipped on his robe, gathered the necessary coins, and went to the Great Hall. He stood at the end of a long table and dropped a small leather bag before Doran, who was finishing his breakfast.

"I believe this is what we agreed upon."

Doran picked up the bag. He lifted it up and down estimating the correct weight, looked toward the Lord of Holbrook, and nodded approvingly.

"Glad to be of service." He stood and tied the bag of coins to his belt. "Thank you for the night's stay. Good day."

Lord Burton watched Doran leave the Great Hall before returning to bed.

When he arrived at the stable, Doran climbed atop his ready horse and rode through the bailey and gatehouse. Once outside the village, he spurred it into a gallop toward Morton.

*   *   *

Mina finished washing the last tabletop in the Great Hall. The midday meal was finished and nearly tidied. Looking to the balcony, she knew Lady Averly had yet to receive her breakfast. She hoped what she had prepared on the tray the night before would sustain her for the time being. She had asked several of the cleaning women for a key to her lady's chamber. They said Lady Miriam had confiscated all of them. Out of concern, Mina dropped the rag into a bucket of soapy water, went to the tiny chamber, and tapped the door lightly.

Lady Averly rose from the chair and returned her mother's portrait under the bed.

Mina whispered.

"My lady, is all well?"

"Mina, is that you?"

"Yes. Is there anything you need?"

The tray of food and tankard of ale were both empty. Her stomach grumbled.

"Something to eat would be nice. Is there any way you can open the door?"

"No, Lady Miriam has all of the keys. I'll have to ask her to open the door."

Lady Averly cringed.

"That's unfortunate."

"I'll return shortly." Mina headed toward the solar in search of Lady Miriam.

Lady Averly paced her tiny chamber as the minutes ticked by slowly. She looked out the small window often, but the view was nothing more than the side of a tower. At least she knew the day was sunny and pleasant and wondered how Lady Mary's garden was responding to the lovely spring weather.

The jingling of keys and the click of the lock preceded the portal opening. Expecting to see her stepmother in the doorway, Lady Averly was pleasantly surprised to see Mina, but standing behind her was a man hated by one and all, especially her. It had been years since she had seen Merle. Her legs trembled. The memory of the cruelty she endured many years ago was brought to the forefront of her mind. He ducked beneath the doorway, taking a step into the room. Considered a giant by many, he was the tallest and broadest man in the kingdom. Dressed in black leather, he carried a two-headed ax, one of many intimidating tools of his trade.

Mina carried a tray of food, a pitcher of ale, and a tankard. She set aside the past evening's tray on the bed and placed the meal on the table.

"Perhaps you would like to stretch your legs and accompany me to the garderobe before you eat, my lady?" Mina winked as she reached under the end of the bed for the chamber pot.

Lady Averly glanced toward Merle, who blocked in the doorway.

"Yes, that's an excellent idea."

With the smelly vessel in hand, Mina held it before her. Merle backed into the hallway and allowed the women to precede him. His heavy footsteps echoed in the hallway as he followed closely behind them.

A rhythmic slapping caused Lady Averly to look over her shoulder. The administrator tossed the ax back and forth between his large hands with each step.

"I dare say, Mina, he can't kill me. Lady Miriam would have his head if she lost the dowry."

"That may be true, my lady, but they could still wed you with a missing hand or prominent limp."

Overhearing the conversation, Merle sneered.

As the women entered the garderobe together, Mina turned her back to give her lady some privacy. Lady Averly looked toward the closed portal.

"It's difficult to piss knowing that brute probably has his ear pressed to the door.

"I could sing." Mina chuckled. With her tension eased, Lady Averly was able to relax enough to relieve herself.

After Mina threw the contents of the chamber pot down the chute, she pulled the door open. Merle nearly fell into the room but righted himself and stepped backward.

As they strolled back to the chamber, Lady Averly tilted her head toward her friend.

"Is there any word as to when I'll be wed?" She entered her chamber.

"I've heard nothing. Lady Miriam walks around the Keep with a smirk on her face as if she's a cat that swallowed his master's pet bird." Mina pulled out the chair to allow her lady to sit.

"I feel as if I'm being led to an execution." Lady Averly glanced toward the hulking man in the doorway as she sat.

Merle snorted at her comment.

Mina filled the tankard with ale.

"Perhaps it would be better if you kept yourself occupied. I'll fetch your needlepoint."

"You know I lack the proficiency in such a task."

"Then practice."

While Mina went to retrieve her embroidery, Lady Averly selected a slice of meat pie and took a mouthwatering bite. She made the mistake of glancing toward the doorway where Merle stood. A drop of spittle dangled from his lip as he stared at the food on her tray. She looked away, hoping her food would settle within her stomach as she swallowed and took a drink from the tankard.

The key tied on Merle's belt swayed as he stepped aside to allow Mina to enter.

"Here you go, my lady." She set the needlepoint, thread, and a tiny pair of scissors on the end of the bed. "Well, if there is nothing else you need, I must get back to the kitchen. I'll return later with your evening meal." Mina picked up last night's tray.

Lady Averly wished her friend could stay longer. The solitude was unbearable.

"Thank you, Mina."

The cook left the room. Merle closed and locked the door.

Alone once again, Lady Averly smothered a wedge of bread with jam while eyeing the embroidery. *It matters little the length of time I remain locked within this chamber and sew, for no amount of practice will improve my ability to create lovely stitching.*

*   *   *

A week had passed since Lady Averly was escorted by Doran from Tildenham. Many put the sad event behind them and resumed their duties.

At midday, a lone rider rode into the castle and reined his horse before the stable. Bryce held the bridle of the stranger's horse as he dismounted.

"Where may I find the Lord of Tildenham?"

The stableboy saw his lord pass by the stable on his way to the Keep only moments ago.

"Lord Edwin should be inside." Bryce pointed to the doorway. He watched the man enter the Keep before leading the horse inside the stable.

The messenger stepped into the Great Hall. Women were busy washing tables, sweeping the floor, and spreading new rushes.

Isabel turned away from her supervisory duties. The man's clothes were quite dusty as if he had ridden for many days.

"Good day."

"Good day. May I speak with Lord Edwin?"

"For what purpose?"

"I'm to ensure this missive is delivered into his hand." The messenger pulled the wax-sealed document from his cloak pocket and held it for Isabel to see.

"Let me see if I can find him. Wait here please." She motioned to an empty bench for the messenger to sit before whispering to one of the women to fetch a tankard of ale for the man. She ascended the staircase, stood before the closed door of the solar, and knocked.

Lord Edwin looked up from his account book.

"Enter."

Isabel opened the door and was met by Rand, who trotted forward and waited for an affectionate pat on the head. She smiled and complied with a gentle touch of her palm. Rand closed his eyes and raised his nose as her hand glided on his silky fur to the back of his head and patted his shoulder.

"My lord, a messenger is in the Great Hall. He insists on delivering a missive directly into your hand."

Lord Edwin shut the account book on his desk and rose from his chair.

"Maybe he carries a reply from the baron."

Isabel stepped aside to allow her lord and the gray wolf to proceed ahead of her.

The messenger lowered his tankard and stood as he watched a young man at the top of the stairway descend, followed by the servant woman. He stared at the gray wolf as it passed him on the way to the kitchen.

Lord Edwin stood before the messenger with his feet shoulder width apart and his arms crossed over his chest.

"You have a missive for me?"

The messenger looked to the young lord.

"If you are the Lord of Tildenham, then yes."

"I am." Lord Edwin displayed his gold ring with its seal for verification.

"My lord." The messenger handed Lord Edwin the sealed missive, turned, and addressed Isabel. "Thank you for the ale. It was greatly appreciated."

"You're welcome." Isabel smiled as she watched the messenger leave the Great Hall.

Lord Edwin broke the wax seal and unfolded the missive. It was a contract. His father's signature was on the document. It was legal and binding. His eyes widened as he realized the contract entailed his betrothal. The amount of the dowry was specifically listed, payable upon his arrival to collect his bride, with the ceremony performed the same day.

Lord Edwin lowered the missive, sat upon the vacated bench, and exhaled as if the wind had been knocked out of him. If there was any hope of sharing his life with Lady Averly, it no longer existed. To uphold his father's good name and reputation, he would honor his final wish and follow through with the betrothal.

Isabel watched as Lord Edwin's face turned pasty white.

"My lord, is there something I can help you with?"

"Apparently, my father." He hesitated. "My father arranged my betrothal. I'm to leave immediately to collect my wife."

Isabel stared. *Did I hear him correctly?* She sat next to him on the bench, so their conversation would remain private.

"Betrothed? You, my lord? How?"

"Father must have made the agreement sometime after I had left with Sir Garrick and prior to the attack." He handed her the contract, even though he doubted she could read it.

Isabel had little knowledge of Lord Kester's signature but trusted her lord to recognize it as authentic.

Lord Edwin sighed.

"I know what you're thinking, Isabel. Let's not forget that Lady Averly is also bound by a betrothal as well. I'll do what must be done and honor my father's last decree. While I'm away, please prepare my mother's bedchamber for my wife."

"Yes, my lord." She handed the missive back to him. "Will you be leaving immediately?"

"No. I'll wait until Sir Garrick returns." He stood.

"Very well, my lord." She rose from the bench. "Please let me know when you plan to leave so I can ensure you have enough food for your journey."

"Thank you, Isabel." Lord Edwin ascended the staircase with the open missive dangling in his right hand. Rand followed on the heels of his master.

Once in the solar, Lord Edwin closed the door and sat at his desk. Rereading the contract, he stared at his father's signature. *Father, did you believe I was incapable of choosing a suitable bride?* He tossed the missive onto the desk, slouched in his chair, and stared at the contract. *Perhaps I should go to confession and beg forgiveness for whatever sins or transgressions I have committed to having caused such disappointing events in my life.*

Rand placed his head on his master's lap and received a reassuring pat on his head.

A knock sounded at the solar door.

"Enter."

Sir Garrick stepped into the room with a proud grin upon his face.

"Greetings, my lord." The knight's grin faded as he noted his lord's unsmiling face. "Are you unwell?"

"No, I'm just trying to come to terms with recent events."

"What recent events?" Sir Garrick pulled up a chair and sat across from his lord.

"Much has happened during your absence. A transient came to Tildenham, produced evidence of Lady Averly's betrothal to another, and escorted her away to fulfill her commitment. I, on the other hand, have just received a contract with my father's committal of my betrothal." He reached across the table, grabbed the missive, and tossed it to his knight.

Sir Garrick read it, recognized Lord Kester's signature, and set the missive on the desk.

"Do you intend to honor it?"

"Yes."

"The turn of events is unfortunate for you both."

Lord Edwin nodded his head in agreement.

"Please tell me you've brought good news, Sir Garrick." He looked to his knight and tried to smile.

"I can see the fields have been plowed for planting. That's good, for I was able to negotiate a good price for seed."

"And the missive for Baron Vinson?"

"I was able to find a messenger to deliver it to him. Let's hope he grants our request to rebuild our garrison soon. I returned with a friar as well. I'll have him placed in residence within the chapel."

"Well done."

"When do you plan to retrieve your bride?"

"Now that you've returned, I'll leave tomorrow morning." Lord Edwin grimaced internally. "Please inform Isabel of my departure."

"Yes, my lord." The knight left the solar, closing the door behind him.

Lord Edwin rose and entered his bedchamber. He went to the armoire and pushed his clothes aside, pressed the center-right diamond to open the back panel, and lifted the latch on the door to the hidden chamber.

He gathered the value of coin stated in the contract and secured it in a small brass chest. Closing both portals, he exited the armoire, set the chest on the bed, and looked back to his clothes.

"Now, what should I wear to wed a stranger?"

Chapter 36

LORD EDWIN STOOD before the armoire with his fisted hands upon his hips. He scanned his clothing in search of something appropriate to wear for the wedding ceremony. In truth, he cared little for what he donned for the occasion but needed to represent his title and kingdom properly. Selecting the royal blue tunic with silver stitching, he held it at arm's length and examined its condition. *Good enough.* He rolled it neatly and tucked it into his satchel. He packed an extra shirt and pair of breeches before closing the leather bag and buckling it tightly. Exhaling, he looked toward his bedchamber door as he listened to the echoing activity of the Great Hall. *The evening meal must be ready.* With plans to leave early the next morning, Lord Edwin left his room with Rand leading the way and joined everyone below. He took his usual place at the end of a long table with his knight sitting across from him.

Sir Garrick stared at his lord, who had remained quiet throughout most of the meal.

"You seem troubled, my lord?"

"My mind is preoccupied. Reluctantly, I leave early tomorrow morning."

Glenna overheard her lord. She sat to his right and looked toward him.

"Will you be coming back?" The little girl held Henry in her lap and gave him a bit of meat from her plate.

"Yes, Glenna, I'll come back."

"Do you promise?"

Lord Edwin smiled.

"Yes, I promise."

"Because Lady Averly isn't coming back."

"I hope she'll return someday to visit."

"But not as our lady."

"You're right, Glenna. Not as our lady."

*   *   *

Lady Averly sat in the chair at the small table with its single lit taper. She heard the lock click and watched as the door opened. Mina stood in the doorway with a wedding dress draped over her arm and a tray of food in her hands. Merle peered over her shoulder.

"My lady, I thought you should try your wedding dress on to see if there are any necessary alterations." Mina made a silly face, hoping her flimsy excuse for her visit seemed viable to the hulking man behind her. She stepped into the room.

Lady Averly looked to the brute in the doorway. A drop of spittle dangled from his mouth as he hit the palm of his hand with a sharply pointed metal rod. He had changed weapons.

Comprehending the cook's subtle motive, Lady Averly nodded.

"Yes, we must ensure it fits properly."

Mina set the tray upon the table and the dress on the bed. She picked up the midday meal tray from the table.

"I'm sorry Merle, but we need some privacy. On your way down, please be a dear and take this to the kitchen." Mina attempted to hand him the tray.

He scowled.

"I must wait here."

"Very well." Mina set the tray on the hallway floor and closed the door in the torturer's stern face. She turned to her lady, who suppressed a giggle.

"Mina, I'm not in the mood to try on that ridiculous dress. Perhaps tomorrow."

"Very well, my lady. I doubt adjustments are needed anyway."

"Any news?" In truth, Lady Averly hoped there was none. She was dreading her life with a presumably old, wealthy man with a bulbous belly and bad breath.

"No, my lady. Your stepmother is her normal shallow self, your half-brother continues to stuff himself with sweet cakes, and your father seems remorseful. Perhaps he's feeling guilty for allowing his wife to sell you off to the highest bidder."

"Maybe." Lady Averly looked toward the tray filled with a wedge of meat pie and two sweet cakes. There was plenty for two. She stood, pushed the table and chair toward the bed before sitting on the bed and pulling the table toward her.

"Sit and join me." She motioned toward the chair. "I could use the company."

"Very well." Mina sat as Lady Averly broke the meat pie in half and presented a piece for her friend to eat.

Chapter 37

AFTER EATING A hearty breakfast in the Great Hall, Lord Edwin squatted to bring himself eye level with Glenna. He stroked the top of Henry's head before giving the little girl a hug.

As her lord pulled away from their embrace, she placed her tiny hand on his cheek.

"My lord, you'll come back as you promised?"

"Yes, I'll return and bring my bride with me." He smiled and tapped her on the tip of her nose before rising.

Isabel stood in the kitchen doorway, wiping her hands on her overskirt.

"May angels watch over you, my lord, until you return safely."

"Thank you, Isabel." Lord Edwin nodded to his knight, who rose from a bench and followed him out of the Keep with Rand trailing behind. As he passed the garden, he paused momentarily near the roses. They were in bloom.

Tethered to the post, Fulton pranced, drawing his master's attention. Attached to his saddle was a leather bag of provisions. The small chest containing the dowry was covered with an oilcloth and secured behind the seat of the saddle. Lord Edwin patted the betrothal contract in his tunic chest pocket to ensure he had not forgotten it. He turned to his knight.

Sir Garrick extended his hand and they clasped forearms.

"It would be wise for me to accompany you."

"I need you here. Besides, it will be a good experience for Bryce."

The men turned toward the stable door to see the stableboy atop a horse. He ducked his head as he exited and sat tall in the saddle with his chest puffed like a strutting rooster.

"Ready when you are, my lord."

Lord Edwin nodded in acknowledgment.

Catching sight of a rodent darting under the stable, Rand pounced and began digging at the edge of the wall.

Fulton pawed the ground as his master went to his side.

"Sir Garrick, I leave Tildenham in your care."

The knight watched as his lord climbed atop his horse.

"My lord, I'll do my best. Safe travels."

Lord Edwin urged Fulton forward. Bryce reined his horse and followed his lord over the drawbridge. With a whistle from his master, Rand looked toward the gatehouse before breaking into a full run.

*　　　　　*　　　　　*

Mina circled Lady Averly, who stood still in the center of the small bedchamber. She straightened the wrinkled wedding dress skirt and examined the waist. It was loose. She pinched the material at her lady's sides.

"My lady, you seem to have lost weight. I'll need to take in your gown."

"I truly don't care. You could dress me in a gunny sack. In fact, I would love to see the expression on Lady Miriam's face as I walked down the aisle in a gunny sack." She looked down at the ugly dress designed by her stepmother. "My word, I believe she made this dress as distasteful as possible out of pure spite."

"My lady, it will be a picture etched within the mind of your husband as well."

Lady Averly's grin faded. Her friend had a valid point. As Mina pinned the alterations, her thoughts drifted to the impending marriage and husband.

"I imagine he's paid a large dowry for my hand in marriage and resides in a vast estate. He's probably older than Father and quite tight with his coins, a miser. His face may be pockmarked, his teeth rotted, and his rancid breath so odious that it causes even a maggot to gag." Lady Averly flailed her arms as she exaggerated each repulsive flaw.

"Please hold still, my lady. I don't want to prick you. My time is limited as well. I need to finish so I may return to the kitchen to oversee the serving of the evening meal."

"Sorry." Lady Averly stood like a statue.

Mina inserted a pin into a fold, marking the alteration.

"I must admit, you paint an awful picture of your future husband."

"The picture I paint could very well become a reality. Heaven forbid I marry such a beast."

"You don't know for certain he's such a man. He could be handsome." Mina moved to the opposite side of the dress.

Lady Averly scowled.

"But it would be highly unlikely for one so young to be so wealthy."

"He could have inherited his wealth." Mina chuckled. "Perhaps you're correct. If he's old, he may not live for any great length of time. Then you could marry a man of your choice."

Lady Averly looked to the door. *I wish I could escape this prison and ride Nelly back to Tildenham. Surely, a man of the cloth has arrived by now.* She sighed.

"I would prefer to marry the man of my choice and forego marrying one who isn't."

*   *   *

With darkness closing around him, Doran sought a suitable spot to camp for the night. The flickering of a distant campfire caught his attention. Curious, he decided to investigate. He directed his horse toward the light, tied the reins to a tree, and tiptoed toward the camp, hoping to remain undiscovered. He crouched behind a fallen tree and peeked over the mossy bark to see men, many men, who wore layers of animal fur as clothing. Their horses were tied on the opposite side of the camp. Doran listened to the conversations of men sitting around a campfire. Even though he knew several languages, what was spoken was unfamiliar to him. *Barbarians.* He circled the camp and examined the ground, looking for upturned soil from the horses' hooves. As he rounded the camp, his foot twisted on a divot. Doran lowered himself to his hands and knees and placed his cheek near the ground. He saw shadows from the depressions in the turf leading away from the camp. The barbarians had indeed traveled from the direction of Morton. If they continued to travel in the same direction, Holbrook would be their next target.

He returned to his horse, climbed atop, and made his way to the road where he reined it to a stop. He paused and looked in the direction of the barbarian's next target. *Holbrook's walls are strong and should hold until assistance can arrive.* He spurred his horse into a gallop and would ride all night if necessary to inform Baron Vinson.

Chapter 38

IT WAS NEAR dawn when Doran's horse galloped through the village of Kendrickham. Peasants paused and stared at the frothy, sweaty horse and the urgency of its rider. Once recognized by the guard at the gatehouse, he was permitted to pass through it.

Several garrisons were gathered in the bailey. Some waited in line at the blacksmith, who sat at his honing stone with his foot going up and down on the foot pedal of the grinding wheel. Sparks spattered and flew as he held an ax to the spinning stone.

Doran dismounted at the stable and entered the Keep. The baron sat at a table with several lords. He waited next to the baron's chair for a break in the conversation.

"Baron Vinson, I've news."

"Ah Doran, what news do you bring?"

"I discovered the barbarian's camp and can verify that they came from the direction of Morton. If they continue in the same direction, I predict the next kingdom to fall victim to their cruelty is Holbrook."

"Go to the gatehouse and tell the garrisons to ready. We shall leave within the hour."

Doran nodded his head and exited the Keep.

*   *   *

Eager to return to Tildenham, Lord Edwin traveled at a rapid pace and stopped only for a short time during the night to sleep. Rand reveled in the freedom. He easily stayed alongside his lord and even found time to chase a few rabbits. Unlike the wolf, Bryce often found himself several horse-lengths behind his lord. He fought the temptation to close his eyes in fear of falling from his horse and prayed the journey would end quickly.

As they rode through the village, Lord Edwin noted the architecture of the buildings and wondered if his carpenters could construct something similar. He presented the contract at the gatehouse and received the approval of the guard for the trio to proceed. They passed by shops in the bailey and rein their horses before the stable.

The stableboy clasped the bridle of each horse. Looking toward the man's hand, he spotted a gold signet ring.

Lord Edwin unstrapped the chest from the saddle.

"Please see the horses are given water and fed."

"Yes, my lord. I'll unsaddle them as well." The lad tugged on the reins encouraging the horses to follow him into the stable.

Bryce looked to his lord.

"Shall I stay with the horses, my lord?"

"Come with me." Lord Edwin looked toward the Keep, scanning its walls upward and sighed.

Bryce stepped beside his lord and glanced toward his face, wondering the reason for his hesitancy.

Lord Edwin glanced toward the stableboy, nodded, and walked toward the Keep with Bryce and Rand following. They stepped through the threshold and into the Great Hall.

A servant saw them enter and approached.

"May I be of service?" She curtsied before them and watched the wolf warily.

"I'm here to see the lord, make my dowry payment, and collect my bride." Lord Edwin's face was grim and unsmiling. He reached in his tunic, withdrew the contract, and gave it to the woman.

"Very well, I'll fetch him." The servant scampered away, briefly stopping by the kitchen to announce the arrival of the bridegroom.

*   *   *

Lady Averly looked up from her embroidering as she heard the click of the lock and watched the door open. Mina entered and closed the door in Merle's face.

"My lady, your future husband has arrived."

"Already? Have you seen him?"

"No, but..."

The bedchamber door flew open. Both women turned to see Lady Miriam in the doorway. She threw the altered wedding dress upon the bed.

"Averly, get dressed and get to the chapel immediately!" She slammed the door shut.

"Good lord!" Mina stared at the door before looking to her lady and shrugging her shoulders. "At least you'll be away from her once you're married." She smiled. "Let's get you dressed."

*   *   *

Lord Edwin turned toward the nicely dressed couple as they entered the Great Hall. Bryce and Rand stood next to the kitchen door while the transaction took place.

The woman stepped forward with the folded contract in her hand.

"I assume you're the bridegroom."

"Yes."

"And the dowry?"

Lord Edwin placed the rectangle box on the table. He removed the oilcloth and opened the chest. The couple peeked inside. The woman ran her fingers through the coins before closing the lid.

"Excellent." She nodded her head toward a servant, who stepped forward, picked up the chest, and ascended a staircase.

"This way to the chapel. Your bride will join us there." The woman led the way with her guests following.

Lord Edwin looked toward Bryce and nodded for him to follow.

The chapel was small and dark. A pair of stained glass windows donning one wall. Candelabras with their flickering flames projected a golden glow on the crucifix above the altar. The priest stood at the end of the aisle with his leather-bound book in hand as if he was forewarned of the ceremony.

Looking down at his dusty tunic, Lord Edwin realized he had failed to change into the one he brought for the ceremony. *It matters not.*

He walked to the end of the aisle and stood unsmiling before the priest. Bryce took his place to the right of his lord. Rand sat obediently next to the stableboy.

*   *   *

"You look beautiful, my lady." Mina straightened the skirt of Lady Averly's wedding dress.

"Thank you." Lady Averly's chin quivered. *It's just nerves.* She took a deep breath, trying to calm her rapid heartbeat. *This was supposed to be a happy day, a day I've dreamt of since I was a little girl. Will the stranger I marry be kind? Abusive? Force himself upon me?* She cringed inwardly. *I wish mother was here.*

Mina looked to her lady.

"It's time."

Lady Averly looked down at the unstylish dress. Her bottom lip quivered again.

Mina clasped her friend's hand.

"Oh, come now. Chin up."

Lady Averly exhaled and tried to smile.

"Yes, chin up."

They walked to the chapel and stopped in the hallway outside the open door. Mina turned to her lady and friend.

"I wish you happiness."

"Thank you, Mina." Lady Averly took a deep breath, let it out slowly, and kept her eyes downcast to the floor as she stepped through the doorway.

Lady Miriam turned to see her stepdaughter enter the chapel. Her mouth twisted into a sneer. She was quite pleased with the large dowry, but even more pleased to be rid of her stepdaughter. *Once she's wed, I hope to never see her again.*

A twinge of guilt pulled at the heartstrings of Lord Burton as he watched his daughter walk toward the altar. He had agreed to the betrothal, knowing her life with another would be better than the one she had within Holbrook. *Oh Averly, you're so beautiful, just like your mother. I hope you know how much I truly love you.* He sighed and hoped she would forgive him for what he had done.

Knowing all eyes were upon her, Lady Averly refused to look up from the floor. The last thing she needed to see was her gloating stepmother. She assumed her future husband stood before the priest at the altar.

Mina tiptoed into the back of the chapel and watched her lady bravely face her uncertain future. The cook had to admit, however, from the broad shoulders and tall stature, the man she was marrying looked as though he could defend and protect her from any danger that came her way. *I just hope he's kind to her.*

*　　　　*　　　　*

Lord Edwin heard soft footsteps behind him. He raised his chin as he prepared to pledge his life to a woman he did not love. His face was stern, unsmiling. He stared at the cross above the altar. *Father, I hope you have chosen wisely and she is tolerable in character.*

As she stepped beside him, he presented his left hand and waited.

*　　　　*　　　　*

Lady Averly watched as her future husband's hand raise. She lifted her right hand to place it upon his. She hesitated as she noticed the ring on his pinky finger. It was gold with a ruby on each side with the crest of a lion. *Could it be true?* She looked to the profile of her future husband, placed her hand atop of his, forced her fingers to intertwine, and squeezed tightly.

Lady Miriam's sneer faded as she saw the change in her stepdaughter's demeanor.

Lord Edwin thought it odd for the woman, a stranger, to boldly entwine her fingers within his. He stared at her hand in disbelief.

Rand sniffed the air, stood, and wagged his tail. Bryce tried to settle the wolf, but Rand crossed in front of his lord and sat on the opposite side of the bride.

Lord Edwin looked to the face of his future wife. He was greeted by the sweetest, most radiant smile of Lady Averly. He returned her smiled and clasped her fingers tightly. Rand nudged Lady Averly's left hand for an affectionate pat on his head. Curious, Bryce leaned forward to catch a glimpse of the future Lady of Tildenham and whispered, "Lady Averly, I'm so very pleased to see you."

"And I you, Bryce."

Lord Edwin and Lady Averly looked into each other's eyes as they listened to the priest's Latin words resonate within the chapel.

Sarah stepped into the chapel and stared at the bridegroom.

"My lord?"

Lord Edwin looked to the back of the chapel.

"Hello, Sarah."

*   *   *

The peasants in the fields were first to hear the thunderous hooves approaching. They dropped their pitchforks, left their plows, and ran toward the village. Women gathered their children. Everyone raced toward the gatehouse of Holbrook, hoping to squeeze through the portal and inside the protective walls of the castle. The garrison began to lower the portcullis, the drawbridge would be raised momentarily, and those unable to cross it in time would have to fend for themselves.

Emmet came out of the stable to see the cause of the commotion. People were rushing into the bailey. He recognized the protective actions of the garrison as he watched the bowmen climb the steps to the top of the walls. He ran into the Keep and saw a peasant woman in the Great Hall.

"Where's Lord Burton?"

She pointed toward the chapel. Emmet ran to the doorway.

"We're under attack!"

The priest stopped talking. Everyone turned toward the stableboy. His chest rose and fell rapidly as he tried to catch his breath.

Lady Miriam glared at the priest.

"Finish the ceremony!"

Emmet ran up the aisle, his eyes wild with panic as he searched for Lord Burton in the dimly lit chapel.

"My lord! We're under attack!"

The priest glanced at Lady Miriam's stern expression before rushing through the remainder of the ceremony. He pulled the Lord and Lady of Tildenham onto the altar, quickly dipped a quill in ink, and pushed it into each of their hands to make their marks on the registry recording their marriage. Lord Burton exited the chapel to assess the threatening situation with Emmet following.

Lady Miriam sneered at the couple before leaving the room to find Alger and ensure his safety.

Lord Edwin turned to his bride.

"What a pleasant surprise to find you as my betrothed." He brought her near and looked into her eyes. "And now my wife."

"And you as my husband." She smiled.

He cupped her face within his hands and kissed her tenderly.

Lord Edwin put his hand on the small of his wife's back, guiding her toward the stableboy.

"Bryce, I need you and Rand to watch over my wife. Keep her safe."

"Yes, my lord."

Lord Edwin pointed his index finger at his pet to convey his command.

"Sit, stay."

He patted the wolf's head before addressing his wife.

"My dear, I must see what I can do to help. Until this battle is won, we're forced to delay our return to Tildenham." He wrapped his arms around her waist and kissed her forehead. "Please remain in the chapel with Bryce and ensure Rand stays with you."

"I will, but only until I'm needed to aid anyone who may become wounded." She squeezed his forearms before he released her and watched him hurry toward the door.

Lord Edwin paused near the doorway and turned to look at her.

"They're red."

Confused, Lady Averly tilted her head to the side.

"What?"

"The roses, they're in bloom and they're red."

She smiled, thankful for the minor distraction of the danger he may face once he left the Keep.

"I look forward to seeing them."

Mina watched Lord Edwin rush past her before hurrying to her lady.

"My lady, you know him?"

Sarah joined them.

"Yes, she knows him."

Lady Averly could hardly contain her happiness.

"Mina, Lord Edwin is the very same lord who took me in when I ran away from Holbrook."

Sarah grinned as she clasped Lady Averly's hand.

"My lady, I can't think of anyone more deserving than you. Everyone in Tildenham will be so pleased."

With her father preoccupied and her stepmother absent, Lady Averly took charge.

"Quickly, we must barricade the sally port and prepare the Great Hall for the injured." She turned to the stableboy. "Bryce, I'll return shortly." The three women exited the room.

"But, my lady..." The stableboy looked to Rand. They were alone in the chapel. "You heard our lord, we must keep watch over Lady Averly."

Rand darted after the three women with Bryce trailing behind.

Chapter 39

LORD EDWIN EXITED the Keep. His attention was drawn to the top of the castle walls where a red-headed man shouted orders while putting on a helmet. *A knight.* Longbowmen strung their bows as pages climbed the stone stairway carrying quivers filled with arrows, spears, and other weapons. In the bailey, people scurried in all directions, trying to seek shelter inside craft houses. Lord Edwin pushed his way forward like a salmon swimming upstream. He wove between peasants, climbed onto a wagon bed, and looked to the portcullis to see people reaching through the grating, screaming and begging for entry. The drawbridge, weighted down with fleeing people, had yet to be raised.

Lord Burton stood in the gatehouse doorway listening to Sir Thomas's commands and observing the chaos. He scanned the bailey, spotting his son-in-law above the crowd.

Spying Lord Burton, Lord Edwin pointed to the gatehouse opening.

"You must open the portcullis and let them in!" He jumped to the ground and forced his way through the crowd.

The Lord of Holbrook looked to the portal. The peasant's arms waved wildly as they reached toward the bailey. Their faces smashed against the bars of the portcullis conveyed panic and fear. He turned to his son-in-law as he approached.

"They're just peasants." He inhaled to shout the order to the men in the gatehouse to raise the drawbridge, but Lord Edwin interjected.

"Exactly, who will work your fields, provide food for the winter, and earn profits for Holbrook. If they're gone, you'll lose the ability for your kingdom to prosper."

Lord Burton scoffed. *Daft young lord.*

Sir Thomas's voice resonated within the bailey as both men looked up at the knight.

"The barbarians are within sight! Hold your fire until I give the command!"

Urgency pushed Lord Edwin to try again.

"Lord Burton, I know of what I speak. Nearly everyone in Tildenham was killed by these very same men who attack now. Without peasants to do the work, everyone suffers. You must let them in."

The cries from the peasants grew louder as the village was set ablaze. Lord Edwin persisted.

"Now! You must open the portcullis now while there's still time to save them!"

Lord Burton scanned the bowmen who lined the crenel topped walls of the castle.

"Sir Thomas, hold them at bay!" He stepped into the gatehouse. "Raise the portcullis enough for them to crawl beneath! Raise the drawbridge!"

The iron barrier cranked upward. The bowmen fired their arrows defending the innocent as the barbarians returned fire and rushed the drawbridge before it closed.

Cries of agony pierced the air as both barbarians and peasants sustained injuries. To avoid impalement, Lord Edwin helped guide the peasants under the sharp spikes of the portcullis. Lord Burton stood next to his son-in-law and assisted a woman who stumbled forward and fell.

As the drawbridge edged upward, those standing on it tumbled forward. An arrow sailed past Lord Edwin's head as he bent to grab a fallen woman's wrists and pull her into the bailey. More arrows followed as the drawbridge rose, enclosing the fortunate safely inside the castle.

Lord Burton stumbled backward, teetered, and dropped to his knees. Bewildered, he looked to his son-in-law before lowering his line of vision to the arrow lodged in his chest.

Lord Edwin caught the Lord of Holbrook as he toppled forward and laid him upon his back. The shot was fatal.

A few of the peasant men gathered around. Lord Edwin thought of his wife.

"Quickly, carry him into the Keep."

Supporting Lord Burton's shoulders, Lord Edwin led the way to the Great Hall where he instructed the men to place him on a table.

"Averly!"

Bryce and Rand emerged from the kitchen.

"My lord, she's in here."

Hearing her name called, Lady Averly emerged from the kitchen carrying a basket of bandages. Mina followed with a pot of hot water, linens, and other supplies.

Lord Edwin took the basket from his wife's arm and set it on a table before guiding her to one side of the room. "Averly, your father has taken an arrow." He drew her near as he kissed the top of her head. "I'm sorry. His time is limited."

As her husband released his arm from around her shoulders, Lady Averly looked to the table where her father lay. She stared at the arrow that rose and fell with each labored breath. Hesitantly, she went to his side, sat on the bench, and touched his blood-soaked tunic. His face was drained of color.

The Keep's staff was drawn to the commotion within the Great Hall. They stood watching silently.

Sarah stepped toward Lord Edwin.

"My lord, is there anything I can do to help?"

He leaned toward the servant and spoke quietly.

"There's nothing anyone can do. He's in God's hands now." Lord Edwin needed to return to the battle. Before he left, he hoped to put his father-in-law's conscious at ease. He approached the table and whispered into Lord Burton's ear.

"My lord, I promise to honor and protect your daughter with my life on this day and always."

Lord Burton opened his hazel eyes lethargically and looked toward his son-in-law. He nodded his head slightly before closing his eyes.

Lord Edwin glanced at his wife, who was staring at her father's pale face. He sat on the bench before her and placed his hand on her hands clasped within her lap.

"My dear, I'll return soon." He sensed his words had not registered within her mind. He squeezed her hands gently before rising and exiting the Keep.

Standing silently behind Lady Averly, Mina placed her hand on her friend's shoulder.

Lady Averly watched the rise and fall of her father's chest, expecting each breath to be his last. She looked over her shoulder.

"Mina, perhaps you should fetch Lady Miriam."

"Yes, my lady." Uncertain of where to find the Lady of Holbrook, Mina hurried up the stairs, hoping she may find her in the solar or Alger's bedchamber.

Lady Averly scooted forward on the bench until she peered down at her father's face. He turned his head toward her and raised his hand, extending his fingers toward her cheek. She entwined her fingers within his and pressed the back of his hand to her cheek.

"Father." She whispered. Her bottom lip trembled.

Lord Burton gasped as he cringed.

"I'm sorry...the betrothal."

Lady Averly grinned, as a tear trickled down her cheek.

"Oh, Father. You've chosen a kind husband for me. In all honesty, I'm very fond of him." She brushed a strand of his charcoal hair away from the side of his face. He smiled.

"It's all...I ever...wanted for you...I'm sorry for...." He gasped for air, turned his head away from her, and grimaced in pain.

"Shhhh, Father, don't..."

Lady Miriam peered over the balcony.

"Oh, what's happened!" She hurried to her husband's side, pushing Lady Averly off the bench and onto the floor.

Supportive arms from several concerned peasants reached around Lady Averly's waist and lifted her to her feet.

Alger stuffed the last bite of sweet cake into his mouth as Mina led him down the staircase. Lady Miriam looked toward her son.

"Alger, sweetheart, come and sit by your father." Lady Miriam patted the bench beside her. The chubby lad waddled to his mother and sat.

A silent vigil began as those within the Great Hall made the sign of the cross and prayed. They watched as Lord Burton's chest fell for the last time.

Lady Miriam stood from the bench, yanking her son to his feet and placing him before her.

"Lord Alger, the Lord of Holbrook!" Lady Miriam lifted her chin as she waited for everyone in the room to kneel or curtsy.

Standing across from Lady Averly, Mina saw her friend cringe at the thoughtless announcement, for her father's body had yet to grow cold. She went to her and clasped her hand.

"I'm sorry for your loss, my lady."

Sarah stepped forward.

"My lady, you have my heartfelt condolence."

Bryce joined the three women.

"Mine too, my lady."

"Thank you, all of you." Lady Averly wiped a tear from her cheek.

Lady Miriam seethed.

"Well, aren't you going to kneel to your new lord?"

The Keep's door flew open and two men entered the room, drawing everyone's attention. One cried out as he held his hand up with an arrow through his palm. Blood trickled over the eye of the second man, down his face, and onto his breastplate.

The chaos from the bailey echoed into the Keep. Bryce closed the door.

Lady Averly grabbed the poker leaning against the fireplace and inserted it into the hot embers as the injured men were helped to separate benches. She hoped to avoid searing the wounds, for the smell of burnt flesh upset her stomach. She went to the nearest injured man, reached for his bloody wrist, and examined the entry and exit wounds. The arrowhead's barb, wider than the shaft, made it impossible to withdraw the weapon from the direction it entered without causing additional damage.

"Mina, go to the kitchen and get the ax." She searched the basket to ensure she had needles, thread, and the mortar and pestle. "Oh, and wine too."

"Yes, my lady." Mina hurried to the kitchen with Sarah following.

Lady Averly turned to the second injured man, dunked a linen in the pot of water, and wrung out the excess. She dabbed away the blood. *Not the eye, God, not the eye.* She discovered a deep gash across his forehead. She would need to match up the loose edges of the skin as best she could and stitched it. The eye remained unscathed.

Sarah returned with the wine and set the uncorked bottle on the table next to her lady.

"Here's the wine, my lady."

"Thank you, Sarah." Lady Averly picked up the bottle and turned to the soldier.

"Close your eyes."

Once his orbs were shut, she sprinkled the wine onto the wound. Selecting a spool of thread from the basket, she pulled off a length and bit it with her teeth to cut it. The man watched as she threaded the needle and scrutinized the wound, trying to determine which end to begin sewing. She looked into his eyes, exhaling to calm herself.

"I do apologize. My stitches may not be very even under the circumstances."

"My lady, I appreciate your effort in mending my scratch."

Lady Averly stitched quickly and tied off the thread. Unable to find scissors in the basket, she used the man's dirk to cut the thread. Turning to the basket, she retrieved a small crock of salve, untied the cord, and removed the linen top before dipping her finger into the gel. She smeared the goo on the man's wound before binding it with a bandage.

Nearly out of breath, Mina stepped beside her with the ax in hand.

"Here you go, my lady. I had to wash the blade. It had chicken feathers and dried blood on it."

"Thank you, Mina." Lady Averly accepted the weapon and dripped wine over its blade.

Bryce stepped forward.

"May I help you, my lady?"

She looked to the eager stableboy.

"Are you squeamish at the sight of blood?" She would have little time while treating the injured to address her stableboy fainting.

"No, my lady."

Lady Averly handed the ax to Bryce, who accepted it with a nod of his head. She looked to the arrow in the man's hand and then to his face.

"I need you to lay the end of the arrow upon the table with your palm braced against the edge."

He did as she instructed.

She clasped the arrowhead in one hand and pressed her fingers against the back of his hand.

"Bryce, swing with force, but keep your distance from his hand, and mine."

"Yes, my lady." The ax came crashing down upon the arrow's shaft and embedded in the wooden tabletop.

Lady Miriam turned toward the noise.

"Quit chopping the table! You're ruining it!"

Lady Averly turned to see her stepmother's scowling face glaring at her. Lady Miriam stood with her arms protectively upon Alger's shoulders.

A loud bang resounded outside the Keep, causing everyone to look toward the door.

Lady Averly's thoughts turned to her husband and his safety. As the activity in the room resumed, she glanced at the table where her father laid. All that remained atop it was a pool of his blood. Assuming his body had been moved to the chapel, she looked back to Lady Miriam, who was still glaring at her. Lady Averly tightened her fists, clenched her teeth, and returned her stepmother's stare unwaveringly.

"Perhaps you should go to the chapel and pretend to grieve for your husband. You're of no use here." Lady Averly continued to stare, tempting her stepmother to object to her suggestion. Others in the room paused in their tasks and looked at the Lady of Holbrook.

Lady Miriam scanned the room. Her face blushed with embarrassment.

"Come, Alger, let's go pay our respects to your father." Lifting her nose in the air, she tried to regain what little pride she had remaining as she left the Great Hall with her son in tow.

The door to the Keep slammed open, drawing everyone's attention. They watched the injured men enter. Lady Averly glanced at each individual as they were helped to a bench or laid upon a tabletop. She breathed a sigh of relief, for her husband's face was absent.

Men groaned and screamed as Mina, Sarah, and the other women administered to the injured as best they could.

Lady Averly brushed her fingers across the end of the chopped arrow, inspecting it for loose splinters. There were none.

"Bryce, I need you to hold his hand in place." She grabbed a bandage from the basket and wrapped it around the arrowhead. Bryce pressed his hands on each side of the arrow, holding the man's hand against the table's edge. He looked at his lady. She nodded, gripped the arrow with both hands before informing the injured soldier of her plan.

"I'll try to pull it through swiftly." Lady Averly waited for the man to nod in understanding. "I'll count to three." She braced her feet to gain leverage. "One, two." She pulled with all her might.

The man cringed but did not cry out.

"What happened to three?" He watched as she pressed a bandage to each side of his hand to stop the bleeding.

"It's better to pull on two. If I'd pulled on three, you would have tensed in anticipation of the pain. Sorry."

A cry of agony echoed within the room. She turned to see its source. Mina was helping a man onto a table. He appeared to have a stomach wound.

Red blotches on Lady Averly's wedding dress drew the stableboy's attention.

"My lady, your gown."

Lady Averly looked down at her skirt and scoffed.

"We've more important things to worry about than this ugly dress. I need you to hold these bandages in place until I return."

"Yes, my lady." Bryce placed his hands on the bandages to hold them in place.

Lady Averly stepped to the opposite side of the table and helped Mina lower the injured man to the tabletop.

"I took one to the stomach, I did, my lady." The man's face was white. His bloody hands shook as they protected his injury.

"Let me take a look." Lady Averly pulled open his blood-soaked tunic. The left side of his abdomen was split open. The wound was deep. His organs remained unscathed. She jerked her head toward Mina indicating she should follow her.

"Rinse the wound with wine before stitching the muscle together. Sarah can push the skin together while you stitch it with a curved needle. When you've finished, get the honey from the kitchen and apply it to the wound before bandaging it."

Lady Averly returned to her previous patient and removed the bandages from the man's hand. It had stopped bleeding. The wound appeared to have closed, but she feared it may become infected. She rinsed both sides with wine and patted them dry with a clean bandage.

"Can you move your fingers?" She watched closely as the man moved each digit of his hand. Hearing a wooden bowl being dropped upon a table, she looked to the vessel. *The honey.* Lady Averly reached for the bowl and fresh bandages. She spread the honey on each side of the wound and wrapped it securely.

The man stood from the bench.

"I'm grateful, truly, my lady, but I must return to see if I may be of use." He exited the room.

Lady Averly looked around the Great Hall as she took a moment to catch her breath. There were nearly a dozen injuries needing her attention.

"How am I ever going to keep up?"

Chapter 40

THATCHED ROOFTOPS CRACKLED and snapped as flames reached skyward like greedy fingers. A cloud of smoke swallowed the village. As advancing barbarians magically appeared through the grayness, Holbrook's bowmen rained arrows down upon them. As one attacker fell, another jumped over the fallen body and charged forward. Their number seemed endless.

The drawbridge and portcullis remained secure with their chains locked in place.

Holbrook's men stood ready with long poles. Protected by their shields, barbarians advanced carrying tall ladders. They braced them against the castle wall and began to climb.

Lord Edwin walked along the battlements with his sword ready. As a ladder crashed onto the wall next to him, several men rushed to place the forked end of their poles on the top rung of the ladder and push it away from the wall.

A thundering battle cry caused Lord Edwin to turn around to see an ax-wielding barbarian charge over the top of the wall and strike down several men. Sheathing his sword, Lord Edwin grabbed a long pole that lay upon the battlement floor and rushed forward. He jabbed the man in the neck as one of Holbrook's knights struck him down with his sword. The barbarian's lifeless body fell to the bailey below. The men climbing the ladder were picked off by Holbrook's longbowmen before it was pushed away from the wall.

Lord Edwin looked to the sky. The sun was past midday. Glancing toward the Keep, his thoughts drifted to his new bride. He prayed they both survived.

*   *   *

The sounds of battle echoed through the door of the Keep as it opened, and more injured men entered. Rand was acutely aware of his master's absence. He sat obediently near the kitchen doorway. His ears perked, listening to the chaos beyond the portal, hoping to hear his voice. Lady Averly glanced at the faces of those who entered the Great Hall, grateful her husband's face was still absent.

Lady Miriam emerged from the chapel. Her mouth hung agape. She surveyed the injured, the dying, and the dead that crowded the room.

"There's blood everywhere. How many more can possibly fit into this room?"

Lady Averly tied a bandage in place before standing with her bloody hands fisted upon her hips.

"As many as necessary! They're fighting to keep you safe!" Lady Averly exclaimed as she brushed away a loose strand of hair from her line of sight.

"Don't you raise your voice at me." Lady Miriam looked at the carnage surrounding her. "I've lost my husband..."

"And I've lost my father and may lose my husband as well!" Lady Averly narrowed her eyes and stared at the stepmother. "You ungrateful, selfish hag! I'll no longer listen to your ranting. If you're going to do nothing but complain, then leave the room now!"

Sensing Lady Averly's distress, Rand crept to her side while curling his lips to display his teeth. He lowered his head and growled as he kept a watchful eye on Lady Miriam. His mistress reached down and patted his head.

Lady Miriam's face turned several shades of pink before becoming scarlet. She took a deep breath, trying to compose herself as she straightened her spine and lifted her chin.

"I was just on my way to get Alger another sweet cake." Keeping as much of her dignity as possible, she marched toward the kitchen.

Mina walked past Lady Averly as she went to get another bandage from the basket.

"Well done, my lady."

Lady Averly looked to her friend, exhaled, and hoped her pounding heart would calm.

"I must admit, it felt pretty good to put her in her place." Her stomach grumbled. "Perhaps we should start a large pot of stew and take inventory of the bread. No telling how long the siege will last, and we need to ensure the strength of the men."

"Yes, my lady." After bandaging a wound, Mina gathered a few of the women and led them toward the kitchen. They passed by Lady Miriam, who scowled at them as she exited carrying a heaping platter of sweet cakes.

Hours passed. Daylight turned into darkness. Lady Averly grew weary. Unable to find time to eat, her stomach ached, protesting its emptiness. She looked through the odorous steam rising from a wound she was searing with the poker to see the priest blessing a body. She returned the poker to the embers in the fireplace and watched as the corpse was carried away and another injured soldier lowered himself upon the bloody tabletop.

Becoming acutely aware that something was amiss, Lady Averly paused and scanned the room. She looked toward the Keep's portal, hastened her effort to finish bandaging the man's seared wound, and walked to the entry. She pressed her ear to the door and listened. *It's quiet. Is the battle finished?* The door flew open, causing her to shriek in surprise as she tumbled forward.

Lord Edwin caught his wife around the waist.

"Averly, stay away from the door. A stray arrow may strike at any moment." Lord Edwin stepped over the threshold, protectively guiding her away from the portal as he pulled it closed behind them.

Hearing his master's voice, Rand's ears perked, and his head tilted to one side. He ran into the hallway, greeting his lord as he pranced about his feet and lifting his nose under his master's hand. Lord Edwin petted the wolf, reassuring him that all was well.

Thankful for the moment of privacy, Lady Averly turned and scanned her husband's body.

"Are you injured?"

Lord Edwin clasped his wife's blood-stained hand as it touched his chest.

"No, I'm fine."

Lady Averly looked to the closed door.

"Why is it so quiet? Is the battle over?"

"No, the barbarians have pulled back and set up camp for the night."

They strolled the length of the hallway hand in hand and entered the Great Hall. Lord Edwin scanned the injured men and those attending them before remembering his reason for entering the Keep.

"Is there anything to eat?"

Lady Averly looked about the room. The flow of injured had decreased. Much like her husband, she had yet to eat.

"Yes, come with me." She led him to the kitchen with Rand following, took a tray from the shelf, and set it on the table. He looked about the room as she washed her hands in a bucket of water, ridding them of the soldier's blood. Dodging a woman, she grabbed a loaf of bread from a basket and took two wooden spoons and bowls from the shelf. She filled the bowls with stew from the pot hanging over the fireplace and placed them on the tray. Lastly, she grabbed two empty tankards and a pitcher of ale from the table. She tossed Rand a bone from a tray.

"If you would be so kind as to..." Lady Averly began.

Lady Miriam entered the kitchen.

"Why wasn't a meal brought to Alger and me? The poor child is starving." She stood with both fisted hands on her hips and stared at Lady Averly.

Lord Edwin opened his mouth to speak but hesitated as his wife touched his arm, indicating she would handle the matter.

"I'm no longer a servant of Holbrook. I'm the Lady of Tildenham. With the kitchen staff attending to the injured, you can take two bowls," she pointed to the shelf, "and fill them from the pot hanging in the fireplace. Once you have done so, please leave the kitchen. I would like to eat in peace."

Lady Miriam gasped. She looked to Lord Edwin.

"Are you going to allow your wife to talk to me in such a disrespectful manner?"

Lord Edwin looked to his wife and then back to the Lady of Holbrook.

"With all due respect, I was advised by my father to never argue with a woman, especially when she's in the right. I believe you're perfectly capable of getting the food yourself."

Lady Miriam scowled as she seized two bowls from the shelf and ladled the stew. She shoved a spoon into each bowl, tucked a loaf of bread under her arm, and stormed out of the kitchen.

Lady Averly sighed.

"I need to get away from this carnage and chaos. The quietest chamber that I can think of is mine." She handed him the pitcher of ale and tankards and placed the tray of food on her shoulder.

Lord Edwin placed the mugs on the tray before relieving his wife of the burden.

"My dearest wife, lead the way."

They crossed the Great Hall, ascended the staircase, and crept past the solar. Lady Averly paused before her chamber and opened the door.

"Place everything on the table while I light the candle."

Candlelight spilled in from the hallway, allowing Lord Edwin to locate the small table in the dark room.

Lady Averly picked up a rush from the floor, lit it from the hallway candelabra, and cupped her hand protectively around the flame as she entered her chamber. She set the candle alight, illuminating the room. Her husband rotated as he inspected the tiny chamber with its sparse and crude furniture.

"This is your bedchamber?"

"Yes. It has been so for many years." She shut the door, sat upon the bed, and pulled the table toward her.

Her husband lowered himself to the chair and sat across from her. The puzzle of her past life was beginning to take shape within his mind. *It's beginning to make sense.* But he probed to complete the picture.

"This has always been your bedchamber?"

She set a bowl of stew before him.

"No. After my mother died, my father remarried. Lady Miriam insisted I relinquish my bedchamber and become one of the servants." She broke the bread in half and gave him the largest piece.

A scratching at the door drew their attention. Lord Edwin rose and opened the door. Rand wandered into the room and sat by the table as his master resumed his seat.

Lord Edwin dipped his bread in his bowl of stew.

"How many men have succumbed to their injuries?" He hoped the number to be low as he ate the moistened crust. He spooned a chunk of meat from his stew and dropped it onto the floor. Rand ate it in one bite and looked to his master for more.

"Several dozens, maybe more. In truth, I was too busy to keep count." Lady Averly dunked her bread into the stew, placed the sodden bread in her mouth, and bit into the crust. Broth ran down her chin.

The golden glow of the candlelight danced upon the features of his wife's face. Lord Edwin leaned over the table, wiped her chin with his thumb, and kissed her forehead. He displayed a devilish grin, raising his eyebrows up and down as he ate a heaping spoonful of stew. She smiled, but then became serious.

"How long do you think the battle will last?"

"It's difficult to say. Holbrook's walls are strong. With a large number of men in the garrison, the battle may be a long one unless we run short of supplies and water."

"I wish we could leave for Tildenham and let my stepmother fend for herself." Lady Averly looked to her husband.

He reached across the table, clasping her hand within his, pressed it against his lips, and kissed it gently.

The gentleness of his lips upon the back of her hand brought a smile to her face. Even if she was in a kingdom filled with horrid memories, this moment she would cherish and remember.

Weariness settled into their minds and bodies as they relaxed and finished their meal. Assuming the attack would resume close to sunrise, Lord Edwin emptied his tankard and set it upon the tray. He rose from the table and pulled it away from the bed for his wife to rise. She tidied the dishes while he removed his sword and dirk.

With her back toward him, he wrapped his arms around her waist, pulled her next to his body, and kissed her neck.

"Care to join me for a nap?"

She chuckled as she placed her hands upon his and leaned her head against his chest before looking up into his alluring eyes.

"Something tells me we won't be sleeping." She rotated to face him.

"You're probably right." He traced his finger along her chin before tilting it upward to meet his and kissed her tenderly. She coiled her arms around his neck, pulling him closer. Their kiss deepened, heartbeats became rapid, and Rand barked before wedging himself between the couple, forcing them to come apart. Lady Averly tried to catch her breath.

"Perhaps Rand is right. As much as I look forward to becoming your wife in the true sense, you need some rest. I need to see to the injured and ensure everyone is fed."

Lord Edwin ran his hand through his hair as he stared at his lovely wife. He plopped down on the bed, laid down with his ankles crossed, and put both of his hands behind his head.

"Are you sure you won't join me?" He raised his eyebrows teasingly.

Lady Averly laughed.

"Rest. I'll return shortly." She picked up the tray of dishes and exited the chamber.

Lady Averly tiptoed around the moaning men lying on pallets and tables and stepped over the bloody bandages littering the floor of the Great Hall as she passed through to the kitchen. She set the tray on a table before returning to the makeshift infirmary and inspecting the wounds of several of the men.

Mina hurried through the room to the kitchen.

"My lady, I thought you had retired for the evening."

Curious as to why her friend was in such a hurry, Lady Averly followed.

"I wanted to check on the injured first. Mina, what are you doing?"

"Feeding the garrison. The men have rotated their responsibilities and are eating in shifts. They're lined up at the door. I came to fetch more bread."

"Do you need any help?"

"I have help. Please rest yourself, my lady." Mina rushed out of the kitchen with a basket full of bread.

Curious, Lady Averly followed and peeked over her friend's shoulder. Men were indeed lined up at the Keep's door. She looked to the torch-lit crenels and walkway. Some of the men sat with their backs against the wall sleeping while others may have found a cot in the gatehouse in which to rest. Men patrolled the walls ready to call out a warning if a night raid should occur. Lady Averly placed her hand upon her friend's shoulder.

"Thank you, Mina. Please alert me of any developments."

"Yes, my lady."

Lady Averly ascended the staircase, paused before her chamber door, and listened for snoring. As tired as her husband looked, she hoped he was able to sleep. Her ears were met with silence. Unlatching the door ever so slowly, she tiptoed into the room. Laying on the floor, Rand lifted his head to see his mistress before returning it to the floor as she closed the door. Her husband lay fully dressed upon the small bed. She listened to his rhythmic breathing before petting Rand on the head. Removing her slippers and blood-stained wedding dress, she stood beside the bed dressed in her chemise and watched her husband's chest rise and fall. His face, shadowed by the candlelight, was peaceful.

Lord Edwin opened his eyes as if he was aware his wife stood near. He lifted his hand toward her.

She placed her hand within his and lay on the bed next to him.

"I know this is our wedding night, but aren't you tired? I know I am."

He traced the shadowed profile of her face with his finger.

"Mmmm…yes, but one never knows if there will be a tomorrow." He rolled toward her and draped his arm over her waist, pulled her near, and kissed her.

Rand lifted his head and looked toward his master.

Lord Edwin lifted the corner of his mouth from Lady Averly's lips.

"Rand, stay."

The faithful wolf laid his head down and went to sleep.

Chapter 41

THE SUN HAD yet to breach the horizon. After being on patrol most of the night, a soldier along the battlements of Holbrook peered into the distance. He thought he saw dark shadows moving amongst the rubble of the village. In his exhausted state, he did not trust his eyes. He nudged a sleeping soldier with his foot.

"Aye, look. Tell me what you see."

Wiping the sleep from his eyes, the man rose and peered into the distance. He spied the outline of a man appearing from behind a dilapidated fireplace. His eyes widened as he turned toward the bailey.

"Attack! They're attacking!"

The barbarians let out a bloodcurdling battle cry as they charged forward.

*   *   *

Lord Edwin opened his eyes as the sound of battle reached his ears. The candle sputtered, and the flame flickered as he lifted his head from the pillow to see Rand standing next to the bed staring at him. *His ears hear the sounds of battle as well.* His wife lay next to him sleeping protectively within his arms. He brushed a blonde tress away from her eye.

Lady Averly lifted her heavy eyelids to see her husband staring at her. A pleasant grin conveyed her happiness as she snuggled closer to his warm body, wishing she could remain within his arms for the entire day.

He kissed her forehead.

"They attack. I must go." He untangled his arm from beneath her as he climbed over her to the opposite side of the bed and sat upon its edge. He ruffled the top of Rand's head before getting dressed and buckling his belt with his sword and dirk attached. He leaned toward his wife.

"Perhaps you should rise too. There may be injured men soon."

"Let's pray they are few in number."

Lord Edwin pressed his lips to his wife's cheek before leaving the chamber with Rand following.

Lady Averly watched the door as it closed. She sighed as she looked about the room. *Tildenham, I long to return.* But for now, she would do her best to aid those who defended everyone within Holbrook's walls. She dressed in her peasant attire before leaving the chamber to confront whatever the day may bring.

*   *   *

The thundering of hooves resonated from the narrow passage of the valley. Flapping banners bearing the baron's red and yellow colors were held high. The towers of Holbrook came into view above the treetops. Baron Vinson held up his fisted hand signaling the garrison to come to a halt. The horses pranced nervously as they inhaled the thick, acrid smoke. Their riders reined their steeds as they listened to the sound of battle in the distance.

Baron Vinson turned to his informant, Doran, needing information for their attack.

"Tell me what you know of Holbrook and those who attack it."

Doran dismounted and made a crude map on the ground with rocks to represent the castle and village.

"If the barbarians are creatures of habit, they have destroyed the village and are attempting to breach the castle. Holbrook is built strongly, but their walls may be scaled. If the garrison surrounded them on three sides and trapped them against the castle walls, with our vast garrison and Holbrook's attacking from above, our success is highly probable." He stood and looked to Baron Vinson for his approval.

Baron Vinson stared at the crude map before looking in the direction of Holbrook. He had grown tired of the death and destruction, and he was determined to put an end to it once and for all. He shifted his line of vision to Doran, nodded his head in approval, and began to call his knights by name. He divided his garrison into three groups. Each knight led their men into position and waited for the baron's signal to converge simultaneously and trap the barbarians.

*   *   *

Several rooftops within Holbrook's bailey were burning. Peasants formed a line to shuttle buckets of water from the well to douse the flames. Lord Edwin paced the battlements. He searched the smoky sky trying to locate the sun. The hazy orb directly over his head indicated it was midday.

He froze in place as the ominous sound of a battering ram pounded against the drawbridge, a crude forewarning of the barbarian's entry.

Sir Thomas peeked to the moat below. The barbarians had advanced under the protection of the leather roof of the battering ram. The attackers pushed

385

the log back and forth, allowing it to swing across the moat and strike the drawbridge.

"Aim and strike true!"

Holbrook's bowmen aimed toward the invaders while men within the gatehouse carried large pots of hot tar up the spiral stairs and positioned them above the portcullis. They would pour their contents through the murder holes, scalding the attackers once they breached the drawbridge. The barbarians who survived the hot dousing would enter the bailey after prying the portcullis open with a wedge and lever and engage the garrison in hand to hand combat.

Lord Edwin scanned the bailey for able peasant men. Most of them had armed themselves with pitchforks, hammers, or whatever else they could find. He spied several barrels, surmised a plan, and ran down the stone steps two at a time.

"Quickly now, push wagons, carts, and barrels toward the portcullis. We need to build a barrier."

Lord Edwin helped push a wagon onto its side as a board of the drawbridge splintered and fell. He looked toward the Keep. *Averly*. An arrow sailed through the bailey, grazing his shoulder. He placed his hand upon his cut tunic and pulled it away to see blood on the palm of his hand.

Sir Thomas paced the battlements.

"Let the arrows fly, m..." His voice was silenced.

Lord Edwin watched Sir Thomas fall from the battlements and land near his feet. He had taken an arrow to the throat, piercing his spine. His blank orbs stared skyward.

Lord Edwin raced up the steps to the battlements and took command.

"Bowmen! Set the arrows aflame before you release!" He hoped the protective hide of the battering ram would catch fire, weakening enough to allow arrows to pierce it and kill the men inside.

*   *   *

Baron Vinson's men were in position. He nodded to his banner-bearer, who lowered the colors to the ground, signaling the forces to advance. The three divisions charged forward in unison surrounding the barbarians.

The men on the castle battlements cheered. A young page turned to Lord Edwin.

"We have reinforcements! My lord, we have reinforcements!"

Lord Edwin peeked from behind a crenel at the battlefield below. He saw the charging garrison on horseback encircling the castle and recognized the baron's colors. As an arrow sailed past his head, he ducked behind the crenel.

"Aim at the men closest to the castle wall!"

Threatened by entrapment, the barbarians doubled their efforts to scale the wall with their ladders, hoping to find safety within. Lord Edwin saw a brawny barbarian with deerskin draped over his wide shoulders climb onto the battlements.

"Damn."

The warrior wielded a large poleax through the air, impaling several of Holbrook's men.

Lord Edwin reached for his sword as he charged forward. His ankle twisted to the side as he stepped on a long spear lying on the walkway. Sheathing his sword, he stooped to pick it up.

Turning toward the invader, a bowman released an arrow toward the next barbarian cresting the ladder, killing him instantly. He continued to shoot and kill the men who climbed the ladder as Lord Edwin charged forward.

The poleax twirled over the barbarian's shoulder before swinging toward Lord Edwin, who ducked his head. As it crashed into the crenel, Lord Edwin thrust the spear forward, jabbing the barbarian in the shoulder. Without hesitation, the barbarian attacked aggressively, forcing Lord Edwin to retreat a step as the poleax came toward his face. He turned his face as the weapon sliced his cheek. Placing the spear's handle on the battlement floor next to his foot, he braced it with a stiff arm to block the momentum of the poleax as he pulled his sword from its sheath, aimed for the warrior's chest, and pierced his heart. As he withdrew his sword, the man dropped his weapon and collapsed. Holbrook's men pushed the body off the walkway and into the bailey below.

Lord Edwin looked to where the man had breached the wall. The ladder was no longer there. Bowman continued to shoot as additional ladders were pushed away, freeing the castle walls from the threat.

With the two garrisons working as one, the merciless battle was over quickly. Barbarians who managed to escape the entrapment were hunted down and killed.

As the sound of battle subsided, Lord Edwin peered over the castle wall. The ground was littered with the dead and the dying. The baron's garrison combed the battlefield. Barbarians found alive were put out of their misery with a quick jab to their chest with a sword.

Lord Edwin descended the stone stairs and helped dismantle the barrier blocking the gatehouse entrance. The portcullis was raised, and the damaged drawbridge lowered.

Curious, Bryce opened the door of the Keep and peeked into the bailey. Rand scooted around the stableboy, pushing the portal wide as he darted toward his master. Realizing the portcullis was raised and the drawbridge was lowered, Bryce ran into the Great Hall.

"It's over!"

Busy hands paused as everyone listened for the sound of battle. It had subsided. Wanting to witness the aftermath for themselves, many went to the open doorway and stepped into the bailey. Lady Averly finished bandaging a wound, hurried to the portal, and entered the bailey. She gasped upon seeing the many bodies on the ground. *Where's Edwin?* Her heartbeat quickened as she looked from body to body before scanning the garrison. She walked forward, dodging bodies as she searched. The broad shoulders and mahogany hair caused her heart to skip a beat. She sighed with relief and she smiled with pride as he helped upright a wagon and pushed it aside.

Lord Edwin turned to see his wife's sweet smile as she wiped her bloody hands upon her overskirt and walked toward him. He reached out his hand and drew her into his embrace. Rand pranced around his master, who playfully rustled the fur on the wolf's head.

Lady Averly touched the cut on her husband's cheek before noticing his blood-soaked sleeve.

"You're hurt?"

Hoofbeats sounded behind him.

"Ah, a mere scratch. You can tend to it later." He placed his arm around his wife's waist as he turned to see Baron Vinson and his knights ride into the bailey. Everyone in the bailey knelt upon one knee. The baron and his men dismounted before raising his hand, indicating all should rise. Lord Edwin stepped forward.

"It has been a while since our last visit, Baron Vinson." Lord Edwin greeted as he extended a hand and they clasped forearms.

"Yes, it has. I received your missive. I've sent men to Tildenham to rebuild your garrison. My condolence on your father's death."

"Thank you. May I introduce to you my wife, Lady Averly of Tildenham."

Lady Averly curtsied. Baron Vincent reached for her hand and brought it to his lips before releasing it.

"It's a pleasure to meet you, Lady Averly." He looked to the young lord. "Your father chose wisely. If you hadn't have married her, I may have snatched her up myself." He chuckled.

Lady Averly blushed.

"Baron, you are too kind."

Her husband's protective arm pulled her a little closer toward his side. She smiled as she looked into Lord Edwin's eyes.

Baron Vincent cleared his throat.

"Doran discovered the whereabouts of the barbarians and determined their next attack. Once informed, we set out immediately for Holbrook. It looks as if we arrived just in time."

"Your good timing is appreciated." Lord Edwin looked to the gatehouse to see Doran ride into the bailey. "The Lord of Holbrook was killed during the battle." He glanced to his wife.

Baron Vinson looked to Lady Averly as well.

"My condolence, my lady."

Lady Averly nodded her head in appreciation.

"Thank you." She sighed. "If you'll both excuse me, I'm needed elsewhere." She curtsied before walking to the Keep. Once over the threshold, she rushed into the Great Hall and ordered the High Table washed and tidied. She sent a woman to alert Lady Miriam that the baron had arrived.

Lord Edwin motioned with his hand toward the Keep as he began to walk with the baron and his men.

"The kingdom's only knight died in battle as well. The Lady of Holbrook and her son are safely within the Keep."

Baron Vincent cringed.

"I'm well acquainted with Lady Miriam." He paused. "Excuse me for being rude." He motioned to the men following them. "My knights, Sir William, Sir Bruce, and Sir Robert." Lord Edwin exchanged a handshake with each man. Baron Vincent continued toward the Keep.

"I've heard you've made great progress with the reconstruction of Tildenham. Well done."

"Thank you." Lord Edwin reached down and patted Rand's head as he walked beside him.

Lady Miriam met the men at the entrance to the Great Hall.

"Baron Vinson, how good it is to see you again." She curtsied and pushed Alger forward.

"My son, Lord Alger." She announced loudly. The chubby boy smiled.

Baron Vinson raised an eyebrow as he glanced at the child.

"I'll send an advisor and steward to help manage the estate."

"But Baron..."

Baron Vinson raised his voice, talking over Lady Miriam.

"And someone to educate and groom your son to be a proper lord."

"But I'm quite capable of..." Lady Miriam placed her hands upon her son's shoulders.

Baron Vinson raised the palm of his hand, ordering her to cease her defensive chattering.

"Nevertheless, this is how it shall be." He turned to Sir Bruce. "I believe this 'young lord' needs a thorough understanding of the finer techniques of battle. He must begin his training immediately to determine if he is worthy of this kingdom."

"Yes, Baron. I'll remain behind and see that his training meets your expectations." Sir Bruce stared at the chubby lad, assuming a daily workout and proper nutrition may be necessary.

With the baron's orders stated firmly, arguing any further would only anger him. Lady Miriam turned and motioned toward the makeshift infirmary.

"As you can see, I've everything under control."

Upon hearing her stepmother's falsehood, Lady Averly looked up from the wound she was stitching. She looked to her husband and then to the ceiling. He smiled.

The baron stepped onto the dais, sat in the Lord's chair, and challenged the Lady of Holbrook.

"That's good to hear, so asking for a meal for myself and my men before we return will be of little inconvenience."

A mask of shock covered Lady Miriam's face. She looked to her stepdaughter, who shook her head, denying her assistance as she finished with her patient, wiped her hands on her overskirt, and went to her husband.

"If possible, I'd like to leave Holbrook immediately. I'll only be a moment while I pack my belongings. If you approve, I'd like to have Mina and Emmet join our staff at Tildenham."

Lord Edwin looked at Lady Miriam.

"I think that would be wise and also charitable."

Lady Miriam's face became flushed with color.

"But she's my cook."

Baron Vinson joined in.

"Lady Miriam, how much longer must we wait for something to eat?"

The Lady of Holbrook clenched her teeth, glared at her stepdaughter, and headed toward the kitchen.

Lady Averly raised her eyebrows and smirked before turning back to her husband.

"I'll inform them of your decision, my lord."

Lord Edwin watched as his wife crossed the room and talked to a woman who was changing a bandage. He joined the baron in conversation.

Lady Averly handed her friend a clean bandage.

"Mina, when you are finished, I need you to pack your belongings. You'll be residing with me in Tildenham."

Mina paused in wrapping the wound.

"Truly?"

"Yes, you, Sarah, Bryce, and Emmet. Please go and tell them to pack their things too. Have Bryce and Emmet ready the horses. When you have finished, meet me in the kitchen to prepare food for our journey. We'll leave as soon as everyone is ready."

"Yes, my lady."

Lady Averly went to the chapel. Staring at her father's motionless body lying on the floor before the altar, she wondered if his soul was at peace. She knelt upon a kneeler, stared at the cross upon the wall, and entwined her fingers in prayer.

"Heavenly Father, please embrace my father's soul as he crosses over from this world to yours."

She crossed herself, rose, and walked down the aisle, pausing in the chapel doorway. She looked back.

"Goodbye, Father." Lady Averly could hear the panic in Lady Miriam's voice as it echoed from the kitchen. She couldn't help but grin as she passed through the Great Hall, ascended the staircase, and went to her chamber to pack.

She changed into a clean peasant dress before using a cloth bag that hung from a peg on her wall and packed the few clothes she possessed. She reached under her bed and withdrew her mother's portrait. Looking at her chamber one last time, it was so very small, meek, and filled with memories she would just as soon forget. She closed the door and returned to the Great Hall with her bag in hand.

Lord Edwin looked to the staircase as his wife descended. She motioned for a moment of his time.

"If you will excuse me, Baron."

The baron nodded before Lord Edwin went to his wife's side.

Lady Averly set the bag and portrait on a clean bench before examining the gash on her husband's cheek.

"I'll only be a moment longer while I prepare food for our journey, but first let me tend to your wounds."

Lord Edwin looked to his bloody tunic.

"Very well."

After ensuring her husband's wounds were cleaned, stitched, and properly dressed, she looked up from tying the last bandage to see Bryce step into the room.

"Bryce, please take my items to the stable. Where's Sarah and Emmet?"

"They are waiting at the stable, my lady."

"Good, once Mina and I finish packing the food, we'll join you and depart for Tildenham."

"Very well, my lady."

Lady Averly stepped into the kitchen. She paused to scan the disheveled, chaotic scene. Lady Miriam shouted orders as she slammed a tray upon a table. Confused women scurried about trying to anticipate their mistress' needs before receiving a reprimand.

Rolling her lips inward, Lady Averly pressed them together to refrain from laughing. She went to the storage room and found Mina inside. Working together, they filled several pouches with food and flasks with wine. As they stepped back into the busy kitchen, Lady Averly met the glare of her stepmother and refused to look away.

Lady Miriam glared at the provisions.

"What do you think you are doing? You're not entitled to that."

"I'm not asking for your permission. I'm taking it, leaving, and hope to never return." Lady Averly watched as her stepmother's mouth dropped open. She grabbed two loaves of bread from the center table, tossed them into a satchel, and marched out of the kitchen.

Mina picked up a rolled bundle and a tiny package both wrapped in oilcloth from a table in the Great Hall.

"The larger parcel belongs to you. Emmet had given it to me when you returned. When I looked inside, I hid it from Lady Miriam. The smaller one is mine. It's all I have, my lady." Mina held the items before her mistress.

"Very well. Please take them to the stable with these." She gave Mina the food for the journey. The cook hurried away.

Lord Edwin stood before the dais addressing the baron. Rand sat obediently next to his master. Lady Averly patted the wolf's head before joining her husband.

Lord Edwin extended his hand to bid the baron farewell.

"Baron Vinson, it has been a pleasure to see you again."

The baron stood and grasped the young lord's forearm.

"Lord Edwin, keep me informed of the progress of Tildenham's reconstruction. I have the highest expectation for your success."

"Thank you, Baron. I shall."

Baron Vinson looked to Lady Averly.

"I'm certain your husband will depend on you greatly to put Tildenham in order. From what I have seen, it will be a task you accomplish quickly."

"Thank you, Baron Vinson."

The Lord of Tildenham put his hand on the small of his wife's back as he escorted her through the Keep. He slapped his thigh. Rand obediently followed. They went to the stables where the small party awaited them.

"Bryce, is all in accord?" Lord Edwin inspected the saddle straps on Fulton.

"Yes, my lord. Between the two of us, the horses were saddled quickly." Bryce looked to Emmet and nodded his head.

"Indeed, my lord." Emmet smiled as he looked to his new friend.

"Then let's be on our way to Tildenham." Lord Edwin cupped his hands and boosted his wife onto her saddle. Lady Averly was pleased to see her mother's portrait strapped securely to the side of the palfrey. She planned to display the painting above the fireplace in her awaiting bedchamber.

Lord Edwin boosted Sarah easily, but it took him several tries to lift Mina and ensure the stout cook sat securely on her saddle. He climbed atop Fulton and looked to everyone's eager faces.

Lord Edwin urged his warhorse through the bailey and out of the castle. He looked skyward for the placement of the sun, hoping to travel a good distance before nightfall.

Chapter 42

WHEN THE CURTAIN of darkness met the horizon, it was necessary for the Lord and Lady of Tildenham and their party to camp for the night. Bryce and Emmet unsaddled the horses and secured their reins to a rope tied between two trees before gathering firewood. A campfire was built to take the chill off the night air. Everyone gathered around the fire and enjoyed their prepared meal.

Lord Edwin tossed Rand a scrap of dried meat.

"I'll keep watch. The rest of you should get some sleep."

Bryce and Emmet looked to one another.

"My lord, would you like us to relieve you for a few hours so that you may sleep as well?"

Lord Edwin looked at their eager faces.

"If needed, I'll wake you a few hours before daybreak. For now, sleep."

The stableboys lay upon the ground and covered themselves with their horse blankets.

Mina, Sarah, and Lady Averly secured the remaining food in the pouches and readied their beds. Mina looked toward her new lord as she sat beside her saddle.

"My lord, thank you for allowing Emmet and I to reside within Tildenham."

Lord Edwin looked toward the cook.

"Both of you are welcome and, in truth, are needed at Tildenham."

Mina grinned, laid her head upon her saddle, and watched the dancing flames of the fire.

Lord Edwin watched his wife as she spread a blanket upon the ground, sat, and draped her husband's horse blanket over her shoulders. He stoked the fire before sitting next to her, wrapped his arm around her waist, and pulled her toward him. Lifting her hand from her lap, he kissed it before entwining his fingers within hers.

"It'll be a few days before we reach Tildenham."

"A journey I've become quite familiar with traveling." She grinned. "I'm eager to see its progress during my absence."

"Sir Garrick understands the importance of providing housing for the arriving freeman. I hope he has been able to keep pace with the demand." He chuckled. "Glenna asked me to bring you back to Tildenham."

"She did?" Lady Averly traced her finger along the back of her husband's hand.

"I told her I would return with someone she didn't know. She's going to think I lied."

Lady Averly smiled, but it faded quickly.

"I've missed her, and Henry too."

Lord Edwin sighed. He released her hand.

"You must sleep. We have a long day ahead of us tomorrow." Lord Edwin lifted her chin upward and kissed her. "Good night, dear wife."

Lady Averly covered herself as she lay down, yawned, and looked into his eyes. She smiled sweetly.

"Good night, dear husband."

Lord Edwin went to a nearby tree, sat, and leaned against its trunk. Rand sat next to him with his ears perked. The crackling fire, croaking frogs, and hooting of a distant owl coaxed the Lord of Tildenham to lower his eyelids. He dozed, knowing Rand would alert him of any danger. His head tilted to the side. Lord Edwin forced his eyes open to ensure all was well. Rand lay with his head between his paws. He looked to his wife. The rise and fall of the blanket indicated she slept soundly. He added wood to the fire before allowing his eyes to close once more.

Rand rose and scampered away. Lord Edwin opened his eyes and looked to the horizon to see the pinkish hue of the morning sky. *Morning so soon?* He rose from the ground, knelt next to his wife, and kissed her warm cheek.

"Good morning, Lady of Tildenham."

She opened her eyes, stretched, and glanced at the morning sky. She sat up, pulling the horse blanket around her shoulders to ward off the chilly morning air.

"Good morning. Did you sleep?"

"Some, while Rand kept watch." He winked, before rising to stand.

Lady Averly retrieved the food and wine while Lord Edwin woke the others. Emmet and Bryce readied the horses. Unaccustomed to traveling on horseback, Mina moaned as she rose from the ground and limped toward the backside of a distant tree to relieve herself. Sarah rose and stretched before doing the same.

After a quick breakfast, Lady Averly watched from atop her horse as Lord Edwin and the stableboys pushed Mina up into her saddle. She looked away from the comical sight to hide her smile. Once astride their horse, they continued their journey toward Tildenham.

Even though they traveled at a slow pace, Mina struggled to stay atop her horse. From the painful expression on her face, Lady Averly assumed the cook suffered from saddle sores.

It was necessary to camp another night before reaching their destination by midday.

As Tildenham came into view, Bryce and Emmet spurred their horses ahead to announce their arrival. Lord Edwin was pleased to see freshly plowed plots of land and workers in the fields.

The Lord and Lady of Tildenham rode into the village with Rand prancing proudly by their side. Sarah and Mina followed their lord and lady.

Lady Averly looked from one side of the road to the other at each new dwelling they passed.

"Oh, my. Look what they've accomplished."

The village was a beehive of activity. Men, lots of men, were carrying boards, hammering and sawing, climbing ladders, and finishing rooftops.

A man atop a ladder waved and shouted.

"It's Lady Averly! Look! It's Lady Averly!"

She looked in his direction, smiled, and waved.

Peasants lined the street of the village to greet their lord and lady. They shouted merry wishes and cheered. Upon seeing Sir Garrick standing on the roadside, Lord Edwin reined his horse and his wife did the same.

Sir Garrick reached toward Lord Edwin and clasped his forearm.

"Welcome home, my lord."

"Thank you. It's good to be home."

"I see you've returned with a lovely and familiar bride. All will be pleased, as I am."

Lady Averly's cheeks became pink as she smiled.

"Thank you, Sir Garrick."

Lord Edwin held up his hand. The crowd quieted.

"I'm pleased to see the progress you've made during my absence. When I set out to collect my betrothed, I did so remorsefully. However, all is as it should be. For my heart was joined with a kind and loving woman that many of you know." He looked toward his blushing bride, picked up her hand, and pressed a kiss upon it. "Our kingdom has endured much and remained resilient. I believe it's time for Tildenham to celebrate our accomplishments and our new lady. But if you don't mind, I ask that you allow me a few days alone with my wife, and then I promise you a grand celebration!"

Many in the crowd chuckled at their lord's implication. Lady Averly's blush intensified.

The couple urged their horses forward.

People continued to line the street and cheer as their lord and lady rode through the gatehouse and into the bailey.

A familiar ringing of metal echoing from the blacksmith's shop was music to Lord Edwin's ears. The couple reined their horses at the stable. Bryce and Emmet came forward to take their horses. Anticipating the tasty treat he would receive in the kitchen, Rand went directly through the open door of the Keep.

Lord Edwin dismounted, went to his wife, and helped her down from her horse. He held her close as he whispered.

"Welcome home, my Lady of Tildenham."

"It's good to be home."

He looked over her head and saw something he knew would please her. He placed his hand over her eyes, turned her around, and guided her forward.

Lady Averly laughed as she took an apprehensive step.

"What are you doing?"

"It's a surprise."

The couple walked several steps before stopping. He removed his hand from her eyes and watched as his wife's mouth dropped open. She touched the lumber and discovered the sturdiness of the fence that guarded the perimeter of the garden. She stepped into the garden and scanned the flourishing plants. She spotted the roses. They were in bloom.

"The roses are such a lovely shade of red." She looked back to her husband who remained outside of the fence. "Thank you, Edwin."

"You're welcome."

As she went to his side, she placed her arm around his waist. He placed his arm upon her shoulder and they turned toward the Keep.

"Lady Averly!" Glenna emerged from the doorway with Dolly in one arm and Henry in the other. "I'm so happy to see you."

Lady Averly picked up the little girl, placed her upon her hip, and hugged her tightly.

"I'm happy to see you too, Glenna."

Her big brown eyes looked toward her lord. She tilted her head to one side.

"I thought you said you wouldn't be bringing Lady Averly back with you."

Lord Edwin laughed.

"Glenna, I didn't know my betrothed was Lady Averly. It was a surprise to me as well." He patted the little girl on the head.

Glenna kissed the top of Henry's head and looked to Lady Averly.

"Henry got bigger. I'm taking good care of him, see." She lifted the kitten toward Lady Averly.

"I can see that you are. He is bigger."

Lord Edwin stroked the kitten's fur and smiled. Surprised by his affection toward the feline, Lady Averly looked to her husband.

"I thought you didn't like cats."

"I don't like cats. Henry is a kitten." He smiled at his admission.

Looking at the doorway of the Keep, Lady Averly saw Isabel and other staff members waiting to greet her. She set Glenna on the ground, clasped her wrist, and threaded her arm through her husband's offered arm. The trio walked toward the staff.

Isabel stepped forward.

"My lady, it looks as if our prayers have been answered. Welcome home." The staff nodded their heads in agreement.

"Thank you. It's good to see all of you again."

A whooping holler came from the stable. Everyone looked toward Mina, who was delighted to set foot on solid ground once again. She stepped away from her horse and walked awkwardly toward the Keep with Sarah leading the way.

Lady Averly chuckled as she turned back to the cook.

"Isabel, I'm reassigning you, along with Sarah and Mina, to be my ladies in waiting."

Mina waddled next to Sarah.

"What's this?"

Lady Averly smiled and looked to her friend before motioning Isabel to step forward.

"This is Isabel. From this day forward, the three of you will be my ladies in waiting."

Mina stared in disbelief.

"No more working in the kitchen?"

"Only when necessary, or for pleasure."

Isabel, Sarah, and Mina huddled to greet each other.

Sarah composed herself to speak.

"We're honored. Thank you, my lady."

Lord Edwin released his wife's hand from his elbow before scooping his bride into his arms.

"And your first responsibility is to draw a warm bath for our bedchamber, gather food, lots of food, and plenty of wine. Do not disturb us for three days. When we emerge, we expect a grand feast for everyone in Tildenham to celebrate our happiness!"

The staff laughed and cheered as they watched their lord carry their lady through the Keep's doorway. Many hurried to the kitchen to ready the hot water for their bath, gather their food and drink, and plan the celebration.

Chapter 43

LADY AVERLY STROLLED through the flower garden, admiring its colorful blossoms. She sat upon the limestone bench and tilted her face skyward while she waited for Bryce to saddle Nelly. She was certain her face blushed as she recalled the intimate moments shared with her husband during the three days hiatus within his bedchamber. Smiling, she remembered the way the lovely wedding gown of her design seemed so special and the reaction of everyone in the Great Hall as she descended the staircase wearing it for the celebration feast. Everyone had a splendid time. The food was delicious with many overindulging until their stomachs ached, dancing the first song of the evening with her husband as he held her closely, and twirling around the room with every man in attendance. *Oh, how my feet ached the next morning.*

Bryce held the horse's bridle.

"My lady, Nelly is ready."

Lady Averly looked to the stableboy, rose, and climbed atop her mare.

Familiar with his lord's policy, Bryce offered his service.

"May I accompany you, for your safety, of course, my lady?"

She preferred to go alone but knew her husband would want her to have an escort.

"Very well." She waited for the stableboy to saddle his horse. He joined her moments later, and they left the castle.

Lord Edwin was overseeing the construction of another building in the village. Lady Averly waved to her husband to reassure him that all was well as she rode past him.

The Lady of Tildenham and the stableboy rode toward the mill. Keeping their distance, they reined their horses to watch men stack freshly cut lumber as the demand for the wood had increased.

Lady Averly encouraged Nelly forward. She reined her mare and entered the full green foliage of the forest. Weaving her way into the shadowed woods, she reined her horse in the clearing and stared at the angel statue. Lovely wildflowers of yellow and orange were in bloom at its base. Green ferns on the fringe of the woods circled the clearing and a pathway of lush moss lead to the bench.

Lady Averly dismounted, stepped along the pathway, and sat upon the bench. Bryce, respecting his lady's privacy, remained atop his horse a distance away.

She looked to the angel's face. Even though the day was warm, an icy breeze brushed her cheek. As sunlight parted the foliage of the trees, she saw Lady Mary standing in the beam of light next to the statue.

Lady Averly smiled and bowed her head graciously. *You knew all along, didn't you?*

Lady Mary smiled.

"Yes, all is as it should be."

Lady Averly looked toward Bryce. He seemed oblivious to their silent conversation. She turned back to Lady Mary, who looked upward toward the source of light and then back to her.

"I must go home now." Lady Mary disappeared as the light faded.

Goodbye. Lady Averly looked around the perimeter of the shadowed clearing. She glanced at the angel's face before rising from the bench and retracing her steps back to Nelly. She mounted her horse and followed Bryce through the pathway to the mill.

The pair rode back to the village and Lady Averly reined her horse where her husband was working with Rand by his side.

"Thank you, Bryce, I don't want to keep you from your duties."

"Very well, my lady." The stableboy encouraged his horse forward.

Lord Edwin approached his wife as he wiped the sweat from his brow.

"Is all well?"

She smiled at her husband and leaned close enough for only his ears to hear.

"All is as it should be." She brushed aside a strand of his hair from his cheek before kissing it gently.

A few of the men elbowed each other and whistled teasingly at the young lord. He looked toward them smiling mischievously, pulled his wife from her saddle and into his arms, dipped her backward over his left arm, and kissed her.

Rand tried to wedge his nose between his master and mistress.

Breaking their kiss, they both looked toward the wolf and stated a command simultaneously.

"Stay."

I hope you enjoy reading
A Lady's Destiny.
If so, your review on Amazon.com
would be greatly appreciated.

For further information about
Brenda Hasse Books, please visit
www.BrendaHasseBooks.com.